Morrissey Jarrett is fresh out of prison and back on the streets of his hometown Cardiff.

During his enforced absence the city has been re-developed to within an inch of its life and a disoriented Morrissey falls back into old habits as he scams, schemes, and steals whatever he needs to survive.

Morrissey has big dreams though. Dreams of making one last huge score, dreams of leaving his life of crime behind, dreams of reuniting with the love of his life and dreams of walking off into the sunset with her. Happy. Ever. After.

All he needs is a plan.

Luckily, the circles Morrissey frequents provide ample opportunities for ill-gotten gains and soon the perfect job literally falls into his hands.

And so, along with a hastily assembled crew of misfits, Morrissey embarks on planning the perfect heist. With all their eyes fixed steadily on a payday that could change their stars forever, all they have to do is keep their heads down, play it cool, and follow the plan to the letter.

What could possibly go wrong?

This edition first published 2022 by Fahrenheit Press.

ISBN: 978-1-914475-43-6

10 9 8 7 6 5 4 3 2 1

www.Fahrenheit-Press.com

F 4 E

Cash Rules Everything Around Me

By

Rob Gittins

Fahrenheit Press

For Suzanne Phillips

PART ONE

'Offerings At The Feast of Tabernacles'

Numbers, 29

1. WELCOME TO CARDIFF DOCKS

Nine forty-five, Friday night, and Morrissey Jarrett, 29, thin and wiry, finds this foot in a bag. The bag's canvas, a drawstring at the top. The foot's standard issue, five toes, one big, the others not.

Next afternoon, Morrissey's in a bar, south end of Bute Street, sitting in front of an upturned diving bell that's moonlighting as a table, trying to explain all this to Diesel only he's not getting through, and that's not just because Diesel's two years older but has always been ten years behind, it's because the bar's introduced entertainment.

First, it was topless dancers, now it's a stripper and Diesel's eyes are fixed on a leopard-skin thong a few inches from his face which is just covering a stretch-marked arse but which, in a few moments, won't be.

The topless variety were real dancers, as real as students AWOL from a local drama school can be anyway, and the routines were pretty classy once you ignored the bits that bounced. The stripper's a class-free act, but a lot more successful in packing in the punters. The bar itself used to be dying on its feet until the manager packed it full of salvage masquerading as collectables and artefacts from the golden age of sail.

Welcome to Cardiff docks.

But none of that's bothering Morrissey right now. All that's on his mind is the foot, and Morrissey's trying to set the scene like he's heard you should in all good stories.

'So we were on that bit of waste ground just down from Atlantic Wharf.'

'We being?'

Only Morrissey's not ready for that bit yet.

'The music's on low, the heaters on full and she's wearing these heels, high.'

'How high?'

'Only now she's taking them off because they keep getting caught in the cloth.'

'On the seat?'

'On the roof.'

Diesel nods, approving.

'Class.'

Across the bar, Slippery, another of Morrissey and Diesel's old mates from the even older days, is now approaching the stage and is trying to paw the stripper as Morrissey reaches what you might call the first complication.

'Your dog?'

Morrissey nods back.

'You took your dog on a date?'

'He can't get used to it. Me being out. Maybe he thinks I'm going to go away again, he follows me everywhere.'

Diesel's eyes go back to the stripper who's ignoring the distraction and is toying with her audience now, pulling at her thong. Slippery reaches out to grab her arse only to get his ear kicked by one of the stripper's flailing heels, which is when a couple of her tom mates at the bar detach themselves from their punters. And now they're eyeing him, hard, first, because he's getting to his feet and, second, because he doesn't look in the mood to take even a kick to the left ear as any sort of signal to stop.

A bit like Morrissey's dog.

'He's yelping outside the door so I try turning up the music, only the song's one of those power ballads.'

'Celine Dion?'

'The other one.'

'Don't like her so much.'

'And this singer's really hitting the high notes and outside, Yorkie'

'Yorkie?'

'My dog, he's matching her note for note. So now I've got this singer on the CD giving it her all –'

'She's still no Celine Dion, don't matter how much she's giving it.'

'And my dog.'

Morrissey takes a swig of lager.

'So now it's ultimatum time. I get rid of the dog or she puts those heels back on and walks.'

Back on the stage, Slippery's still circling and now the stripper's getting pissed, professional pride beginning to kick in seeing as he's starting to get more cheers than the star attraction.

'So I get out of the cab and try shooing him away, just a couple of gentle prods to begin with, only he thinks it's some sort of game and he goes back a few paces, then charges right back up again and puts his nose on the windscreen.'

'Irritating.'

'So now I'm mouthing at him, just sit, keep quiet, no singing and definitely no howling, 'cos Leanne –'

'Leanne?'

Morrissey shifts in his seat as Diesel stares at him.

'Leanne as in Looner's Leanne?'

On stage, Slippery's just made a sudden dash for the stripper as she starts toying with her thong again only she dances out of the way, getting a big cheer as she does so. So now she's thinking maybe Slippery's not such a problem after all, maybe she can even use him in her act and she starts to play with him, just as a moment before she was toying with her thong.

> *Come on Slippery -*
> *Come and get it, Slippery -*
> *Too slow Slippery –*

But Diesel's still staring at Morrissey.

'Have you got some sort of fucking death wish?'

But Morrissey shakes his head. OK, he's a chancer but he's on no date with the self-destruct button, not yet and maybe, if he plays his cards right, not ever.

'Phil The Travelling Greek?'

Diesel looks at Morrissey for a long moment, his point, slowly, as slowly as everything with Diesel, sinking in.

On stage, the stripper's moving on from the thong to taunting the stumbling Slippery with flashes of naked arse.

'And it seems to work. Yorkie flops down by the front wheel. The next thing – bang.'

Diesel nods, approving again.

'Double class, Morrissey.'

'No, bang outside. On the windscreen.'

'Your dog had jumped on the windscreen? What did you do, Morrissey, take away his bone when he was a kid?'

'Dogs aren't kids, they're puppies, and anyway, this wasn't my dog, it was the Professor.'

'The Professor had jumped on your windscreen?'

'The Professor and his Mate were walking past, chucking around all these lanterns.'

'What sort of lanterns?'

'Chinese lanterns.'

'Why the fuck were the Professor and his mate chucking around Chinese lanterns?'

Only Morrissey's not ready for that bit either, but in any event, a scream from the stage suddenly sounds. Slippery's now on all fours and has just grabbed the stripper's thong with his teeth.

'For a moment it looks like everything's going to be OK because now Yorkie's joining in, and I'm thinking that after two years, forty-eight days and ninety-three minutes I am finally going to get my rocks off.'

'You know how long to the minute it's been since your last shag?'

'It's a nice round number.'

On stage, the stripper's act is in tatters, much like her underwear, and now Slippery's got a very pissed-off stripper, still in her bra, but without her leopard-skin thong, looking down at him.

'Then it all goes quiet.'

'The Professor and his mate had gone?'

'That's what I thought. Leanne lets out this little moan.'

'How little?'

'First of many sort of little.'

'My favourite number.'

'Then she rolls her eyes.'

'Rock and roll.'

'That was the problem.'

'Not another fucking problem?'

Diesel shakes his head.

'I'm beginning to think you're accident prone, Morrissey.'

Back on the stage, the two toms are now approaching, maybe because the leopard skin thong has sentimental value, or maybe because they just don't like Slippery. Maybe there's lots of reasons one of them now brings a scull retrieved from a recently discovered wherry, not a clinker as the inscription proudly states on the side and not a tilt-boat and not a peter and not a sculler or a whiff, but an actual, working wherry, whatever the fuck that is, down on Slippery's head as he chews, dreamily, at the thong.

'The problem now was the Shogun.'

'What Shogun?'

'Looner's Shogun.'

5

'You borrowed Looner's Shogun to shag his girlfriend?'

'No, I nicked Looner's Shogun to shag his girlfriend.'

'Triple Class with a cherry on top, Morrissey.'

'The Shogun's rocking now, just like it should, laws of physics and all that because all that energy has to go somewhere, only that's what the Professor and his Mate are looking at now, this Shogun that's rocking, and that's why it's all gone quiet, not because they've gone away to play with the lanterns or mess about with Yorkie, it's quiet because they've decided to investigate which is when Leanne opens those rolling eyes of hers.'

'Rolling 'cos of the laws of physics, right?'

'No, rolling 'cos after two years, forty-eight days and ninety-four minutes I am finally about to get my fucking rocks off.'

'Which is when she sees the Professor and his mate?'

'And my dog. Looking in on her.'

'And she goes ballistic?'

'That's one word for it. There are others. Like totally fucking bananas.'

'That's three words.'

'Never mind the fucking word count, she hated my dog copping an eyeful, so the Professor and his Mate were always going to be a no-no.'

'That's no-no 'cos there's two, the Professor and his Mate?'

Morrissey ignores that.

'She pushes me off, kicks open the door of the Shogun and yells, top of her voice, and this is exact Diesel, this is word for word.'

Morrissey pauses, building the moment.

'Will you pair of cunts fuck off and let me and Morrissey have a shag in peace.'

'Indiscreet. I mean, you, Leanne, and shag in the same sentence.'

'Phil the Travelling Greek?'

Diesel nods.

Point made.

Again.

Around the stage, a sense of fair play's beginning to kick in. Slippery's a twat and the stripper's every right to be aggrieved, her act's gone south and her thong's got teeth marks, but a close encounter with a large piece of wood from a wherry is still striking most in that bar that day as more than a touch excessive by way of payback. And the now-prone Slippery's still getting a pasting from the two toms which is when one steps in, getting a glass in his forehead for his trouble.

Meanwhile, Morrissey's hunching closer to Diesel.

'Only the Professor and his Mate aren't getting the message although it really doesn't help that Leanne's stark bollock naked right now.'

'34, that's the easy bit, but D or E – '

But Morrissey's not debating breast cups, not now he's got this far.

'So with verbals not having too much in the way of impact, Leanne picks up one of the lanterns to chuck it back at them, only something falls out of this bag inside.'

'This something being?'

Diesel starts to turn back to the entertainment on and around the stage which is now kicking off big-time.

'A foot.'

Diesel turns back just as a glass sails past his head. Slippery's mate does not appreciate getting glassed and he's grabbed the tom by the throat, but the tom's just kicked him in the balls while the stripper glasses him again, but Diesel isn't watching that anymore.

'A foot?'

Morrissey nods.

'An actual?'

Morrissey nods again.

'As in toes, toenails?'

Morrissey nods for the third time. This was becoming Biblical.

'A fucking foot.'

Morrissey hunches forward. This is selling a story and if she wasn't so busy trying to gouge out one of Slippery's eyes right now that stripper could actually be learning something.

'And now Leanne's screaming her head off but I'm still trying to rescue this.'

'Because it has been two years, ninety-eight days - and how many minutes are we talking about by now?'

'Add another five, maybe ten.'

'Even so, a fucking foot.'

'So I'm telling her how this is a high crime area and she's got to have seen the odd unpleasant sight every now and again working for Looner, and she is calming down. She's even beginning to see the funny side which is where the Professor and his Mate are helping out because now the Professor's haring out of there, bat out of hell time and his Mate's being sick and with them being so flaky it's starting to put a bit of steel back in her.'

Morrissey pauses.

'Until.'

'There's more?'

'A lot more.'

'Another foot?'

'Same foot. But something we hadn't seen before. Yorkie started to drag it away, well, he didn't know it was a foot did he, it could be a big bone for all he knew.'

'It is a bone, sort of, there's bones in feet.'

'But up to now it's been one side up.'

'Which side?'

'Doesn't matter which fucking side, the point is now it's the other side up and now Leanne's seen something, just by the ankle.'

'That's another bone too, the ankle.'

'A tattoo.'

Diesel pauses.

'What sort of tattoo?'

'A name.'

'His name?'

'Whose?'

'The guy - the foot.'

'Diesel, people do not put their own names on their foot, they put other people's names or their Mum.'

'So what name did he put there?'

'Why do you think it was a bloke?'

'Wasn't it?'

'Well, yeah it was, but he'd chosen a football team.'

'Which one?'

'Sunderland.'

And now Diesel's eyes widen.

'Oh fuck.'

Morrissey nods as Diesel keeps staring at him.

'It's Billy, isn't it?'

Morrissey nods.

'Billy as in Leanne's cousin?'

Morrissey nods again.

'It's Billy's foot.'

Diesel exhales, troubled now.

'That's not an easy one, Morrissey. I mean, you've always had a gob on you the size of just about any fucking tunnel you care to mention but this one is going to stretch even you a bit.'

Diesel hunches forward, intrigued, as Morrissey stares at him.

'How do you get into some top totty's knickers when all the time she's got her own cousin's foot looking at her, well, not looking, feet don't look, but you know what I mean.'

Morrissey keeps staring back at him.

'Is that it?'

'What?'

'Is that all that's running through your tiny fucking mind?'

Suddenly, from behind, there's an explosion. Another of Slippery's mates has just set fire to the stage and it's ignited a fake gas lamp that's been keeping all those old docks collectables and curios company.

But Morrissey's still staring at an uncomprehending Diesel.

'I'm telling you all about this face we know who seems to have become detached from his fucking foot, and all you can think about is my shag?'

Diesel nods back.

'Yeah.'

2. GUN-METAL GREY

An hour later the bar's a smoking ruin, and it's all down to Slippery and a leopard skin thong. Slippery himself, the stripper and her two tom mates are now in the nearest nick which these days is in Ely which isn't near at all.

Morrissey's not in the pub now either, no one is apart from a few fire boys, hosing down, making safe. Morrissey's in Looner's office trying to explain, via a strictly censored version of everything he told Diesel, how he came across a severed limb belonging to one of the fat fuck's employees.

'Billy?'

Looner repeats himself, blinking all the while.

'Billy as in?'

Looner gestures across the office towards Leanne, now in tight white jeans and an even tighter red top, trying to look like in sudden shock at all she's hearing, actually looking at Morrissey's trim arse, then at the walking piece of whale meat that's Looner and beginning to wonder whether she didn't maybe over-react just a bit back in that Shogun?

But Looner's thinking something else and what he's thinking he doesn't like, although Looner doesn't actually like a lot of things. He doesn't like the people he grew up with, including Morrissey. He doesn't like the neighbourhood that raised him and which he still calls home. He doesn't like what he has to do each day to earn his daily crust. But all that's fitting somehow, as no one he grew up with, no one from his neighbourhood, and no one who helps him out in earning that crust, could give a flying fuck about him either. If he hadn't made a small fortune over the years employing most of his old acquaintances along the way, no one would even piss on him if he started to smoke.

But he has made that small fortune and he does employ a lot of faces and so, and shagging his girlfriend aside, that does tend to make people keep up at least the pretence of a grudging respect.

'Why's someone chopping bits off Billy?'

Looner looks down from his first-floor office onto a collection of portacabins tucked into a rat run of railway arches, his business empire spread out below. One portacabin for this, one for that, and some for the other, Leanne having been known to use a fair few in her time.

There's also a paint shed at one end, formerly used for cut and shunt jobs for the dodgier dealers who used to line City Road. That market collapsed but the paint shed remained, now performing a much more useful function than blowing over old Transits because the pulleys are just the right height to suspend bodies which need to be hit, making that rusty old paint shed a shortcut to answers, and it's where the Professor and his Mate are right now.

Looner opens the door to his office, and now the Professor can be heard yelling his head off. His Mate's not making a sound, he's got low BP and being suspended like that is making his erratic blood supply loop around his body in fits and starts and he's already starting to lapse into what looks like the first of a series of convulsions.

'It's a message.'

Looner clatters down the metal staircase towards the paint shed, another of the faces from the firm, Tonto, talking ten to the dozen all the while. Tonto's a DVD buff, working his way, more or less alphabetically, through the shelves of a large repo store that's just opened up over in Grangetown. He's already done A to H which means G is very much in recent memory.

'What is?'

From the paint shed, more yells sound from the Professor along, now, with gurgles from his Mate.

'Like in The Godfather.'

'What the fuck's he talking about?'

'The horse's head in the bed.'

Looner's not exactly film literate, or any sort of literate, so this is sounding like serious double Dutch to him.

'What the fuck has a horse's head in someone's fucking bed got to do with Billy's foot in a Chinese fucking lantern?'

'It's the same thing.'

By now they're at the door of the paint shed.

'Well, apart from that being a head, and this being a foot, and that being in a bed, and this being in a Chinese lantern.'

Looner opens the door, staring back at Tonto all the while.

'Someone's trying to tell us something.'

Looner turns, grim, towards the Professor.

'Someone's going to do more than fucking try.'

Looner hits a button on the wall and the Professor shoots skyward, the problem being he's a tall sort of fuck and his head cannons against a metal girder running the length of the roof. That knocks him out and with his Mate already near-comatose on account of his failing blood pressure everyone's got to wait twenty minutes for the dazed Professor to come round by which time Looner's in even more of a mood.

'What were you doing with my driver's foot?'

Looner's face is now inches from the Professor who's blinking which is the good news because it means his eyes are open again. Nothing's coming from his Mate who's turned a strange sort of yellow, a half-interesting colour on a wall or a ceiling, but none too healthy on a human being.

'We didn't know it was his foot.'

Looner stares, stumped by that one.

'We just thought it was some rubbish.'

Looner keeps staring.

'Well it's not much use to Billy now, wherever he is, but I still wouldn't call his foot a piece of fucking refuse.'

The Professor's shaking his head, trying to get himself back under some sort of control, but it's not easy when he's seeing the world upside down.

'So you picked up this foot?'

'We didn't pick it up.'

'And you said to your Mate, oh look, it's raining fucking feet - should he be that colour?

The second bit's Looner breaking off, not Looner paraphrasing any previous conversation to which he actually wasn't any sort of part and now Diesel's eyeing him too.

'He's all yellow.'

Morrissey shakes his head.

'That's browner than yellow.'

Morrissey casts round for inspiration.

'That's more ochre - or taupe.'

'What the fuck's taupe?'

'For fuck's sake!'

Looner glares at them, this is no time to be debating colour charts.

'We found it in a skip.'

Looner looks back at the Professor.

'Everyday sort of sight I suppose, someone's foot in a fucking skip.'

'Chang's doing a refit.'

Which is a new element in the story and for a moment it's overload time. Looner still can't get his head around rubbish which turns out to be a foot so he definitely can't take in this one.

'Chang?'

The Professor nods back, or maybe it's an involuntary spasm

'What the fuck would Chang have Billy's fucking foot?'

'He was chucking all these lanterns out, the skip was full of them and that's why we didn't know it was a foot, 'cos it was in a lantern, well, in a bag in a lantern, so we didn't see it, not till it fell out, and anyway we were looking at – '

Then the Professor stops as he stares at a now-shifty-looking Morrissey, alarm bells ringing even in his weakened state, visions of Phil The Travelling Greek swimming before his now-panicked eyes.

But Looner doesn't even notice because now the world really is beginning to turn on its axis.

'Billy's foot was in one of Chang's skips?'

Diesel chips in, trying to be helpful.

'He might have had some kind of accident I suppose.'

'What, Billy got his foot chopped off and thought, well, no need for that anymore, so he lobs it in one of Chang's skips?'

The low gurgles from the Professor's Mate are now turning into strangled mumbles. Much more of this inverted existence and he's going to be off anything down under for life.

Tonto cuts across again.

'I told you, it's a message. Like the horse's –'

Which is as far as the exile from Planet Hollywood gets. Looner swings the side of the bag that still holds Billy's foot against his head which smashes, in turn, against a big purple lever, a large sign above it reading, Do Not Touch, and it reads Do Not Touch because it activates the paint spray process. In the old days that paint spray process took various shapes and sizes of sheet metal panels through a cycle of applications that, first, under-coated them and then rust-proofed them before sending them out into the world in a not particularly fetching shade of gun-metal grey.

Today there aren't any panels to spray, just the Professor and his Mate and now the Professor suddenly starts screaming blue murder because he does not want to be sent back out into the world in a not particularly fetching shade of gun-metal grey, let alone being under-coated and rust-proofed first.

Looner doesn't give a fuck. All that's on his mind is a Chinese business acquaintance and his possible involvement in a plot to remove bits from one of his employees which, given certain recent events is striking Looner as very definitely, and most decidedly, iffy with a capital fucking F.

'Looner!'

But then the Professor stops as the undercoat hits his lungs which is rule number one if you ever find yourself on the wrong end of an industrial paint sprayer. Try, at all times, to keep your gob shut.

'Looner!'

A strangled moan sounds as Looner strides away, suggesting the Professor really wasn't learning the lesson.

3. LOONER'S COUSIN'S RUBY WEDDING

Chang's arse is surprisingly hairy for a man of Oriental extraction. A smooth body, largely devoid, would have been Morrissey's admittedly-cliched expectation, but Cha
ng's covered in the stuff.

Right now it's in full view too as he's lying on top of a waitress in the kitchen of his upmarket diner, a bijou little place just a few steps away from Morrissey's old flat but a world away in every other sense. The old names on the even older wharves might still be there, *St John's, The Sun and Swan, Olivers and the Orient*. Echoes of a famous trading past still maintain a ghostly presence, the old alleyways there too and some of the old boozers do still ply their trade. But Chang's restaurant very much caters for a new clientele and he's doing well too. No wonder he's bobbing away, not a care in the world, with an arse that's definitely on the hirsute side.

But it stops bobbing pretty quickly when Looner puts a gun to one temple and Tonto puts a gun to the other, although it does give one last, almost involuntary, bob when an unsure Diesel, wanting to get in on the action but unsure how, rams his gun right up Chang's arse, which doesn't please Looner one little bit and isn't tickling Chang's fancy much either.

'What the fuck did you do that for?'

Diesel stares back, aggrieved.

'Where else was I supposed to put it?'

The door opens behind and, Fomo, Chang's head waiter and general jack of all trades, walks in, stopping as he does so. His boss pumping the latest recruit from the land of the temps, fair enough. Par for the course, to borrow a foodie phrase. Fomo's been known to cop for the odd bit of itinerant himself when he's not obsessing over his all more all-consuming passion which is Persian whites and long-haired tabbies. But his boss, diverted from his habitual leisure pursuit by a piece of hot metal inserted in his surprisingly hairy anus, is something else and he's just about to turn right around and head back out again when Morrissey grabs him.

Which is when Chang, finally, finds his voice.

'What the fuck's going on, Looner?'

But Looner's still eyeing Diesel and the gun which is putting Looner off his stroke and it's not going to do much for Chang either, Looner's not going to get answers with his main suspect distracted by a shooter in the rear passage. There are aids to concentration and distractions, and right now Diesel's well and truly providing the latter.

'Take that out of there.'

Morrissey and Fomo both wince as Diesel does so, using as little finesse as the original insertion and to the accompaniment of a loud and painful-sounding pop. For a moment, as the minor explosion sounds, it's as if Diesel has, albeit accidentally, fired one up him and if the Chinaman's arse wasn't so tightly clenched right now because he's, metaphorically speaking, shitting himself there'd be nothing metaphorical about it at all.

'And wash it.'

'What?'

'We swap these shooters all the time. I'm not picking that thing and honking Chang's arse every time I want to take a pop at someone.'

Diesel, with increasingly bad grace, heads for the nearest sink. Underneath the still-rigid Chang, the temp starts to whimper. Her English isn't too good, and she doesn't know what the fuck's going on here. Chang's English is perfect and neither does he.

But Looner's still staring at Diesel.

'And don't put it near any food preparation areas either, my cousin's got her ruby wedding here Sunday.'

Looner waves his gun around the kitchen, taking in the wires hanging from the ceiling and the sacks of sand and cement on the floor, all of which is a welcome relief for Chang who was getting very nervous about it being pressed to his temple.

'And you'd better be fucking ready too.'

Fomo, still being held by Morrissey, cuts in.

'The builders are on a bonus. Complete on schedule, they're on time and a half.'

'More money than fucking sense.'

Which is when Chang cuts in, wanting to know, and for the second time of asking -

'What the flying fuck is going on?'

Behind, Diesel's heading for a standpipe just outside the rear door as Looner turns back to Chang.

'What's going on? Well, let's see.'

Looner starts ticking off items with his fingers, shopping list-style, which is something of a dangerous tactic seeing as how he's still got a loaded gun between at least two of those gesticulating digits. Morrissey and the rest of the entourage start ducking and diving every time the nozzle points their way. Chang follows suit only his ducks and dives are turning into thrusts, and his new girlfriend is now looking up at him in something approaching wonder. From now till the day she dies she's going to be telling all her nephews and nieces back home about this crazy little fucker who didn't even let a gun to each temple, not to mention one newly extricated from his arse, take his mind off humping her.

'I've just spent the last two weeks waging war on assorted Itis, Erics and Frogs, trying to find my stuff.'

'Not to mention –'

Diesel cuts in from the open door, gesturing with his gun hand skywards, letting off an inadvertent shot as he does so. On the table, Chang now clenches those buttocks even harder than he clenched them following the previous introduction of six inches of cold steel. Which is when his new girlfriend clenches too and now Chang's eyes are really beginning to bulge, and from now till the day he dies, which at the moment is looking pretty fucking imminent, Chang's going to be telling the whole of his extended family all about this wacko waitress who didn't even let three gangsters and a waving Luger belonging to Looner distract her from her internal grip on Chang's rapidly deflating rod.

Looner nods back, his eyes now misting over.

'Not to mention –'

Looner's gun gestures skywards too and now there's a second bang as Looner inadvertently fires one off as well, before he turns back to the sweating Chang.

'And now I'm wondering whether all that has been so much wasted fucking effort.'

Looner pushes his face close to Chang's, stopping, seemingly surprised to find the girl still there as well, although where she could go with Chang, two guns and two heavies in close attendance fuck alone knows.

'Seeing as how all the time you've been chopping bits off my fucking employees.'

Looner takes Billy's foot out of its bag and plonks it down at a safe distance from any of the preparation tables, but inches from a now-gasping Chang's head.

'What's that?'

Which in one sense is a pretty stupid question, but in the circumstances, you'd really have to be unreasonable to rub it in.

'A kangaroo.'

But a sulky Diesel, still by the door, is in no mood to be reasonable at all. He's scraping and digging and doing his best, but there's still deposits of what looks suspiciously like shit inside the barrel which even the crafty volley he fired off a moment before hasn't shifted.

'Whose is it?'

Chang, finally getting his brain more into gear, is beginning to ask at least halfway sensible questions.

'Billy's'

Looner nods down at him again.

'As in my driver, Billy.'

Then Looner stops, a new thought striking him.

'As in my one-fucking-legged driver, Billy.'

And Looner's cars are mainly manual too, a fact not lost on Diesel who's still scraping shit out of the gun but who now points that out.

But Tonto, still pressing his shooter to Chang's left temple, shakes his head.

'There's the purple Shogun.'

'That's automatic too.'

'Yeah, but it's got those paddle things on the steering wheel.'

Diesel looks over at Billy's foot, a new thought striking him as Looner stares at them both.

'Which one is it anyway? Right or left?'

'What the fuck difference does that make?'

'You can drive an automatic if you've still got your right foot but he's going to be a bit fucked if it's the left.'

'He's going to be a bit fucked anyway if we can't find the rest of him.'

'Will you two shut the fuck up!'

Looner turns back to Chang again.

'Yes, Billy. Billy of the two feet, now one. And –'

Looner leans closer, the girl whimpering as he does so, Chang tensing again.

'It was in one of your fucking skips.'

'As well?'

'What?'

'As fucking well?'

Looner, Diesel, Morrissey, and Tonto all stare at Chang, who's now removing himself from his traumatised help and is standing up, anger pulsing blood across his pounding forehead, and even Looner's taking a half-step back which is something seeing as how Chang's naked with a rapidly diminishing erection and really doesn't look all that threatening

'Open the freezer.'

'What?'

'Open the fucking freezer.'

From the rear door, Diesel moves across but Looner, health matters, cousin, upcoming ruby wedding, on the big man's mind, signals to Morrissey to do it instead.

Morrissey opens the freezer, staring as he sees a human finger sitting on the top shelf. If fingers sit that is. Lie, maybe. Squat. Perch. But whatever they do, however they sit, lie, squat or perch, what's staring back at him, although they don't stare either, is very definitely a finger.

'Now open the fridge.'

Not even waiting for a signal from Looner this time, Morrissey does, and there it is next to some lentils and green seaweed, another finger which could be a sister or brother to the other one, it's difficult to tell when they're not attached.

Chang climbs down from the preparation table, the girl still laid out on top, still prone, just staring at the ceiling.

'One of the chippies found the first one in his plate of ribs last night. I thought he was just after a freebie. Then this posh tart from Whitchurch, she finds the other one in her salad.'

Still by the fridge, Morrissey looks at him puzzled, really can't work that one out, but Fomo cuts in and explains.

'Pak Choi, thickly sliced.'

Morrissey nods.

Now he's got it.

'It was hidden underneath one of the slices, not very well-hidden mind you, she found it pretty fucking quick once she started moving it around.'

Chang's cock's bobbing up and down now as he jabs the air with his finger, the diminutive Chinaman now every bit as agitated as Looner.

'I had to put the chippie on double time to stop him going to the Environmental Health. I've had to give the posh totty free dim fucking sum for life.'

Chang's cock bobs some more.

'What the fuck's going on?'

4. A FAT PATHETIC FUCK

Chang's cock is still bobbing although it is now covered by twenty-six vertical inches of denim. And it's bobbing because those small legs of his are trying to keep up with Looner's moon-sized strides as he bolts from his Shogun, vaults a chain link fence, rounds the newly pointed corner of a brand-new redbrick links mews and comes out into a communal Square flanked by a whole raft of identical redbrick links mews houses.

Where even Looner, a man on a mission right now, has to pause at the sight before him because all he can see is dripping, blood-red flesh hanging from milk-white bones, and as far as the eye can see cops gorging on it all.

But there's only one copper Looner's interested in right now and he's just seen him, sporting a poncy chef's hat, a blue apron covering his gut and a big smile on his gob and no wonder. Mac's annual barbie is going down a storm, his fencing business, as in goods for resale, not picket, also going down a storm with most of his colleagues, all of whose houses and flats are sporting at least one item of Mac's knockoffs.

Mac's also smiling because he's currently got a watery eye on a new, female black recruit, native of the old Cardiff docks so the story down their home nick has it, but who's going to hold it against her with a pair of bangers like that, and he's thinking that maybe her telling him he's a fat pathetic fuck with zero chance of even sniffing her knicks is some street-speak way of saying she's interested.

Then his smile wipes as he clocks Looner and the now-trousered Chang, that smile wiping completely as Diesel takes one arm, Tonto takes the other and Morrissey grabs a can of lighter fuel from the side of the barbie. Then they all do a quick reverse trip back towards the house and a closed patio door which presents a temporary obstacle but strictly temporary as Looner picks up a metal chair and flings it at the glass which shatters into a million pieces onto a gold and purple shagpile inside.

Across the communal Square, Mrs Mac, chatting to the new ACC, doesn't see a thing and hears even less above the rhythmic gnawing of molars. That new, female, black recruit sees it though and she hears Mac's protests too. And now Carmel's frowning.

Because this is sort of the plan.

Just not exactly the plan.

Which could be a necessary and prudent variation.

Or a fucking great cock-up.

'Talk to me, Mac.'

Everyone's now up in the bathroom, but Mac's not really taking in anything Looner's saying. Right now he's more worried about the lighter fuel being sprayed all over his crotch by Tonto. Then Mac stares, as in really stares, at a lighter that now appears in Tonto's hand, at a low blue flame that starts to blaze steadily from the business end as Tonto wafts it backwards and forwards over Mac's soaked, and now pungent-smelling groin.

'What the fuck?'

That's Carmel, coming in from outside to investigate, and she's grabbed by Diesel who cops a quick feel of her left tit at the same time as Looner repeats the question of the moment.

'Talk to me.'

'What the fuck do you mean, talk to me?'

By the door, Carmel cuts in.

'Stop feeling my tits.'

A shifty Diesel shuffles his feet.

'I'm not.'

'For fuck's sake!'

Diesel ducks as Looner takes a swing at his head with the nearest thing to hand, in this case a wall-mounted towel rail, wall mounted no longer, Looner not wanting any more distractions right now.

'Looner!'

Mac couldn't give a flying fuck about Carmel's tits, although he has fantasised about them on more than one occasion. All he can smell is lighter fuel, all he can see is a naked flame in imminent danger of incinerating his nuts and all he wants are a few fucking answers.

Which, coincidentally, and as he now tells his partner in crime, is what Looner wants too.

'For starters.'

Looner nods at him.

'Why was Billy's foot in one of Chang's skips?'

Mac blinks.

'Billy?'

Looner nods again.

'Billy the wanker who works for you?'

Looner keeps nodding, albeit qualifying that as he does so in the interests of the strictest accuracy.

'Billy the one-fucking-legged wanker who works for me.'

Chang leans forward, getting in on the action now too.

'And why was his finger in one of my plates of ribs?'

Looner leans closer still in turn.

'And his other finger in a pile of dim – fucking - sum?'

'Salad.'

From across the room, Tonto cuts in, in the interests of total accuracy again.

'And we don't actually know it was Billy's finger. I mean, the foot's a cert, fair enough, the chances of anyone else round here having Sunderland tattooed on the ankle, which has to be a million to one.'

Looner stares at him in disbelief again.

'So it's a complete fucking coincidence is it? There's more than one face round here losing bits of their fucking body and getting them planted in and around Chang's?'

'I'm just saying –'

'Don't.'

'It could be a smokescreen. Like in The Godfather.'

Tonto's head now makes a clunking sound as it hits the bathroom wall. But Mac is staring back at Looner.

'So let me get this straight. You've just turned me into a walking, talking, fucking, incendiary device because a foot and two fingers belonging to some local loser have turned up in Chang's?'

Looner nods.

'Are you off your fucking trolley?'

But then there's a diversion in the form of a loud scream from out in the communal Square. Mrs Mac, Christian name Verity, Latin root, veritas, meaning truth which is pretty ironic given her choice of hubby and his lifestyle, not to mention his various and dubious proclivities, is staring at the barbie.

And she's staring at the barbie because in among the steaks and sausages and chops is another item that sort of passes muster on one level with it being meat of a kind, but not on any other because no one, not even a whole posse of rabidly ravenous coppers are going to even think about stuffing it down their gullets.

Another foot.

No tattoo this time.

But very definitely another foot.

Mrs Mac starts to wail, and she isn't going to stop till that thing's off her barbie and maybe not even then. Dozens of coppers begin to crowd round, beginning to register, even after quaffing several dozens of cans of freebie lager, that this really isn't right.

Upstairs, a very jumpy Looner, Chang and Mac are all now looking at each other, three sets of eyes narrowing in dark, mutual suspicion all the while, which is when Tonto breaks in again, albeit a bit more woozily this time.

'This is just like The Godfather too.'

Stubborn to the fucking end.

'Tonto, shut the fuck up.'

'Was it The Godfather?'

Chang's still eyeballing Mac, who's still eyeballing Looner, who's still eyeballing Chang

'I said, shut the fuck up!'

Eyes swivel in sockets as Chang, Looner and Mac don't let each other out of sight, a bloodbath about to kick off.

'The bit when what's-his-face.'

'For fuck's sake!'

'Thinks he's been set up by what's his name.'

'That is fucking it!'

'And they all start shooting each other.'

'Fucking ace idea!'

Looner takes his Luger out of his pocket

'When all the time it's someone else who's set them up instead.'

Looner pauses at that, Chang pauses now too, but Mac's still eyeballing them, partly because of all that lager, but mainly because he's a stupid fuck.

Looner looks back at Tonto.

'Say that again.'

'Was it The Godfather?'

'Not all of it you stupid twat. That last bit.'

Chang cuts in too.

'Just the last fucking sentence.'

And Tonto says it again.

And this time even Mac gets it.

And now Morrissey's beginning to experience the same sinking feeling as Carmel those few moments before.

Because this was all going so well, and now all of a sudden it isn't.

5. SEVERED FEET AND FINGERS

A few minutes later a line of Shoguns scream to a halt outside Looner's portacabin empire.

Looner's ranted all the way over from Mac's. He's still ranting all the way across the concrete yard and up the metal stairs, ignoring the two figures still suspended on pulleys outside the paint shed which would normally excite some sort of comment, but right now the Professor and his Mate aren't even getting a second glance.

Behind Chang, Looner and Big Mac, the second string of arrivals comprising Fomo, Morrissey and Carmel exit another of Looner's Shoguns, Morrissey pausing as he passes another of Looner's employees, Kim, 20's, thin, mixed race, half-Spanish, half-Ghanian.

For a moment there's a look and Morrissey can see that new sinking feeling reflected in her eyes now too.

Up in Looner's office, three pairs of eyes are now staring at two severed feet and two fingers on Looner's desk.

'Possibility number –'

Looner breaks off, having been listing options all the way over from Mac's too.

'What number is this?'

'Does it fucking matter?'

'None of us did for Billy.'

Looner looks at Chang who looks back at Mac.

'Someone's just trying to make it look like one of us did for Billy.'

Mac looks back at Looner and Chang.

'Which means someone's trying to fuck us over.'

Looner looks back at them all

'Set dog against fucking dog.'

Then Looner, Mac and Chang all look towards the door.

Outside, at the bottom of the metal stairs, looking across at the still-suspended Professor and his Mate, but not seeing them either, Morrissey, Fomo and Carmel are in a huddle. Behind Morrissey is a telescope, but no one needs any help in the vision stakes right now, extended or otherwise. Everything's all too crystal clear.

'This is a fuck-up.'

Carmel nods.

'A complete and total arse.'

Fomo nods too.

'Now what are we going to do?'

But Morrissey doesn't reply because he can't. His mind's working overtime and going absolutely nowhere.

Which is when Looner, Mac and Chang appear at the top of the stairs. And the Professor still isn't getting a look in or his Mate despite the fact the whole of their upper bodies are now gun-metal grey. The only thing Looner, Mac and Chang are looking at are the hapless bunch of losers and hangers-on milling at the foot of those stairs.

Morrissey, Fomo and Carmel are looking anywhere other than up at the watching trio, but they know those three pairs of narrowed eyes are burning down into them anyway.

And they really don't need to be told, even though Fomo mutters it anyway, that they are now well and truly, one hundred and ten per cent, in the flying fucking shit.

PART TWO

'Sundry Prayers, Praises and Professions of Obedience'

Psalms, 1119

One Month Earlier

6. SADDEST SIGHT IN CHRISTENDOM

One month. Four weeks. Six hundred and seventy-two hours. Doesn't matter how you slice it, that short time ago Morrissey had no idea any of this was going to happen. If he had he'd never have walked out of that nick, he'd still be clinging to the bars of that cell like there was no tomorrow. Which given how the next month panned out, might just be the case.

It's called the walk of life. Along the echoing corridors, up the stairs, past the suicide nets, the open cell doors, different faces inside, but all delivering the same message right now, all variations on the one single theme.

'Give her one, Morrissey.'

'A long, slow screw.'

'Or a quick one.'

But it doesn't really matter what they're saying, it's all a blur because Morrissey's floating on air. A two-stretch at the age of twenty-seven has taken him perilously close to the big three-zero and he hasn't exactly made a brilliant fist of all the things he'd planned to do by that not-so-little milestone. But now Morrissey's got a chance to do at least some of them, and not even the sad old sicko of a screw who can't resist the sour; 'See you soon, Morrissey' can dampen his spirits right now.

Then light floods the corridor. What sounds like an angel singing a Requiem Mass sounds from outside. It may only be a crappy song on a shitty radio playing from a builder's van parked across the street, but to Morrissey, it's the sweetest sound on God's earth right now. Moving outside the gates, Morrissey takes a deep breath of his first draught of fresh air from the sweet outside even if it is only a gob-full of industrial effluent belched from a passing wagon. Then he looks out on the saddest sight in Christendom, or at least the saddest sight if you're a con who's just become an ex-con.

An empty carpark.

Which is the sight greeting Morrissey right now.
Empty, because there's no one there.

Five minutes later and Morrissey's in a phone box, the airtime contract on his mobile having unaccountably expired in the last couple of years. The phone in front of him needs a card and Morrissey hasn't got one, but that's not why he's standing in that kiosk right now doing an impersonation of a man who's turned to stone. Morrissey's staring into space, his fingers doing no walking and his mouth doing no talking, because that carpark's told him all he needs to know so what's the fucking point?

Outside the phone box, all hell's breaking loose which is why that van's there. The street's being dug up for the third time in a fortnight because all the nearby residents are complaining about the smell from the drains. And this one face ache in particular has really been giving the foreman grief about it, because he can't sleep, can't eat, can't breathe even and it's all their fault, if they'd done their job properly in the first place when they'd laid those pipes etc etc etc.

But the foreman's switched off. He's dreaming about his dingy which is moored a few miles down the coast, just off Barry and a run he's going to make, a few miles further down that self-same coast to visit this fifty-something he met three weeks ago when he was shopping in the Hayes and who might be knocking on but is perfectly preserved and she's been giving off all the right signals too once he'd told her he was this big shot off the tankers.

One ear on the still-complaining punter, his mind much more on the blonde and the contents of her admittedly ample knickers, he hits the water main with his digger. Along the way he inadvertently identifies the problem too, because the main's got raw sewage in there which seeped in after a flash flood the previous week.

Now the water's been released you can literally smell the problem and the complaining face ache can smell it better than most because that first full blast of contaminated shit has just blown him clean off his feet. He'd been told to keep his distance and wear a hard hat if he wanted to stand that close, so fuck him is the foreman's opinion.

Which is when he sees him. A lone figure standing in a nearby phone box, oblivious so it seems to the evil-smelling sludge currently pounding down on its roof from the sky.

The foreman watches as the lone figure inside still doesn't move. Then he realises he isn't actually talking, in fact he hasn't even got the phone in his hand, is just staring into space.

And now the foreman's trying to work out what it is that's so pressing on his mind to drive from it the fact you're slowly being buried in a fast-expanding sea of liquid shit.

7. A HALF-EMPTY LAGER CAN

One hour later, Morrissey's in a high-speed train, the carriage shaking as another high-speed carriage flashes past in the opposite direction.

And suddenly, back before his eyes, there he is.

Anti-Anti.

Anti-Anti was one of Morrissey's old mates, with the emphasis on the was. Walking home one night, he decides to take a shortcut along a railway line. A train approaches and he moves to one side which is when another train approaches from the opposite direction.

Which is no sweat in Anti-Anti's book, there's plenty of room between two passing trains, let's face it they never collide when they shoot past each other do they? So he moves to the middle.

Then Anti-Anti starts to grin as the two trains get closer. Maybe he's even going to cop a bit of extra cabaret watching a few first-class punters spill their complimentary coffees all over their suits when they see his laughing mug grinning in at them from outside.

It's probably the onset of that first rush of wind that gives Anti-Anti the first glimmer of a suspicion that this is a really bad idea. Or maybe he never feels it, maybe he's too busy contorting his face into that weird grimace his little nephew always cracks up at whenever he calls round to cadge some blow, and which more than makes up for having to put up with his brother's wife who's always cursed her bad fortune in marrying into a family with so many losers and hangers-on.

Oddly enough, years later, she's actually going to break down when she takes Anti-Anti's nephew, who's long forgotten his funny Uncle, to a small town in Andalucía and walks past a local butcher's shop, only to stop as she sees what looks like a small fountain of blood dripping from freshly slaughtered meat on a pristine marble slab.

They tried keeping most of the details from the family but there was the inevitable inquest, so some stuff had to come out. So she knows Anti-Anti was literally swept up in the buffeting maelstrom the two passing trains created as they sped past each other, before being tossed backwards and forwards like some demented, human ping-pong ball. Only ping-pong balls stay pretty well white and intact no matter how many times you hit them. By the time the slipstream from those two trains had batted Anti-Anti back and forth in a space no more than two metres wide he looked like he'd been turned inside out which, in one sense he had. They found most of his internal organs spattered on the windows which meant the first-class punters in their suits did spill their complimentary coffees, but that wasn't because of Anti-Anti grinning in at them.

And now, as Morrissey looks out on roughly that same patch of the track he suddenly sees a figure waving at him from a field. It's a kid on a man's shoulders and the man's the same age as Anti-Anti he has the same idiotic grin on his face as well. And Morrissey knows it's not Anti-Anti and he knows what happens next is one of those tricks of the light, but just before the train ploughs out of sight and leaves them behind, the man looks straight at Morrissey and points his thumb down towards the ground, as if he's sending him a silent message.

Turn back, Morrissey.

Don't do this.

Don't go there.

Which is when a voice breaks in from behind.

'Yeah, I'm on my way there now.'

Morrissey half-turns, then stops as he sees a man looking at a laptop, mobile pressed to his ear, a street map open on the screen in front of him featuring Morrissey's home manor. And for a moment Morrissey wonders if his luck's about to turn at last. Maybe this is his long-lost cousin, who emigrated down under years before, come back to distribute his new-found wealth amongst a family who've never been out of his thoughts from the day he left home shores.

'Don't say it like that.'

Laptop man begins swigging from a can of lager, his mobile, which even Morrissey can now see is state of the art, still clamped to his ear.

'They've cleared all the old shit out from them shitty old docks.'

Laptop man's lager wobbles as the train passes over a set of points, and Morrissey reaches out, saves it from falling, but he doesn't even acknowledge Morrissey's intervention, let alone invite him to have a slurp of the amber nectar by way of thanks, just keeps on with his call.

'And most of the low-life losers who used to live there.'

Then everything goes as black as Morrissey's dashed hopes as the train heads into a tunnel. For a few seconds, the lights cut, and he loses reception.

'Fuck.'

That's Laptop man. And in the family carriage too. Then the lights come on again as the train careers out of the tunnel into daylight once more.

'About fucking time.'

Laptop man begins punching buttons on his mobile only to stop dead, a puzzle confronting him, because now he's trying to resume his call via a lager-can, now half-empty, which had been rescued from oblivion a moment or so before by some admittedly-quick-thinking lowlife, and his fancy state-of-the-art mobile is nowhere to be seen.

8. FORTY RED, WHITE, AND BLUE SHOESTRINGS

Ten minutes later the train pulls into Cardiff Central and now Morrissey really feels as if he's landed in some sort of alternative universe where nothing looks real and even less makes sense.

Two short years, Morrissey's been away.

And all because of a cock-up with a . . .

Never mind. Forget it, Morrissey doesn't want to even think about that. His old muckers in the slammer included some serious league villains. Days and nights were spent in cosy chats around the metaphorical fireplace comparing sentences and offences, and Morrissey was very much the cabaret turn once the full details of his own offence came to light, meaning some things never change.

But everything else in the world seems to have.

Morrissey stares out of the train window as they come to a halt overlooking a giant wheel. From inside, different coloured flares pump great plumes of coloured gas in all directions. Silver and gold tassels flutter around the outside. All it needed were forty red, white, and blue shoestrings for Morrissey to feel like he's going to be getting off in the middle of some bad sixties' song.

And that's just for starters. Coming out onto the concourse a few moments later the next thing he sees is a sculpture of two bronze figures locked in what seems to be animated debate. Then Morrissey turns to see a life-size galleon decorated with tapestries of maritime adventures from seven continents. He's going to find out later they're pieces of public art turning the gateway to his old stretch of homeland into a multi-million-pound redevelopment project, but all Morrissey knows for now is that it's a fuck of a change from the tart's boozer that used to stand on the corner by the newspaper kiosk that always used to run out by early afternoon. Of newspapers that is. Never tarts.

Then Morrissey sees a rickshaw. And a few yards away where the dossers used to try and fleece the exiting commuters, he sees a rickshaw park. Morrissey does a slow three-sixty, staring all the while.

Has he taken a wrong turn or something? Where's he just landed for fuck's sake?

Behind Morrissey, Laptop man's also emerging from inside the station and now he's eyeing him, suspicious, mobile and lager-can finally connecting. Then he looks over at a hovering copper who Morrissey expects to be dressed in a sailor suit seeing as how this is all so Alice-in-fucking-Wonderland and, in no wish to be caught in possession of a hot mobile less than three hours after being sprung from stir, Morrissey moves quickly away, no real idea in which direction he's travelling given the way all the old landmarks seem to have disappeared.

But then a toot on a nearby horn cuts across the rickshaws, and the water taxis, and the sculptures, and the giant-coloured wheel, and the life-size galleon, and makes Morrissey feel, for the first time in the last thirty seconds, that maybe, just maybe, there may still be some small part of a foreign field where Morrissey might still just have a home.

A jet-black hearse careers towards him and Laptop man tears his reluctant eyes away from the hovering copper as it comes to a halt by Morrissey. Maybe he's about to finger a soul wrestling with raw grief which just goes to show even pond life have feelings. Then he remembers all the state-of-the-art gadgets crammed into that little silver beauty he's just lost and starts looking at the copper again.

But by that time Morrissey's inside the hearse, which is pulling away like it's jet-propelled which, in a sense, it is. The fuel that powers it is a mixture of industrial vegetable oil, potato peelings and paraffin, which does fuck all for the ozone layer but gets away from boy racers at traffic lights like a crazed cheetah. It also boasts ace brakes too which is double handy given its driver's chief means of earning her crust.

But all that's for later. All Morrissey wants to know for now is what the fuck is going on?

Angel looks back at him

'What are you talking about?'

'This fucking place.'

'What about it?'

'Don't fuck me about Angel, where have I landed, Mars?'

'You haven't seen the half of it, Morrissey.'

Angel inclines her blonde curls across the street towards what used to be their favourite greasy spoon.

'That's Carini's old place, the old man's gone now and all his kids, and the new lot, you'd be hard put to find a waiter in there who don't look as if he's auditioning for the next fucking Bond.'

Angel shakes her head again, carving up a police car as she turns out onto the main feeder road down to the docks.

'And the nosh, Jesus. Go in for a bacon bap, you come out with something that looks like it belongs in an art gallery.'

Angel dabs the accelerator, a new hole opening up in the heavens above them.

'And the squirt shop that used to be above it, that is a fucking art gallery.'

Angel turns down onto Bute Street.

'Apart from that, it's much the same old, same old.'

Which is when out it comes. A question Morrissey didn't know he was about to ask. A question he'd promised himself all the way down from that evil-smelling phone box and that empty carpark he wouldn't ask.

'How's Kim?'

Angel hesitates, then looks back at him, knowing exactly what he's really asking.

'She don't want to know, Morrissey.'

Morrissey stares towards two tower blocks that still, despite the rickshaws and galleons, dominate the skyline.

'It's why she never came to see you when you were inside.'

Morrissey keeps staring, unseeing, at the pair of landmarks he used to call home.

'I tried, I really did.'

And Angel would have done, Morrissey knew that. She might drive a hearse propelled by waste products and have a very dodgy way of making the monthly rent, but she'd always had a heart of gold.

'So did Aidan.'

And so would he.

Angel, shrugs, helpless.

'But you know that sister of mine when her mind's made up.'

Morrissey just keeps staring out over the distant water.

'She just don't want to know.'

9. GERMANIC TOADS

An hour later and Morrissey's staring out of another window, this one eleven floors up.

Below, which is some relief at least, are the same sights he'd have seen before he left, a school, a grassy playground, an evangelical church, The Strangers Retreat, a children's centre, and a single piece of graffiti.

The council had obliterated all the others over the years with vandal-proof paint, but this one example of the street artist's craft had always survived untouched. It appeared one day as if by some strange act of sorcery, a large and perfect circle with five letters inside spelling, CREAM. No one ever saw who did it, and the name of the artist or vandal depending on your point of view, remained unknown. But for some reason the council workmen had always left it alone.

But then, as Morrissey looks down on it, he sees something else pulling up on a Square across what looks like a simple road, but is actually an unbridgeable divide between the haves and the very much have-nots. And have-not Morrissey keeps on looking.

Morrissey's always hated Porsches. Squat. Germanic toads, all of them. Efficient and ultra-reliable, yes, but where's the fun in a life without a little adventure? Give him Brit bangers and breakdowns any day. But now, and with escape in mind, Morrissey's beginning to appreciate the advantages of clockwork transport.

One minute later, Morrissey's down on the street. The Porsche driver's ferrying files from an office that used to be a canning factory because the sign on the front says so, although when Morrissey was growing up Ye Olde Canning Factory was plain and simple warehouse number thirty-three and no one went near. A new nameplate, a massive hike in rent and the punters started queueing. The only problem was access. The block's got a narrow, steep drive leading down from the street to the communal front door. But one man's problem as they say, is a chancer's opportunity.

Porsche boy finishes loading his files into his motor and now he's reversing back up the steep drive, but then he stops. And he stops because some fuck of a workman has only gone and left a dustbin smack bang in the middle of the shitting, fucking, twatting drive. That much Morrissey hears. The rest he doesn't because the bad-tempered Porsche boy has now picked up the offending large piece of black plastic and his voice is now muffled.

Morrissey's pulled this stunt a hundred times, and one hundred times out of a hundred the same rule applies. Take one wanker reversing up a drive, stop him at a newly installed dustbin, they'll curse the council, they'll shoot out of the car, they'll grab the bin, they'll move it out of the way, but they will never, ever, turn off the engine while they're doing all that.

Ninety times out of that hundred they never even close the driver's door which has to make this the easiest way to a carjacking in the history of the internal combustion engine in the opinion of the cop who taught Morrissey this particular trick in the first place.

And it's working a treat all over again.

'Bastards.'

That's Porsche boy, his back now to his dream motor, slamming the bin back down on the ground. Which is when he hears his engine rev behind him and now he starts to freeze. Of course, he's going to embroider this a bit when he retells the story later that night to his wife, lover, girlfriend, boyfriend, dog, whoever or whatever. He's certainly not going to say he kept his back turned all the time like he's doing now. When you drive a Porsche, there's always going to be a nagging suspicion you might be a touch lacking in the trouser department, so it's good to have a fund of war stories to counter the quick, downward look at the front of the Calvins when you flash your car keys across the bar.

Porsche boy remains frozen, his back still turned, as he hears the wheels begin to dig into the tarmac, the tyres spinning a little because Morrissey is a bit out of practice. Time was he could put a motor in gear, engage first, and be a hundred yards down the road, feathering the throttle as light as the proverbial feather, without the exhaust emitting a single burble. One time he'd actually turned the corner and was out of sight, leaving the poor sap with his back still turned, the bin still in hand, and having to explain to his insurers how his luxury, top-end motor had seemingly vanished into thin air. But this time Morrissey has made a sound and Porsche boy, finally, turns.

It's always amazed Morrissey what a smile can do. Give someone a cheery grin and it's a human thing, they smile back. It must be a reflex action or something, flash a grin and back it'll come, straight at you. It might be a little uncertain in certain circumstances admittedly, it might be the kind of smile that has a couple of questions puckering its corners like what the fuck is that total fucking stranger doing in my car? But that first grin does what it's always intended to do. It buys time.

And Porsche boy's a peach because now he's grinning back for fuck's sake. A bin by his handmade brogues, his motor driving away from him and he's still smiling and now Morrissey's shaking his head. Some people would say please and thank you when you hand them the blindfold and tell them to kneel. Just too nice for their own fucking good.

But then Morrissey puts him out of mind as he starts to relax, looks at the CD player, wondering what's on the stack system if cars still have stack systems, looks at the Satnav and wonders how it works, looks at the glove box and wondering if Porsche boy's got any jelly babies in there, yellow ones if he's in real luck, because Morrissey could do with a bit of sustenance for even the shortish journey he's got in mind right now down to the fence over in Gabalfa, time-honoured haunt of receivers for all sorts over the decades.

Then he starts to work out just why Porsche boy had that grin on his gob all the time Morrissey was heading away from him, and why, in all likelihood, he still has.

The first thing Morrissey knows, the nose on the Porsche dips. Morrissey's none too sure why, maybe he's still not massaging that throttle quite as smooth as he should be. Then it's like a great fist hits him, smack in the middle of his chest, pressing him back in his seat. And now the motor's decelerating and fast, only Morrissey hasn't even breathed heavy on the brakes. A second later and the whole motor's grinding to a complete halt which makes no sense at all because Morrissey still has leather to metal on the loud pedal and is still pumping away at it. And now Morrissey's thinking that if he had the front, and in a different world and time maybe he'd have had that in bucketfuls, he'd go back and ask Porsche boy how he can spend sixty grand or more on an upmarket motor and then let the fucking thing run out of petrol? And the gauge's reading full too which means it's not only human failure Morrissey's talking about here, but the dials are dodgy as well.

Which is when Morrissey starts to get a bad feeling, which is not a bad sort of feeling really, in fact it's quite a good sort of feeling in that he's right to have it, but it's not such a good feeling given what happens next.

For a moment there's silence. Then there's a weird sort of whooshing sound as if the motor's clearing its throat or something, and Morrissey's getting more and more uneasy. What is this, a Porsche or Christine's cousin for fuck's sake? He's half-expecting it to talk to him next which is another one of those good/bad feelings, good because yet again Morrissey is sort of spot on, but bad because he really doesn't want to be.

Morrissey tries the door. But the second he touches the handle, the locks hammer shut as deadlocks cut in. The whooshing sound growing louder. Then, and without any sort of warning, but then again what sort of warning would you get, a fierce jet of orange goo fires from the centre of the steering wheel covering Morrissey in what he'll later discover is a large dose of indelible dye.

'Fucking hell.'

Now Morrissey's beginning to seriously go off this test drive. If this is what's in store for prospective purchasers no wonder sales of these kind of motors have gone through the floor.

Then a voice cuts in.

'Stop.'

But stopping isn't the problem is it? Morrissey's stopped already, in fact he's well and truly stuck and going nowhere.

'Stop, thief.'

Which is the next bit that now blares from the onboard speakers and echoes up and down the street. But it's the next message Morrissey really does not want to hear.

'Call the police.'

Outside the car, which is now rocking wildly courtesy of one very panicky Morrissey, a few spectators are gathering and a couple of them are taking out their mobiles which means one or two of them may be about to act the good citizen and do just that, but more probably they just want a pic to flash round the boozer that night, meaning they're in for a double treat now.

A second burst of orange goo hits Morrissey. In something fast approaching real panic, Morrissey looks up, searching wildly for escape, sees the roof, and that's it! It's a fucking soft top! Thank you, Mr Porsche and your passion, for open top, wind in your hair sunshine motoring! All Morrissey's got to do now is open it!

Morrissey looks at the dash, and it's that typical Germanic efficiency again, God bless them, there's a roof symbol staring back at him and even an instruction underneath, Press to Open. Morrissey does so and gets another load of goo in his gob for his troubles and if Morrissey had any dosh in the world, he'd stake the lot he heard laughter coming from somewhere inside his mobile prison right now.

An electronic read-out suddenly appears below the original instruction to press *Malfunction due to unauthorised access*. In other words, a villain is behind the steering wheel and he isn't getting out that way. Only he fucking well is getting out because Morrissey's now grabbing the door handle which, despite the motor's sixty grand plus price tag, is plastic and he yanks at it, breaking it in two, meaning there's now a jagged bit on the end which is just what Morrissey's looking for as he digs it into the roof.

Down the street, those few spectators have decided they're definitely going to have more cabaret watching this rather than reporting it, so Morrissey's got a little time on his hands and he's not going to be needing too much more of it. Within seconds he's turning the hand-stitched hide of that soft top into a crazed patchwork quilt and making a Morrissey-shaped hole.

Know the old adage about one never being there when you need one and one always there when you don't?

That's when the copper appears. At first Morrissey thinks a have-a-go did call them after all, but one look at their disappointed faces as they realise the cabaret's about to end tells Morrissey this is just bad luck, and everyone knows what they say. If it wasn't for bad luck, and all that. Morrissey used to sing that on karaoke night, belting it out to Kim who'd be standing there, three rows away looking at him with that OK, impress me expression on her face that never failed to get him going. But that was in another country and that wench seems to be well and truly swimming with the fishes if the evidence of that empty prison carpark and all Angel had just said to him was anything to go by.

The copper's now seen the wildly-rocking Porsche, the goo-covered toerag inside, a roof that now looks like an exhibit from Tate Modern and he's now also hearing the electronic voice that keeps repeating, Stop, Thief, Call the Police. And the horn's sounding now too, which isn't another security device, but courtesy of Morrissey's foot being jammed up against it as he tries clambering out of the top.

The copper starts running towards him. He's out of condition and the gut he's carrying wouldn't look out of place on a prospective mother of quads, but Morrissey's still got two feet and one shoulder stuck inside the Porsche which is evening things up a bit.

The impromptu audience starts to barrack the approaching copper which makes Morrissey feel like he's getting the popular vote at least, and the barracking gets louder when the copper reaches for his radio to summon back-up because the one thing most punters really do appreciate is a totally level playing field and a strictly fair fight.

Morrissey pushes his foot down, hard, jamming it in the steering wheel as he does so which, for a moment, doesn't look good. Then the wheel breaks underneath him, and the roof suddenly gives way above and just as suddenly Morrissey's out and tumbling down onto the pavement, the copper picking up pace as Morrissey picks himself up.

And now it's game on because the copper's deceptive. Yes, he's wobbling like a jellyfish on speed but he's still shifting. Morrissey's built like a whippet but he's finding it difficult to get going seeing as how his left ankle's still sporting a steering wheel bracelet as one of the have-a-go's he now passes points out. But once Morrissey's freed himself of that, the mobility quotient definitely moves up a notch.

Morrissey runs up the street, putting more and more distance between him and Dunlopillo Man, which is when the backup arrives. One patrol car, two cops inside, one eating an ice cream and it must be the biz as well because he never stops licking away all the time he's eyeing the recently stalled and now-strangely-customised Porsche.

Morrissey looks back towards the distant but still pursuing lump of human lard, up towards the cop with the sweet tooth and what now looks like not-so-sweet eyes, sideways at the manor to which he'd vowed, less than a few minutes before, never to return. But what are vows for if not for breaking?

Morrissey turns tail and heads once again for home.

10. MAN'S BEST FRIEND

Five seconds later, Morrissey's heading for a nearby underpass.

He knows this part of the 'Diff like the back of his hand, has played here a zillion times as a kid. There are five alleys leading off this particular underpass, each one taking you into the rabbit warren that's Morrissey's home estate. Five alleys mean five escape routes. No way will the pursuing coppers know which one Morrissey's going to choose, which is when he hits the first problem.

No underpass.

Morrissey just stands there, blinking for a moment.

No fucking underpass?!

Which is when a forty-something, muscle-bound, tattooed crane driver, real name unknown, that's buried in the mists of time, known now as Lulu on account of his long-established and loudly proclaimed transexual proclivities, pauses as he sees him. A diminutive Somali, locally known as T-Bone for reasons no one knows, is with him, Lulu's current squeeze, and it would be a squeeze too given the difference in physique.

'Morrissey?'

Later, Morrissey's going to wonder how he recognised him given he's all orange right now, and why that little fact isn't even warranting any sort of comment. But for now Morrissey's only got one thing on his mind.

'No fucking underpass?'

'It's boarded up, Morrissey.'

'So where the fuck?'

Lulu turns, pointing out an alternative route around a distant corner and just in time too because the pursuing coppers have now appeared. Morrissey takes off in the direction of Lulu's pointed finger just as its owner frowns.

'Or has that been?'

It has. Morrissey rounds the corner a few seconds later to be faced with a ten-foot-high brick wall with a huge poster pasted on it proclaiming, Save Our City Farm.

Morrissey stares again as three pairs of pounding feet are now heard behind him. Lard and Sweet Tooth have been joined by the spare Plod as well because they all want to be in on the day they nicked the man from Del Monte. This might even get them a mention in The Echo. But Morrissey's always been publicity-shy so he launches himself at the wall.

Ten seconds later, and with his hands and arms well and truly skinned, Morrissey's on the other side. Now he's orange and green, orange from the German goo and green from the slime on the wall and still he's recognised.

'Morrissey?'

Now Billy's staring at him, and Morrissey's really not in the mood for this and not just because he's on the wrong end of some serious attention from Plod. Morrissey's not in the mood for Billy full stop, forever, till hell freezes over and maybe even after that, Morrissey decided Billy was a non-person two years, seventy-eight days and who the fuck knows how many minutes ago when that hanging fucker of a Judge passed sentence on the pair of them, but made Billy's sentence suspended on account of him having nice eyes or something. The last time Morrissey saw Billy he was standing in court, looking across at him big-time guilty and mouthing, Sorry.

Sorry!

For fuck's sake, sorry!

'Fuck off!'

But Billy doesn't fuck off, he just keeps staring after Morrissey now haring away, calling out to his old and now ex-mate as he does so.

'Not that way, Morrissey!'

Only Morrissey is acting on his resolution of two years and seventy-eight days ago and he really shouldn't, on this occasion anyway because now Morrissey's facing a brand-new canal and this is a proper piece of work. The old canal was a rat-infested open sewer decorated with old bits of bikes. This is tiled. If Morrissey had world enough and time he'd have stopped and stared in wonder because this one has edging stones and tiles that go all the way to the bottom and you can tell because the water's almost blue.

But Morrissey doesn't have world or time and so all he's not seeing is a fucking great obstacle where right now he really doesn't want there to be any sort of obstacle at all. But then there's another distraction as

Morrissey's hand suddenly turns all wet. Morrissey stares down at it. Billy's still watching him, hangdog, from about fifty metres down the street, so he's obviously not the culprit and he's not. This time it's a real dog instead.

Morrissey's dog in fact, Yorkie. Absent from his master for two years, seventy-eight long ones and ecstatic now because it's reunion time and to be fair Morrissey's pretty choked too. His former best mate in the shape of Billy can take a running jump, but this is Yorkie and some bonds you just can't break. The problem being that while this particular prospect is ever-so-pleasing, the general aspect right now is well and truly vile in the shape of the three evil-looking coppers who've now also mounted the wall and are gaining fast on an orange and green Morrissey which is not too surprising as right now he's standing totally stock still, but not for much longer because Morrissey now jumps in the canal.

Yorkie stares at him for a moment, puzzled as ever by the occasionally odd, if not downright puzzling, antics of the two-legged members of their home planet. Then Yorkie turns and makes for a footbridge just a hundred metres or so up the newly constructed towpath, having worked out it's going to make any crossing a lot easier.

Morrissey, now swimming, gasping, and having only just spotted it, can't believe it.

A bridge!

A fucking bridge!

Yorkie's halfway across by now and the grinning coppers are haring for it too, which is when Yorkie turns on them, fangs bared, mouth salivating and slobbering, pulling the fearless forces of law and order up short and a good job too because Morrissey's struggling. The water's really not mixing with the goo from the Porsche or maybe it's the green slime from the wall, maybe it reacts or something. All Morrissey knows is by the time he's hauled himself up on the other side, his skin feels like stretched rubber and leaves and twigs are sticking to his head but at least he's got to the other side of the sudden, great fucking obstacle thanks to the still-barking, still salivating and still slobbering Yorkie.

But the coppers are now having serious trouble keeping up their pursuit anyway, Yorkie or no Yorkie, because Morrissey's looking so fucking comical right now. They began by pursuing a carjacker, now they're chasing Catweazle. Yorkie turns back and gives Morrissey a quick congratulatory lick for completing his swim, a gesture even the loyal soul's soon regretting seeing as how now he's got a gob-full of goo, but by now Morrissey's off again.

Morrissey turns left, only there isn't a left and Morrissey hares straight into a former Job Centre that's now an indoor performance theatre space and then on into a block of industrial units that's now a Mosque owned by an old mucker of his who's made his fortune in the time Morrissey's been away knocking out prayer mats each with their own inbuilt compass. Morrissey hares from the rear of the mosque into a schoolyard which, miraculously, does still happen to be a schoolyard and is still attached to a fully functioning school.

Which is when a voice which sounds like fifty aircraft carriers screaming into land cuts through the unresisting air.

'Morrissey Jarrett!'

Vesuvius Hughes, famed local warrior and Headmistress stares at him, and Morrissey slows, instinctive, automatic, earning him an approving nod from Vesuvius because there never has been and there never will be any running in her fucking yard.

Which is when an eight-year-old boy also now stares at the orange and green sticky figure currently slowing to a walk.

'Uncle Morrissey?'

Morrissey nods back at him.

'Yeah, hi Aidan.'

'And you lot!'

That's Vesuvius again, so named because she goes off at periodic intervals, barking now at the pursuing, arriving coppers. And Vesuvius keeps watch as an orange and green villain and three coppers slow to a sedate walk across the schoolyard, all with their heads down and all watching their P's and Q's. Vesuvius's favourite letter always was P closely followed by Q because in her book it's the key to a healthy, happy, and respectful life. And if you don't mind your P's and Q's, Vesuvius always had a big stick handy to beat you black and blue instead.

Aidan's keeping pace with Morrissey, forming a procession with Yorkie, each flanking him on either side, Aidan giving him a pep talk, low voice, all the while.

'Right at the end of the street, Uncle Morrissey.'

Morrissey nods.

'Then the next left.'

Morrissey nods again.

'Right.'

'No, left.

'No, I meant –'

'Then through the big blue door that's right in front of you.'

Morrissey looks at the young boy, lost already.

'Show me?'

Aidan nods back at his grimly watching Head Teacher.

'It's dinnertime. Vesuvius is never going to let us out.'

Then Aidan stops at the white line marking the playground off from the outside world, Morrissey springing into life again as he does so, the frustrated coppers still proceeding at their own funereal pace under Vesuvius's watchful glare because they know a funeral's the next thing they'd all be attending if they don't.

Meanwhile Morrissey, miracle of miracles is actually remembering Aidan's instructions and is turning right, then left and now he's heading through a big blue door in front of him and all of a sudden he really is in Wonderland or at least what it would be Wonderland if it had suddenly become a zoo because everywhere Morrissey looks, animals are looking back at him. It's disorientating and it's bewildering, but it's also a perfect hiding place as Aidan had already sussed. Only Yorkie now starts barking at all these potential competitors for his master's affections, making him an all too voluble guide to said master's present whereabouts for the coppers who have now taken up the chase again and are now following them inside.

Morrissey takes off again, and now he sees the old waste ground where he used to play on as a kid, only now it's a cinema, a multiplex, sixteen screens with some good stuff on too from the admittedly hurried inspection Morrissey's got time for right now.

Then there's a road leading to what used to be another underpass, but this underpass houses a florist which is selling the sort of flora and fauna that looks like it's come straight from the Brazilian rainforest. It's also, as Morrissey can see only too clearly, another bricked-up, boarded-up dead end.

Beyond that Morrissey can see a new traffic island with an ornamental fountain in the shape of a swan, water cascading from its beak onto a set of coloured tiles each one depicting different varieties of seabirds on their migratory way south. An old tramp's currently pissing against one of the tiles, maybe because he's taken against it for some reason, or maybe because he just needs a piss. So Morrissey next scales the wall that's in front of him, not knowing what the fuck's on the other side. The Hanging Gardens of Babylon maybe.

Wrong.

A mirror.

A sixty-foot long, twenty-foot-high fucking mirror!

As Morrissey stares at it, a million Morrisseys stare back at him, a fat Morrissey, a thin Morrissey, an oblong Morrissey and the real one's already beginning to wonder if he could have picked anywhere more fucking obvious to try and hide.

The coppers are still following, but now they're getting more than a bit disorientated by seeing a phalanx of coppers suddenly appear in front of them, as well as now getting seriously out of breath.

So now Morrissey's making for one last wall at the far end of the mirrored monstrosity and if the Hanging Gardens of Babylon really are waiting for him then Morrissey's just going to lie down, right in the middle of them and fucking die.

Morrissey scales the wall, crashes down the other side, and it's not the Hanging Gardens of Babylon, and it's not another mirror or a piece of sculpture or a fountain or another pissing tramp either.

It's a taxi. Brakes squealing, the driver frantically trying to avoid the sudden apparition that's appeared in front of him, and maybe Morrissey's getting more than a little jaundiced right now but to his eye it doesn't look as if the hapless driver's going to make it. And Morrissey's already beginning to wonder whether life wouldn't be just that little bit simpler if he didn't.

But he makes it. It may only be with an inch or two to spare but that really makes all the difference sometimes as some of Morrissey's old girlfriends had occasionally been heard to say.

Actually, only the one ever said that. And it was the only one that ever counted and always will. And that's the face that flashes before Morrissey's eyes right now as he hears the brakes squeal and waits for an impact that never comes.

And when he opens his eyes, Kim's face has gone, which is one reason to regret he's still in one piece. The other is that he's now staring at a Vietnamese pot-bellied pig.

'Fucking hell, Morrissey.'

For a moment Morrissey thinks the pig has the power of speech, but then a face appears from behind the staring animal, the driver's large hands wrapped around the pig's arse to stop it smashing into the windscreen during the emergency stop.

Oz, another of Morrissey's old, if not his oldest, friend, eyes him more closely.

'What the fuck have they been feeding you in that prison?'

Morrissey scrambles to his feet, diving into the back of the cab as three still-disoriented coppers slide down the wall behind him and start looking around.

'You're all different colours.'

'Just drive, Oz.'

'Orange – green –'

'Just fucking drive!'

11. OZ AND MRS OZ

One hour later and Morrissey's in Oz's yard, old taxi parts stacked to one side, even older docks memorabilia on the other, and not the fake tat on view down in the new bars lining the water, this is the real thing, a tea clipper's ensign, circa 1830, a prop shaft salvaged from a banana boat scrapped in 1868. But it's still nothing that added up to much according to the bored valuer down the local auction house whenever Oz's long-suffering wife made her annual pilgrimage down there in the vain hope of clearing some much-needed space.

Oz and Mrs Oz only argued once a year and it was always about salvage, scrap and space. Then, one year, they didn't. The day after her funeral, Morrissey and the rest of his old mates had to form a human shield to stop Oz from throwing the whole lot into a skip that had guilt written all over it, but which shouldn't have had anything but hero marbled through like a stick of rock.

Right now, Morrissey's looking like a pratt and feeling like a pratt, courtesy of the high-pressure water jet currently being trained on him, ace for removing oil and slime from the underside of motors, but not so hot when it comes to orange dye.

'How's it looking?'

Oz doesn't reply. He just switches the pressure jet on again and for the next few moments the whole world's water. Then the water clears, steam stops hissing, and all of a sudden the world has something almost resembling a smile on its face, and that's nothing to do with the fact Morrissey's now just that little bit less orange or the fact those coppers haven't appeared anywhere on the manor for the last hour or so, having obviously lost interest in Morrissey's abortive attempt to have it on his toes with one of Germany's finest.

It's all to do with the small face peering at Morrissey from the other side of the yard, and a pair of eyes that had always looked on Morrissey like the dad he'd never had, but always wanted. Which is something of a happy coincidence because if Morrissey had ever had a son then this is the one he'd always have wanted too, although knowing Morrissey's spectacular talent for always fucking up even the simplest of things, the real-life version would probably turn out to be the spawn of Satan.

'You missed a bit.'

Aidan, newly released from Vesuvius's not-so-tender clutches, peers at Oz's handiwork as Morrissey stares back at him. He's just out of stir. The last thing he wants is to leave a trail everywhere he goes.

'Where?'

'There, look.'

Morrissey nods back at the pressure jet, still in Oz's hand.

'Sort it will you, Aidan, this old sod's eyesight must be shot.'

Morrissey closes his eyes, waits as Aidan takes the pressure washer from the old sod and so misses that old sod's grin. But the now-industrial-strength jet of water doesn't miss him, the one that hits him straight in the gut and by the time he's realised it's a wind-up, a giggling Aidan's already halfway home.

12. ONE SHIT-LOAD OF PENGUINS

Another hour later and a now-dry Morrissey and a still-grinning Oz are passing a trucker's café, now an All-American diner with a life-size Pluto waving at them from the window. Here and there Morrissey's still seeing other dimly recollected landmarks but it's still like one of those dreams when a gorgeous blonde glimpsed from the back slowly turns her head and turns out to be a penguin because Morrissey is coming across one shitload of penguins right now.

'Seen anyone else?'

Oz grins wider.

'Apart from your new mates in the local constabulary, and me and the wind-up kid?'

Morrissey shakes his head, still hearing faint whooshes of water swilling around inside his ears.

'Lulu and T-Bone when I was doing my sponsored dash.'

Then Morrissey's face clouds.

'Billy.'

'Don't be like that, Morrissey.'

'Bit difficult not to be like that.

Morrissey's face clouds some more.

'I get this sinking feeling, pit of my stomach, and I know, I just know, guess what? I'm thinking of Billy.'

Then he stops. There used to be an old boozer in front of them called the Dog and Duck. No one knew how it got the name which probably owed more to simple alliteration than anything else. Who's ever seen a dog with a duck? Only it's not called that anymore. Morrissey's not even sure what it is called, he's too busy staring at a line of fake Hawaiian beauties with even faker tans draping garlands over the heads of a couple of arriving punters.

Oz glances sideways at him.

'There have been a few changes since you went away.'

Morrissey eyes the garlands. He knows and only too well by now too.

'Like this place turning into Hawaii.'

'No. Like this place turning into a wankers paradise.'

'Let's just get a pint, yeah?'

'A pint?'

Oz shakes his head, more in sorrow than anger.

'Cocktails? Can't move for them. Poncy artisan gins? They're lining the walls. But a pint of wallop?'

Oz leads the way towards a different boozer, dodging garlands as they go.

'Something of a scarce commodity these days, Morrissey.'

Ten minutes later, Morrissey and Oz are inside a mini-spaceship, seats shaped like rocket launchers, aluminium thrusters in place of tables. And best, or worst, of all, are staring across at waiters dressed in silver space suits with mirrored helmets.

And they're all wearing boots. Moon boots that someone probably did die for. Something had to explain the weight dragging at their heels, which is why Morrissey and Oz have been waiting ten minutes for their drinks because self-service is very definitely frowned on seeing as how they've got a specially designated assistant-operative making his way over to them from the bar instead.

'So what are your plans?'

Morrissey looks across the room at a poster of Spock.

'I was going to get away.'

'You've only just got back.'

'You know me. The human Yo-Yo.'

But Oz just eyes him again as if he's heard all this before. And maybe he has, like maybe a million times.

'Got any dosh?'

Morrissey doesn't reply, doesn't need to. And Oz smiles, gently, a smile Morrissey's seen a million times or maybe even more too.

'Why not hang about a bit?'

Morrissey stares out over the aluminium floor.

'Get some folding stuff together first, fresh starts are always easier with a bit of that in your back pocket.'

Then Oz hesitates.

'Looner's looking for drivers.'

'That fat twat?'

'He's started up a couple of new lines, doing well he is too.'

'Fucking toad.'

'This is one of his places.'

Morrissey shakes his head as across the floor the space-suited waiter continues to make his laborious approach.

'Might have known.'

Oz hesitates.

'Kim's working for him these days.'

Which is when Morrissey pauses, the bar wiped, the waiter wiped, the aluminium floor wiped, and it could do with it too. All those moon boots dragging over it probably. It's not much of a pause, just a second or so, but to Morrissey it feels like forever, and now there's this casual note which he thinks he's getting into his voice, but really isn't.

'She with anyone right now?'

Five words.

And the universe, or at least Morrissey's part of it right now, hanging on the answer.

And Oz is trying to strike a balance now, he's trying to be kind although it really would have been a lot better if Morrissey hadn't actually asked. But he has to be honest too.

'Tonto's been sniffing around.'

Morrissey's face creases in disgust.

'Tonto?'

Oz struggles a moment longer. He could tell Morrissey that Tonto's a knob, always has been and always will be, but at least he's been here, unlike the convict kid. He could also tell him that maybe Morrissey should really stop flogging this terminally ill horse. But Oz being Oz, doesn't. Instead, he just settles for the strictly truthful, strictly factual response as, behind, the space-suited, leaden-booted waiter makes what looks like his final approach.

'But no. No one serious.'

A second later Oz is wishing he hadn't been so scrupulously fair and truthful, because now Morrissey's got something like hope in his eyes.

13. WHEN THIS DOG RUNS OUT

An hour later again and Morrissey's smelling sweeter than he's smelt in a long time, which isn't saying a lot given he's been banged up in a cell with assorted scrotes and lowlifes for the past couple of years. Not to mention, even more recently, being showered with liquid shit, assaulted with orange German goo, and baptised in a canal.

He's also mugged up on an up-to-date, street map and wonder of wonders has managed to negotiate his way around his home turf's new layout without getting lost more than the thirty or so times he managed just three hours before.

Morrissey pauses as he comes up to a small house, coach lamps, both new and white, on either side of a plastic door. It's not exactly designer chic, but it's still a lot better than the shitty high-rise Kim used to call home a few streets away. A step up in fact, even if did involve a move fifteen stories back down to earth.

Morrissey rings the bell which actually works. He used to have to squat down and bellow through the half-open letterbox in the old place. But that used to bring Kim running to the door. Just that one yell. Sometimes not even that. A yelp, a sniff, a raspberry, even a fart. But no one's running now. All he can hear is a voice from inside.

'When all of a sudden this dog runs out.'

Which is Angel in the middle of dictating to Aidan her latest accident report, all ready for forwarding onto her latest set of insurers, although you'd have thought she could just be photocopying them by now.

Angel stops as she hears the bell, looks across at Aidan who looks back at her, the expressions on both their faces saying the same. They know who's there, have been expecting him for the last few hours in fact, but no way are they answering that door. They're holding on, like Morrissey's holding on right now, for Kim.

Angel begins dictating again.

'Right in front of me.'

Which is when the bell rings again.

Outside, Morrissey's actually growing hopeful. Maybe Kim's standing there on the other side of the door, wondering, do I answer, thinking, what do I say, how do I play this? Which means she's bothered. And if she's bothered that means she still cares.

Morrissey rings the bell for a third time which is when the door finally opens and the woman of the moment stands there, hair soaking wet, a towel pulled tightly across her chest, dripping water onto a floor which looks like wood but is actually some sort of photograph and which shouldn't actually get water on it all as Kim is now reminding Angel and Aidan at the top of her voice, at the same time as wanting to know why no one in this flaming house is answering the frigging door!?

Then, finally, she turns her attention to Morrissey. And there's something in that look that not even the most eternal of optimists could mistake for a heart leaping in joy.

'There's this story going down, Morrissey.'

Kim eyes him.

'Some car-jack that went belly-up after this chancer gets covered in goo.'

Morrissey looks back at her.

'Word is the cops never got near they were laughing so much.'

Morrissey looks beyond Kim to Aidan and Angel who've now appeared behind her in the hall.

'So I hear about this monumental fuck-up.'

Kim nods at him again, level, cool.

'And then I see you.'

Morrissey stares at her for another long moment. Then he keeps staring at the door closing in his face. And Morrissey stands there for another long moment, his dreams fracturing and not so slowly into tiny shards.

Maybe Morrissey would have felt better if he'd known that Kim, right at that same moment, was standing on the other side of the door, her back pressed against it, willing Morrissey to go, waiting for the footsteps, hating the moment they'd start, dreading each moment they don't.

Is love a disease? Kim has no idea. All she does know is she thought she was cured, but that doesn't matter now. All that matters is that Morrissey goes, that he doesn't knock on that door again because she's nowhere near the hard-faced bitch she's just pretended to be, even if she isn't ever going to admit that even to herself.

Her sister's still staring at her from the kitchen door. Her son's still staring at her too, but before either can speak, Kim cuts across.

'I can't, OK?'

Then Kim turns, still dripping water on the wooden floor that isn't wood at all, and heads back to the sanctuary of the bathroom.

'I just can't.'

Aidan and Angel keep watching as she bangs the door behind her, and then Angel shakes her head.

'Best shag she ever had too.'

Aidan nods his head in sage agreement at around the same time that Kim leans back against the bathroom door this time, closing her eyes once more because it's true.

Outside, and by the still stationary Morrissey's side, Yorkie looks up at him. Morrissey hadn't even realised he was there. Morrissey looks down as he looks back up at him, steadfast and true. In another age and time maybe Morrissey should come back with four legs instead of two. Then Yorkie rubs his nose against Morrissey's leg, and licks him, all soft and hot and blubbery, and Morrissey decides against reincarnation after all.

Morrissey finally turns and heads for home instead, Yorkie trotting after him.

14. ARTIFICIAL INSEMINATION

Morrissey's most immediate problem had already been nailed for him by Oz.

Dollars, euros, pounds, pence, the denomination didn't matter, Morrissey didn't have any. And not much likelihood of acquiring any either. No address that could be called permanent without invoking the wrath of the truth police meant no benefits, and no inclination on his part to participate in any of Her Majesty's rehabilitation programmes for offenders meant no helping hand from that quarter either. Morrissey also really didn't fancy breaking into any more Porsches with or without any interesting security devices, which only really left one option.

Work. After a fashion anyway. Because there was only one local employer left on his particular manor, every other business in the brave new world to which he'd returned was owned by large corporations in the Far East and Morrissey wasn't talking Harwich. And they'd never been big on ex-cons, with or without an aversion to Porsches.

So Morrissey hauled himself up the next morning and went looking for Looner.

Looner, being Looner, wasn't exactly dressed for the office when Morrissey arrived. There was a big convention of space nuts taking place in a new convention hall near Newport, Trekkies and Star Wars freaks all meeting up to talk about rocket propulsion and solar panels. Enough bull to fertilise an entire artificial insemination plant.

Costume was optional, the only requirement being you check out anything resembling taste at the door. There could be no other reason why a twenty-five stone grown man would forget his string of businesses, his top-of-the-range motors, his blonde bimbo bombshell of an occasional girlfriend and tog himself out in a Storm Trooper's outfit, white with matching decals, inviting scorn and piss-take comments from every passing punter, unless of course, that punter happens to be looking for a job.

Looner, currently dressed in said outfit, stares at his visitor staring back at him from the door.

'Problem, Morrissey?'

Yes, and I'm looking at it you fat twat, probably wouldn't have been the best career move Morrissey could have made right now, so he hesitates, then shakes his head which gets him an approving nod from the watching Leanne. Morrissey nods at the big man's Trekkie decals instead.

'Nice transfers.'

But Looner is looking at Morrissey with something approaching pity in his eyes which is pretty rich considering how he's dressed right now.

'So what's the score, Morrissey? Come to say hello? Chew the fat?'

The bit after that is muffled courtesy of Looner putting on his helmet which means the world's at least spared the stupid grin that's spreading across his face right now, only Looner being the dense fucker he is takes a few seconds to realise that.

'Always you with the ball wasn't it, Morrissey?'

Morrissey stares back at him as Looner finally matches up mouth to the opening in his helmet

'Always you saying who was, who wasn't, in the team when we were kids.'

And it was never you, you useless turd, but that's silent again, which earns him another approving nod from Leanne who seems to have become a mind-reader.

'Well, now it's my team. Now I'm the one saying who's in, who's out.'

Looner turns, and heads for his Shogun.

'Now I'm the one with the fucking ball.'

Leanne joins Morrissey as Looner screams away, foot glued to the loud pedal, back tyres screaming in protest.

'Just the one, mind you.'

Morrissey looks back at her.

'Cock's not up to much either.'

But Morrissey keeps looking at her fast-disappearing boyfriend, himself and Leanne's fellow travellers in a strange new world that now belongs to a loser called Looner.

15. ONE GIRL WALKING IN

Ten minutes later Morrissey's in the office trying not to stare at Leanne's legs which isn't easy as she's sitting on the desk showing acres of thigh. Every now and again she leans forward too, so the only respite Morrissey's being granted from that freebie floorshow is a pair of surgically enhanced 34 Double-Ds.

Leanne's got it and she knows it and she flaunts it too and she'll do more than flaunt it given half a chance, an empty office and a man who's seen no action for more time than he'd care to remember, although tragically he can remember every minute.

'OK Morrissey, it's basically the same old stuff.'

Leanne crosses her legs, hitching up her skirt just that little bit higher again, only all of a sudden it's not working as it should. And it's not working because Morrissey's mouth is now going dry and his heart's starting to pound and while it may have been pounding a bit before, now it's knocking like a steamer on its last crossing to oblivion.

And now Morrissey's not seeing Leanne or her legs or her surgically enhanced 34 Double-Ds because Kim's just walked in. Her hair's off her face, her shoes are flat, and she's clothed head to foot meaning there's not an inch of flesh on view making this absolutely no glamour shoot, in fact it's so far from the top shelf it's way below even bottom drawer.

Still pierces Morrissey's heart though. And the sulky Leanne knows it because now she's wriggling down from the desk, dress sliding down at the same time before handing Morrissey a couple of job sheets.

The next few hours pass in a blur. Faces swim in and out of Morrissey's vision, but none really register. Morrissey hooks up with several old mates, but none penetrate the fog.

And all it had taken was one door opening.

One girl walking in.

The whole world hijacked.

16. SLEEPYHEAD

Repossessions were the first job on Morrissey's new work list. Which was anything the poor fuckers once couldn't resist, but now very definitely couldn't afford. All sorts had focused their eyes and all sorts were vanishing in front of those self-same eyes right now too, including beds, TVs, fridge freezers and enough music systems to stock an entire out-of-town superstore.

The odd thing was that most really didn't seem too bothered that the objects of all that previous lust were being lifted. One punter didn't even wake up as they were loading the sofa on which he was still snoozing into the van. He didn't wake up back at the portacabin either so they left him there for the night. Sleepyhead didn't wake up the next morning either which is when everyone realised why he'd fallen behind with his repayments because the poor fucker was dead.

17. CHEAP CLINGFILM

Driving a limo was the next thing on Morrissey's list or, more accurately, a mobile brothel which was Looner's new thing.

The red light on the roof was a bit of a giveaway and the way the whole thing kept rocking on its springs even when stationary was a bit of a no-brainer too, but it did give Morrissey some much-needed cabaret via the rear-view mirror at least. The only snag was that as well as executive relief Morrissey was responsible for personal protection too. At first Morrissey thought that meant fisticuffs and baseball bats, but then he found a different sort of protection was being talked about. Which was how Morrissey ended up later that night in a local chemist trying to negotiate a discount on two thousand individual little items of personal protection with six tarts sitting back in the limo all pissing their knickers if they'd been wearing any.

The discount wasn't a problem, the quantity more so and Morrissey was having to make do with a thousand now and call back at the end of the night after the hard-pressed man in the white suit made a lightning trip to a wholesaler on the other side of Roath. Only now the girls are kicking off because that sort of discount means one thing and one thing only. Low-grade merchandise, rubbers that feel like cheap clingfilm and taste like even cheaper shrink-wrap and if Morrissey doesn't believe them then why doesn't he wrap that fucking useless baseball bat he brought along in a few of them and try a suck or two, or maybe one of the dom dykes Looner also runs can hold him down while the rest of them insert the bat up his arse.

At which point and without the need for any sort of demonstration, Morrissey begins to see their point. Five minutes later he's escorting six slightly happier tarts back to the moon theme pub, past assorted space-suited extras and into the marbled and mirrored Gents where they congregate before a state-of-the-art condom machine that's the size of the original Apollo spacecraft. As well as condoms it'll also dispense chewing gum and toothpaste which is double-handy if you're into a freshen-up or a snack before or during or after, but that aside Morrissey can't see any other obvious sort of connection. The girls also aren't into chewing gum or fresh breath, they just want rubbers that don't turn cocks into frozen sausages and their insides into mini-freezers and this machine has the lot.

Novelty condoms, flavoured condoms, condoms that play tunes, condoms that glow in the dark, condoms that announce to the world that Daddy's Home as the punter shoots his load in the tip, but it's not novelty the girls are after so much, although several of their regulars have been known to favour the musical variety.

It's the kitemark. The BS-something-or-other. Which means they don't fall off, they don't turn the girls' insides to sandpaper after even the most perfunctory of pumps and they don't turn a formerly half-attractive cock into something that's been mummified.

The only problem being the machine only accepts coins. One-pound coins, two-pound coins or fifty pence pieces, it's not fussy, it just doesn't accept plastic even if Morrissey had any, or notes of any denomination, which means Morrissey's now looking for more pieces of silver than is currently held in the vaults in Threadneedle Street. Certainly more than the Neil Armstrong look-a-like behind the bar is prepared to unload into the pleading Morrissey's pocket despite one of the girls promising a trip to the stars once he's out of his helmet if he does, and one of the dom dykes threatening to break his fucking neck if he doesn't.

Which is when Morrissey finally finds a use for his much-derided baseball bat after all. Ten minutes later, and one quick trip back to his illegally parked and now clamped limo, the condom machine's in pieces on the floor, its contents being scooped up into six eager handbags and Morrissey and his band of infinitely merrier toms are piling back into the limo, freed from its clamp courtesy of that self-same and now not-so-derided bat and are heading back out into the eager night on the trail of even more eager punters.

Morrissey's knight in shining cling-film act means he's now going to cop a five-girl session at the end of the night with any condom of his choice according to the beaming beauties in the back, or a couple of broken fingers courtesy of the dom dyke if that's more his bent.

But Morrissey decides to take a rain check, handsome offers though they are. Maybe he's getting old. Or maybe he's just getting choosy. But none of the girls on offer is the one he actually wants to choose right now, so Morrissey just keeps driving through a night punctuated by the sounds of condoms not only announcing *Daddy's Home* but playing *Light My Fire* and *Hail To The Chief* while glowing, intermittently and often, in the dark.

18. ROYALS CALLED VIC AND BERT

Snakes were the third item on the work list. And nothing to do with the one-eyed trousered variety that were now popping up in all shapes and sizes in Morrissey's rear view mirror either, this was the real thing, an actual reptile.

The reptile in question belonged to Fatman, an ageing trainer who ran a small stable of broken-down wrestlers from an old gym at the far end of Channel View. Fatman used to do well in the old days, even attracting some of the dubious greats to the municipal halls of his old home patch to entertain the grannies and the gullible in the age when wrestling ruled Saturday afternoons and Kellett was King.

Then the Americans arrived with their gyrating dwarves and freaks in cages and all of a sudden Fatman's stable began to look more than a little old hat. The kids discovered satellite and Fatman discovered the DSS at around the same time the municipal halls became Scout huts and the sport of kings slipped down the pecking order, then totally off the radar.

Only what do you do when you can't do anything else? You just keep on going and that's what Fatman did. He kept on going. Fatman and his snake.

Fatman's snake's a fully-grown python which he'd spirit into the ring in his trainer's bucket and bring out at whatever opportune moment in the ongoing contest seemed appropriate, usually when his man was one-fall down and everything looked lost. The sudden appearance of Fatman's python usually had any opponent scattering to all four corners of the ring in something approaching blind panic which was actually genuine on those occasions Fatman forgot to mention this unscheduled addition to the evening's entertainment.

But then the python got old and more often than not wouldn't even rouse itself from its resting place, and Fatman pursuing a bemused opponent around the ring with an old fire bucket just didn't look the same. Not that there was too much in the way of pursuing being done by then anyway because Fatman's knees had begun to go in sympathy with his back which had almost given up the ghost by then too. The rest of Fatman's legs soon followed and the ring became an ever more distant memory. These days Fatman just went out to drink with a dwindling band of muckers who still dreamt of the days when the Royals meant Vic and Bert.

But Fatman still had his snake. His body may have let him down but, the occasional hibernation inside a fire bucket aside, his snake never has. In an uncertain world that's abandoned him on more occasions than he can shake a leotard at, Fatman had always been able to count on his pet and over the years it's become the only thing in the old fuck's life that actually means anything. So now it's the one thing Looner wants as part-payment for the debts Fatman's run up as he struggled to keep his old gym just that one single mark above the Plimsoll line. The python might be worth fuck all by itself, but it's worth the world to Fatman and the way Looner sees it with his snake in one of Looner's storerooms its demented owner might just get off his ever more immobile arse and pay off at least some of what he owes.

Which is why Morrissey's now in an old lock-up, a makeshift wrestling ring inside, Fatman sitting on an old stool in the centre, Diesel on one side, Tonto on the other, a currently absent python the matter of the moment.

'Where is it?'

'Where's what?'

You really would have thought thirty years of faking terror, feigning injury, and fixing stunts would have taught Fatman all he ever needed to know about the ancient art of acting, but the truth is he's just shite.

'Fatman, you know the score.'

Tonto eyes him, balefully, gesturing round as he does so.

'You're a year behind on the rent for this place for the starters.'

'I've got a gig coming up. Some of the faces from the old days are coming along.'

'And Looner wants something on account?'

Fatman looks, desperate, around the ring, wracking his remaining brain cells for inspiration and the early signs aren't looking good.

'Anyway, I haven't got it anymore, it ran away.'

Diesel eyes him, equally balefully.

'How can it, it hasn't got any fucking legs.'

'Slithered away then.'

Which is when Morrissey spots a sudden movement rippling across

Fatman's chest.

'Crawled.'

Then Fatman stops as the ripples get more pronounced. Now Tonto and Diesel are staring too and Fatman's hurrying on, first hunching his shoulders like a consumptive in smog, then spreading his arms wide in heartfelt appeal which isn't the best move right now given his chest's now rippling more violently than one of the more bonzer waves approaching Bondi Beach.

'Haven't seen him for ages.'

'What's that?'

Diesel's always been a total fucking dodo in Morrissey's opinion and is now proving it.

'What?'

'Under your shirt.'

'It's my muscles.'

Fatman nods back at them, urgent, cajoling.

'I can't control them. I've got St Vitus Dance.'

Then three heavies dive behind Fatman's bucket as the head of a six-foot python pokes out from the collar of his shirt and hisses at them.

Ten minutes later, Fatman's tied to a stool, sobbing, his python in the middle of the ring, Morrissey, Diesel, and Tonto eyeing it from a very respectful distance.

'Now what?'

And now Morrissey's beginning to rethink his opinion, because in truth that is a good question from Diesel. The quarry might now be identified and located but their next move really isn't going to be that easy.

'We've got to get it in the bag.'

'How?'

Tonto nods at Morrissey and Diesel.

'Pick it up.'

'You fucking pick it up.'

'I'm not picking it up, I'm holding the fucking bag.'

Tonto gestures at a long piece of black plastic in his hand, heavy duty with an in-built tie, perfect for garden refuse and heavy items of domestic waste as it says on the lettering running down the side, but it's not saying too much about six-foot snakes.

Morrissey holds out his hand.

'All right, I'll hold the fucking bag.'

Which is when the snake moves, just a few inches but the whole thing actually moves and not just the head, its whole six-foot length starts to squirm and shake which makes four living, breathing, squirming, shaking specimens of God's wonderful kingdom in that wrestling ring right now because Morrissey, Diesel and Tonto are doing exactly the same. And now Tonto's forgetting all about who is and who isn't holding the bag because there's more pressing matters of the moment to sort out.

'Fatman, how do we get this snake of yours into this bag?'

'Fuck off.'

Although it took considerably longer to say that than might seem possible given that it was spat out between great, heaving gasps and sobs with a lovelorn Fatman still staring at his now-surrounded companion. Morrissey, Diesel, and Tonto look back at each other having worked out they're unlikely to get too much in the way of practical assistance or advice from that direction.

'We need bait.'

'What?'

'Something to tempt it with.'

'Like?'

'Something to eat.'

'What do snakes eat?'

'I don't know.'

Tonto turns to him again.

'Fatman?'

'Fuck off.'

Morrissey, Diesel, and Tonto contemplate the six feet of scales in front of them once more.

'Anacondas eat people.'

'That's not a fucking anaconda.'

'How do you know?'

'Because it hasn't tried to eat any of us for starters.'

'Anyway, never mind what they eat or don't fucking eat what have we actually got?'

Morrissey cuts across, attempting to bring some semblance of common sense to the proceedings which isn't easy given he's in a run-down old wrestling ring in the company of three scared heavies, one hysterical Fatso and a six-foot snake.

'I've got a packet of crisps.'

Morrissey looks at Diesel in something approaching wonder but he should actually have waited a couple more milliseconds because Tonto now cuts in.

'What flavour?'

And now Morrissey flips.

'What does it fucking matter what flavour? It's a snake! From some fucking jungle somewhere, and I'm no fucking expert but I've never seen anything wrapped in a Golden Wonder packet hanging down from any fucking tree.'

'Smoky bacon.'

Tonto, ignoring Morrissey, turns back to a still-shaking Fatman.

'Fatman, does your snake-like smoky bacon crisps?'

'Fuck off.'

Tonto nods at Diesel.

'Give it one.'

'What?'

'Then we'll see.'

'You give it one.'

'I'm holding the bag.'

'Oh for fuck's sake.'

Morrissey grabs the crisps from Diesel, the bag splitting open as he does so, crisps spilling out all over the ring.

'You stupid fucking –'

Then Diesel stops. So does Morrissey and Tonto and Fatman stops bleating too. In fact the only moving thing in that whole room right now is making a beeline, or reptile-line, straight towards the unexpected treat suddenly on offer. A moment later the first of the crisps is slipping down nice and easy which only goes to show there's always a market for convenience food.

Ten minutes later and Morrissey's in the front seat of one of Looner's Shoguns, Diesel driving, Tonto in the back with a now-writhing black plastic bag at Morrissey's feet.

'We've still got to get it out of there.'

'I'm not getting it out, I got it in.'

'Oh for fuck's sake, just drive will you.'

Diesel doesn't respond for a moment and Morrissey reaches over, ramming the selector shift into D which turns out a bad move. This Shogun's the temperamental type which doesn't like anyone but its Lord and Master touching its private parts and it registers its protest by leaping forward a few feet and then expiring half-on, half-off, the feeder road leading down to the docks.

Remember that old adage again?

That's when the female PC appears.

Morrissey stares at her as she taps on the window. He just has the presence of mind to throw his coat over the basket to hide the incriminating evidence before she leans in through the window but a second later wishes he hadn't. Because that's when the snake wakes up.

So now Morrissey's got a confused python at his feet, one heavy to his side, one behind and a female PC asking if they've ever heard of double yellow lines? Maybe it all added up to a routine morning in some people's lives, but it was all getting a bit warmish for Morrissey particularly when the snake decides to go walkabouts up his leg. Maybe it wanted to see its owner again or maybe it was just plain inquisitive, but the snake had obviously decided it'd had enough of its present surroundings and began to explore new ones, which right now meant Morrissey's ankle.

A foot away the female PC who looked young and fresh but was about to have a few lines added to that young fresh face started rabbiting on about blocking the Queen's highway, while another Queen's pet inched ever closer to Morrissey's groin.

Make no mistake a sight like that is a wonder to behold. The head of a python makes a fair old bulge all by itself but by the time the rest of its body has taken up residence in the region of Morrissey's crotch he looked to have a hard-on that would do credit to a Yeti.

The female PC faltered a few times as the snake's progress became more and more difficult to miss, but then she stopped altogether as the bulge in Morrissey's groin just kept on growing. Then she looked up at him in something approaching wonder. There's a lot of perverts in the world and her home patch certainly had its share but she'd never met anyone who got so obviously excited over the Highway Code.

Then the bulge grew some more as the snake pushed upwards and then the female PC dried up completely as a six-foot python emerged from the vicinity of Morrissey's fly. Maybe she realised it was a snake, maybe she didn't but from the look on her face you just knew her boyfriend was going to have to whistle for his next blow job.

19. FUCK ALL TO DO WITH FRUIT

The next morning and Tonto's recounting the story of Morrissey's ever-expanding cock to an ever-growing band of ever-more appreciative faces in a local boozer.

Meanwhile, Morrissey himself is standing outside a Transit van, its sides now smeared in mud and grime, staring in through the open rear windows at pile after pile of -

'Coconuts?'

Diesel, stacking the last few inside, nods back at him.

'Wasn't a problem then?'

Morrissey just keeps staring at the hairy fruit in front of them.

'All them wanks you must have had back in stir.'

Diesel straightens up from stacking the last one on the pile.

'Eyesight's still twenty-twenty.'

'What the fuck are we doing with a van full of coconuts?'

'Delivering them.'

'Who to?'

'Chang.'

Diesel closes up the van, now stacked to the rafters if vans had rafters.

'Chang?'

'Hearing's OK too.'

From behind, Looner starts to moon across the yard towards them, a big grin on his face having also just heard about Morrissey's exploits with the snake. But Morrissey's still staring at Diesel.

'Why are we delivering a load of coconuts down to Chang's?'

But Diesel doesn't need to reply because a fleshy face pushes itself in front of him, the whiff of last night's curry wafting down Morrissey's nostrils as Looner delivers the only answer Morrissey will ever need to know as long as he's working for him.

'Because I'm fucking telling you to.'

Meanwhile, high above on the roof of one of the two tower blocks, Aidan has a pair of binoculars pressed to his eyes and is scanning the local traffic. Angel's not in her usual hearse, she's in what used to be called an invalid car which moves a lot slower but has the same shit-hot brakes.

Right now she's parked up in a side street with easy access to the main road, ready to swing out at a moment's notice, which is usually all she gets and definitely all she needs.

Less than a few hundred metres away and down on the ground, Morrissey starts to drive away in the van, Diesel alongside him, swinging out of Looner's yard, past the storeroom where they've parked Fatman's snake, past a couple more of Looner's heavies who are also enjoying the ever-more exaggerated tale of the day Morrissey caused a female PC to turn tail and run courtesy of his six-foot cock.

But Morrissey's got other matters in mind.

'Looner and Chang hate each other.'

A bored Diesel just stares out of the window. He doesn't give a flying fuck who they're delivering a whole load of coconuts to or why.

Still in his vantage point up with the eagles, Aidan tenses as he sees an upmarket Merc, S-Class, 500 series, full leather, swinging right onto Lloyd George Avenue from the city centre, and Aidan picks up a mobile, and presses a button.

Angel puts the invalid carriage into gear, and swings past a post van, wobbling dangerously as the driver takes avoiding action but there's no protest. You can't apply the normal courtesies of the road to an invalid car. It's just not right. As the driver of the upmarket Merc with its accompanying full leather is about to find out.

Back in the Transit, Morrissey looks sideways at Diesel again.

'So why's Looner turned greengrocer all of a sudden?'

'Just fucking drive will you, Morrissey.'

Back in her invalid carriage, Angel's now got the Merc looming large in her rear-view mirrors. It's about to turn down towards the Bay, indicator light flicking, and Angel takes her cue from the flashing yellow light and follows suit. The driver of the Merc does debate momentarily whether to give her a blast on the horn to get out of the way but, much like the driver of the post van before him, just about stays his hand. Contenting himself with a muttered curse at cripples who clutter up the conurbation he settles for a minute or so trundling behind a three-wheeled coffin.

Back in the van, Morrissey contents himself with a warning.

'If any of these starts ticking.'

Which is a pretty empty threat in truth because even if they did what's Morrissey going to do? A man more out of options, out of step and out of time would be hard put to find outside the Wild Bunch and look what happened to that fraternity of failed fuckers.

Back in her invalid carriage, Angel's waiting for the Merc to start tailgating her which he now does. Subtly, not too obtrusively, nothing that might draw the odd disapproving glance from any passing punter who might know him or recognise his motor. He just wants to get close enough so the wanker in front of him might get the message and pull to the side and let proper people on proper business pass by.

The Merc's driver's mind drifts. His mind's now running on that nice little oriental place he's about to visit with a party of minted Japs, just landed at what used to be called Rhoose and about to be delivered to said eatery by his secretary who might just get a quick grope later for arranging such a hopefully profitable little repast. So Mr Merc doesn't really pay too much attention at first to the rear brake lights that suddenly illuminate ahead of him. Cripple carriages are like that, all over the road, braking at every imagined obstruction. It's only when the back wheels in front slither to a complete standstill that he starts to pay something approaching proper attention although by then, and as always, it's way too late.

What Aidan, still up in his eyrie, knows but Angel doesn't is that Morrissey's now behind the Merc. And as Angel hits the brakes, he's glancing back at the coconuts again so the first he knows about the unexpected cabaret ahead is Diesel's strangled shout.

'Morrissey!'

'What?'

High above, Aidan's still watching, mobile still in hand and normally this would be extra-special. A Merc and a Transit means double-cover which means two sets of insurance companies for Angel to sue. The problem being that just before the moment of impact, in fact, double-impact, or triple, if you count Angel who's already bracing her back as she anticipates the rearward collision and mentally ticking off the likely noughts on the compo cheque, Aidan spots a face in the window of the Transit that looks a lot like his beloved Uncle Morrissey.

And Aidan does what every young boy, old boy, middle-aged boy, wide boy, and rude boy would do in exactly the same situation all over his home city and his home country.

Aidan closes his eyes.

The next second, maybe even less, a succession of crunches are heard. Not the sort of crunches you get biting into chocolate bars and not the sort of crunches you get when an unsuspecting snail wanders in front of your size tens on a wet Monday morning.

Loud crunches.

Fucking loud crunches in fact.

Accompanied by even louder curses as three occupants of two rapidly decelerating motors realise that this is a battle that is well and truly lost before it's even begun, because while they can decelerate all they want they are not going to be able to do a single thing to prevent what happens next.

But then there's another sound. Suddenly, a whole succession of sharp reports and mini explosions go off, as if the street's turned into the biggest transport carnage outside of The Italian Job. And it doesn't stop after the first or second of the dull, metal twisting crunches either as the Merc runs into Angel and Morrissey and Diesel run into the back of him. It goes on and on, crunch, crash, bang, and wallop, well, maybe not wallop but it's just about the only thing that's missing.

Aidan opens his eyes to see Morrissey now two feet from the rear window of a Merc which wouldn't be such a problem if the boot immediately behind that rear window didn't used to be three feet long.

The Merc is one foot from Gran's rear seat which wouldn't be such a problem if the parcel shelf immediately behind that rear seat didn't used to be two feet long as well.

But it's not the fact those three vehicles have suddenly become conjoined that's causing Aidan to stare out at them right now. It's more that Morrissey and Diesel seem to be buried up to their necks in coconuts.

Further down the street, the Merc driver is extricating himself, woozily, from his upmarket motor, all thoughts of Japs and soon-to-be-prone secretaries far from his mind. Angel's not moving, having learn, long ago that the longer she stays in the car the more panicky the punter's going to get and all the more likely to make any contrite-sounding statement to any soon-to-be investigating Plod.

Neither Mr Merc nor Angel are looking back right now and they should because it's double-cabaret time inside that off-white and now more than slightly bent and battered Transit

'Fuck.'

That's Diesel

'Fuck.'

And that's Morrissey. It's hardly original or even halfway constructive but it does seem to just about sum things up.

'Fuck, fuck, fuck.'

Angel's still sitting in her car, turning doleful eyes on the approaching Mr Merc who's already wondering whether his motor might be a total write-off. It's depreciated ten grand in the last ten months, and he's got a poncy new insurance policy that'll pay out full purchase price if it gets totalled.

Angel keeps looking at Mr Merc, wondering whether he's got legal protection on his policy too, that being something of a bonus in the past because if the punter's got that he doesn't usually give a fuck about court cases and briefs seeing as how it's all paid for anyway.

Behind Mr Merc and Angel, all Morrissey and Diesel are thinking about is how the flying fuck they extricate themselves from a van that's turned into solid coconut.

Morrissey gets one arm free, which isn't without considerable personal cost, coconuts not exactly being the most skin-friendly sort of fruit, which is why you drink its contents, not snuggle up to it under the duvet or rub it, affectionately, over your face. One's just rubbed all the way down Morrissey's exposed arm and he's feeling precious little affection for the ugly little turds or their contents right now.

Diesel's up to his neck in them, still buried and is making no move to get out for now, but he hasn't just spent the best part of three years in some stinking nick so maybe he hasn't got Morrissey's aversion to confined spaces.

Morrissey gets a second arm out and smashes open the door and it's like a pinball machine suddenly paying out, first one coconut, then two, then a whole cacophony of coconuts start raining down from the front of the cab out onto the street, some rolling into the gutter, some running down a nearby land drain.

Apart from one. And this coconut doesn't roll anywhere because it's split in two. And having split in two it just lies there, innards exposed to public view, a thin trickle of white goo draining out into the road, an Orphan Annie sort of coconut, abandoned by all the others as they roll away to explore this brave new world that takes it for rides and then lets them out to play on the way.

But this coconut doesn't roll because it can't. It's too heavy and that's not down to the over-abundance of sweet-smelling milk it's been carrying. In fact, it's not had too much of that inside it for a long time. That's been sucked out and now there are just distant memories of former fecundity left behind. In its place, it's had some non-native substance inserted instead and Morrissey's no idea what it is not being exactly up to date with the latest noxious substances being traded up and down Smack City right now.

All Morrissey does know is that he's finally beginning to understand just why they're delivering a load of coconuts from Looner down to Chang and it's fuck all to do with fruit.

20. REINFORCED HUMMER

A few minutes later and blue lights are illuminating the scene, although why you'd need that sort of illumination in broad daylight is anyone's guess. Maybe the cop behind the wheel didn't have too many presents as a kid. But Morrissey's more interested in that single, stray coconut.

By the side of her invalid car, Angel's beginning to run through a well-rehearsed spiel.

'When all of a sudden this dog ran out right in front of me.'

Most punters would over-elaborate, start detailing the breed of dog, the colour, and where exactly on the street it stopped. Old stager Angel's keeping it succinct, adding no extraneous detail, making sure there's nothing in this initial statement that could trip her up later courtesy of any over-zealous brief.

So far as the rookie cop taking her initial statement is concerned, it helps that she's sitting on the pavement at the time as her legs have apparently buckled underneath her and it also helps that her tear-stained eight-year-old nephew is now cradling her fragile body in his arms. The rookie PC is already debating whether to take Mr Merc round the back of his now-bent motor and give him a kicking for ramming this old sweetie up the arse like that.

The arriving Looner and Chang aren't feeling quite so sympathetic. They've seen her pull this sort of stunt many times before.

'This is a fuck-up.'

Looner surveys the bent Transit, the bent Merc, the misshapen invalid car and the street littered with coconuts, Chang nodding beside him in grim agreement.

'Too right it's a fuck-up.'

But Morrissey's staring. He's just seen another police car approaching.

'Looner.'

But Looner's mind is still on the prime culprit in all this.

'Angel again.'

Morrissey tries once more.

'Looner!'

But Looner's still staring down the street at Angel now picking the PC's pocket as he hands her his handkerchief to dab her streaming eyes.

'If any of my stuff goes missing I'm going to do for that old bag.'

Morrissey stares at a plainclothes older male cop emerging from the cop car, another fat bastard called Mac, well known around Morrissey's home turf. He's even fatter than Morrissey remembered, and even more of a bastard too because somehow you just know these things.

But then Morrissey stops dead as the passenger door opens and he sees Mac's companion.

Morrissey last saw the female DC who now appears when she was swinging in the local playground and Morrissey's not talking about adult pursuits. The only dogging Carmel used to do back then involved throwing sticks for the local hounds when they were kids. Now she's looking like she's about to blush deep red if only her natural sheer alabaster black skin would permit it. Avoiding Morrissey's incredulous stare, his old childhood mucker keeps her eyes cast down as Mac begins to wobble over. Joining the ranks of Her Majesty's Constabulary may not be a hanging offence on most manors, but on this one it's always going to be.

Forgetting about Carmel for now, Morrissey hisses in Looner's shell-like again.

'Looner, it's Mac.'

Looner turns, surveys the approaching officer, then nods down at the coconuts.

'And about fucking time.'

But Mac's not looking at the coconuts which are now attracting the attention of several local hungry examples of man's best friend. In fact he's not remotely interested in the current combination of dodgy villain and equally, and obviously, dodgy merchandise at all. All he's looking at is Angel as well.

'What a fuck-up.'

'Devious old scammer.'

'Can't you do anything about her?'

'Like what?'

'Like make sure next time she pulls this sort of stunt there's a reinforced Hummer up her arse.'

Mac shakes his head, then turns back to Carmel.

'Go back to the car, Constable.'

Morrissey stares at her again. So this isn't fancy dress.

Looner nods at the other two bystanders.

You Morrissey, and you Diesel, go and pick up all them coconuts.'

Mac nods at Carmel again.

'While you, DC Hughes.'

Morrissey keeps staring. No mistake about it, she is, she's a rozzer, a fucking wooden top.

'Go and put one of those nice big cordons of ours round the whole fucking lot.'

A few metres away, Angel's coming to the end of her music hall routine. The rookie PC's got tears in his eyes now as he surveys the carnage Mr Merc's caused by dreaming of wankers from wasabi land when he should have been keeping his eyes on the road.

Diesel and Morrissey begin picking up the coconuts as Mac, Chang and Looner stand and watch looking for all the world as if they're in a re-run of the Three Stooges, which as events are about to pan out is maybe not that far short of the mark.

21. EXTRACT OF SCORPION

An hour or so later and Oz is moving from pen to pen on his city farm, Aidan with him, feeding ten ducks, twenty chickens, one stray deer, not to mention the Vietnamese pot-bellied pig of Morrissey's previous acquaintance, all the time updating Morrissey on yet another recent tidbit of local gossip he seems to have missed in his time away

'Snakebite?'

Morrissey stares at him as Aidan chips in.

'And shark fin.'

Which only adds to Morrissey's current confusion.

'Some sort of extract from scorpion too from what I've heard.'

Oz empties a steady stream of feed into yet another pen and three piglets that Morrissey hadn't seen before scamper towards it, eyes wide, mouths open even wider. One metre away, Morrissey, his eyes even wider, keeps staring at Oz.

'It's Looner's new thing, he's cornered the market in it.'

'I thought it was coke or smack.'

Aidan nods, even though the only coke he should know about should come in cans from the corner shop.

'So did we.'

Oz keeps watching his grateful charges.

'Everyone thought the same. He's jumped on the bandwagon. Everyone around here's either sticking it up their hooter or sniffing it through them stupid bongs so he's getting in on the action.'

Oz shakes his head as he keeps watching the scrabbling piglets.

'Then we found out what it actually was.'

Morrissey blinks, still trying to get his head round this, still largely failing.

'Exotic foodstuffs?'

'We thought he's finally fallen off his rocker. All them years staring up at the stars, he's floated away with the fairies.'

Aidan, now feeding the chickens, cuts in.

'Till all these Somalis started turning up. Then a whole load of Kenyans.'

Oz chips in again.

'Then some weird faces from the other side of the Ukraine or somewhere, all with their tongues hanging out and all waving their wallets.'

Oz empties more feed into yet more grateful mouths, Morrissey's mouth not closing any time soon either.

'Chang knocks it out through his restaurants. Mac makes sure the Environmental Health look the other way and the best thing of all is what's going to happen even if they do get caught. Looner'll probably just have to kick back a bit of VAT.'

Morrissey's beginning, but only just beginning, to catch up.

'You mean they actually make money out of this?'

'Ask the Somalis. Ask the Kenyans. Ask the Ukrainians. They make a fortune, Morrissey.'

Morrissey stares at a doe, next in line to be fed, but he's not seeing Bambi. Morrissey's staring into a future which has suddenly turned coconut instead.

'You've got to hand it to him, no one else saw the opportunity, but he did and now he is raking it in.'

Oz nods across at Aidan, feed time finally over, time now to read the inhabitants of Oz's Ark a little bedtime story.

'Lesson for us all, Morrissey.'

Morrissey keeps staring, couldn't have put it better himself.

22. DREAMS OF LEAVING

An hour earlier, Morrissey had been standing on the cordoned-off road. Mac, Chang and Looner are still by Mac's unmarked cop car, the three of them looking at something that resembles roadkill but, and as Morrissey is about to find out, will soon be knocked out for something resembling a small country's national debt with the sort of quantities Looner's shipping in. Keep on like this and he won't be just staring at the moon, he'll be flying there in his own personal spaceship.

Morrissey picks up another of the coconuts from the road and shakes it. Something shifts around inside and it's once again nothing Mother Nature ever placed there. Which is when something catches Morrissey's eye.

Carmel also has a coconut in hand and she's also shaking it, the same sound coming from inside that one too and she has this strange expression in her eyes as she listens to it, as if she's looking at something far-away, beyond this street, this city, maybe even this country because she already knows that just one of these coconuts would probably get her as far away as that look in her eyes is taking her right now.

Which is when something else catches Morrissey's eye because Fomo's now arrived and he's also doing his master's bidding, is also collecting up the spilt coconuts and Fomo's got the same look in his eyes as he shakes his coconut too.

And then Morrissey realises they're both looking back at him, and they're looking at him for the same reason he's looking at them because they've seen the same expression on his face right now too.

They're kindred souls in fact.

All with dreams of leaving.

And now, all with the same idea just how to do that.

23. WEIL'S DISEASE

Three hours later, dark's settling over the city and a park keeper, closing up for the night, pauses as he hears the sound of a distant splash.

The parkie cocks an ear, and keeps listening, but he doesn't hear anymore, so he turns, and heads away. Not that he'd do anything different if he did hear any more anyway. He's got a date with a pint and a game of dominoes in a pub on the other side of Adamsdown before getting tied up and covered in goose fat in a massage parlour just off Newport Road, and this week they'd better not try fobbing him off with melted lard again, lard's lard and goose is goose and never the twain. So all in all he really couldn't give a flying fuck who's splashing around anywhere.

The parkie wasn't to know it and would have cared even less, but the splash was Lulu piloting a small boat across the park pond to an island in the middle or, more accurately, not piloting the small boat at all because he's just fallen out and he's not happy.

'Whose stupid fucking idea was this?'

Lulu, now sopping wet, drips bits of pond all over the canvas sheet Morrissey's spread out on the only clear patch in the undergrowth, nature, red in tooth and claw having taken over by and large seeing as how lawn mowers are a bit tricky to manoeuvre over there in the pleasure park's wobbly boats.

'I'm going to catch pneumonia.'

Fomo cuts in, shivering too, his legs wrapped up in one end of the canvas which used to be dry but now isn't courtesy of his own premature landing in some reeds which looked like dry land but which, as Fomo's ruined brogues now attest, wasn't.

'Never mind pneu– fucking – monia.'

Which is when Carmel cuts in too, also shivering and also soaked courtesy of her own partial absorption in the liquid stuff as she tried mooring her boat.

'This fucking pond's infested, always has been, what about that rat's thing, Weil's disease, what if I go down with that?'

'Just shut the fuck up will you?'

Morrissey cuts across in turn, actually feeling quite smug on account of his being the only one to actually get to their current hiding place without any sort of detour via murky depths.

'We're not exactly likely to run across Mac, Looner or Chang out here are we?'

'Because they've got more fucking sense.'

'So this place is perfect'

'So would some nice little pub somewhere.'

'Nice, dry little pub.'

'Nice, warm, dry little pub.'

'For fuck's sake!'

In truth maybe this is more than a touch over-elaborate in the precaution stakes, but that's always has been Morrissey's fatal flaw as more than one former friend and enemy, not to mention the occasional and not-so-occasional lover, has pointed out on more than one occasion in a perennially complicated past. But so far as he's concerned the sight of Looner's and Chang's employees chewing the cud, not only with each other but with one of Her Majesty's female DCs would have looked decidedly odd, if not well worthy of further investigation, so it was worth the effort it took to pilot four unwieldy little boats across a parkland pond. Then again Morrissey hadn't fallen in so he would say that.

'What is Weil's disease anyway?'

'Fucking hell!'

Lulu, Fomo and Carmel subside into a grumbling huddle, each grabbing bits of the canvas groundsheet as Morrissey hunches forward, finally getting down to the main matter of the moment.

'Looner, Mac and Chang have got this coconut scam running sweeter than Flo-Jo.'

'Who?'

'Runner.'

'Fingernails.'

'She's dead isn't she?'

For not the first time this evening or the last as it turns out, Morrissey begins breathing very fucking hard.

'It checks out every step of the way, all the way from the first pick-up to Chang's lock up.'

Morrissey hunches forward some more as he gets to what might be called the salient point here.

'The only thing is, it's us doing the checking.'

Morrissey nods at Lulu who's slowly beginning to forget about his soaked tank top.

'I get the docket from Lulu.'

Morrissey nods at Fomo who's also now beginning to slowly wipe all recent memories of his close encounter with bull reeds.

'I deliver it to Fomo.'

Then Morrissey nods at Carmel, who's finally starting to put from her mind all fears of a slow and painful end courtesy of waterborne vermin.

'Fomo delivers the completed dockets to Carmel for Mac to sort out the paperwork.'

'So you're saying?'

And now Morrissey's really beginning to despair. If this lot can't follow even this simple scam maybe he should call it a night right here and now and let them all paddle back to poverty.

'He's saying we each adjust our docket.'

That's Carmel, and it's like light shining in on formerly impenetrable darkness.

But Fomo just eyes her, sour.

'I know that's what he's saying.'

'So why fucking ask?'

'I was mulling it over, that's all.'

Morrissey nods around at his new disciples.

'Say it's fifty-four coconuts next time, we make it fifty. That's-'

'Four coconuts.'

'One each.'

'Hello pussy.'

Fomo looks down at his T-shirt, two kittens lying together in a basket featured on the front, quite cute if you're three when everything else is cute and you are too, fucking sad in a feline-obsessed Chinaman of thirty-three.

For a moment there's silence as Morrissey waits for grateful acolytes to start showering him with saffron rice.

'They'd twig.'

Fomo nods.

'Straightaway.'

Lulu nods back.

'Stupid fucking idea.'

Lulu gestures down at his fifty-four-inch chest.

'I got my tank top soaked for this?'

Fomo gestures down at his own twenty-eight-inch T-shirt.

'This is special cloth too, guaranteed not to fade, as in ever, I bet it fucking does now.'

'Fuck that, have you seen my boots?'

Carmel shakes them in Morrissey's face, water spraying everywhere. And now Morrissey knows how the man from the Holy Land felt all those years ago faced with all those doubting Thomases and the rest of the total tits.

'Yeah, they'll realise the delivery was short at some point.'

'Then we're fucked.'

'Weeks later, maybe even months later, when Looner does some sort of stock-take.'

'It doesn't matter when it is, then he'll start checking up'

Lulu nods.

'And he'll go through all the dockets, matching what was supposed to come in with what was actually delivered and he'll find this one docket that really doesn't look right.'

'I'm out of here.'

Fomo stands, Lulu and Carmel standing now too.

'And the first thing he'll think is it was short coming in, so maybe someone on the ship was working a fiddle or maybe the suppliers in Eurocamp are working a fast one, either way, Looner's going to have loads of faces in the frame to work through before he even begins to think about anyone closer to home.'

Lulu eyes him.

'And when he does think about someone closer to home, Brain of fucking Britain?'

'We'll be long gone.'

Three pairs of feet, about to head back to their pleasure boats, pause.

'Way down the road, well and truly over that fucking rainbow, each one of us with our own little pot of gold in our pockets. Oz reckons there could be the best part of fifty grand in just one of those coconuts, maybe even more.'

Lulu looks at Carmel who looks at Fomo, and then all three look back at Morrissey.

'And what's he going to do even if he does ever work it out? March into Ely nick and make an official complaint? Tell the Duty Sarge that someone's stitched him over this sweet little scam him and Mac have been working? Complain to the fucking Ombudsman?'

'What's an Ombudsman?'

But Carmel cuts in, ignoring Fomo, her mind now working overtime too.

'It'd only be four we'd be lifting I suppose.'

Morrissey nods.

'And he brings in dozens every week.'

Morrissey nods again.

'Fifty, sixty a week, fifty odd weeks a year.'

Morrissey keeps nodding.

'He's maybe not even going to realise they're gone, how many got crushed today when Morrissey smashed into the back of that Merc for fuck's sake?'

Morrissey leans back as they all start talking over each other, now beginning to talk themselves into something that moments before they were all walking away from. In a different universe, Morrissey could have made a fortune in double-glazing.

'We just need a week, two weeks max to set it all up.'

Lulu pauses at that and looks back at him.

'A week?'

'Or two.'

'So we'll all still be here for the elephant?'

Morrissey stares back at him.

24. CAPTAIN HOOK

The next morning and Morrissey's back inside Oz's city farm, staring at a poster he didn't really take in first time round, but he's taking it in now and he doesn't know how he didn't before, given the dirty great elephant staring out at him. Behind, Aidan's feeding the pig, ducks, geese, and the doe again.

'A-?'

Oz nods as Morrissey stares in disbelief.

'A fu–?'

Morrissey glances across at Aidan, stopping himself just in time, and looks back at Oz again.

'An actual, real-life, living, breathing, all-singing, all-dancing?'

'Not singing or dancing, but definitely living and breathing.'

'Oz!'

The smiling Oz brushes a stray piece of feed that's latched itself onto the poster.

'They'll be queuing round the block to see something like this.'

'There won't be a block, not with an elephant on the rampage.'

'It won't be on the rampage, it's tame.'

Oz brushes away another stray piece of feed from a sticker fixed to the top of the poster, Donate Generously.

'This is a city farm, Oz.'

Morrissey gestures round at the inmates, all now tucking into their brekky.

'Ducks, geese, the odd chicken or pig.'

'There's nothing odd about my pigs or my chickens.'

'It was loopy enough getting Bambi.'

Morrissey gestures beyond the trumpeting elephant on the now-pristine poster towards the doe.

'But Dumbo's Dad?'

'Dumbo's son. It's still a baby.'

Morrissey stares back at the poster

'And it's already that size?'

'It only popped out a couple of months ago.'

Oz stares at the picture, evermore entranced.

'Wait till it's a full-grown adult, they'll be lining up all the way back to the link road.'

'Why?'

'Cos it's an attraction.'

'No, why get a fuc –'

Morrissey stops himself again as he glances back at Aidan once more, then turns back to Oz.

'Why get an elephant in the first place?'

Aidan cuts in, now cleaning out the feed bucket.

'The pig was first; the geese were second.'

Oz shakes his head.

'No, second was the doe.'

'I don't give a monkeys what came first!'

'We haven't got any monkeys.'

'Not yet.'

Morrissey steers Oz away from the poster, trying to get all this back on track.

'What I mean is, why are you even bothering?'

'The grant's been cut.'

Morrissey stares again.

'You get a grant?'

Oz empties the last bag of feed over the side of the final pen housing the geese, leans against it and watches his offspring-by-proxy feed.

'It's down half on last year.'

'They gave you one last year too?'

'We've got to do something drastic or we sink.'

Morrissey starts breathing heavily again.

'Well, Blue Riband for community spirit, Oz –'

Aidan cuts across again.

'What's a Blue Riband?'

He's doing it deliberately, Morrissey's sure he is, him and Oz are a fucking double act.

'But look round, the whole place is sinking anyway.'

Oz just keeps staring down at the feeding geese as Morrissey leans closer.

'Don't mean we all have to go down with it though.'

Behind, Aidan picks up a couple of the empty feed bag, heads for the door to dump them outside. He can spot a battle lost before it's even begun, but Morrissey's still hanging in there.

'Something's starting to cook.'

Oz looks back at him.

'I can cut you in.'

Oz keeps looking at him.

'There'd be enough for you to get away, make a fresh start.'

Morrissey nods at a pair of eyes that have seen more in one lifetime than most would manage in ten, and which still believe in happy endings.

'Who'd feed the elephant?'

Morrissey all-but explodes

'There isn't going to be an elephant!'

Morrissey gestures around.

'There isn't going to be anything.'

Oz picks up another of the feed bags and heads for the door, Morrissey following him outside where the air's even worse than inside, which sort of makes Morrissey's point for him right now only Oz still isn't listening.

'There isn't going to be anything.'

Morrissey gestures across at the boarded-up flats all around them, steel shutters barricading every door and window, paper blowing like tumbleweed on open spaces, black bin bags flapping in broken windows where curtains used to hang.

'Look around Oz, look what's happening to the place.'

Morrissey gestures across at the only unrestored canal left on the manor, overgrown with clinging ivy, decorated with bricks, mortar and bags of rotting refuse.

'And have you heard about the latest little brainwave, Vesuvius has been telling Aidan and all the kids in school about it, a brand-new waterway.'

Morrissey's breathing is even heavier now which is actually sort of surprising him because he didn't really know he felt so strongly about all this.

'And you know what's going to be floating on this brand-new waterway? Not needles, not condoms, water taxis, fucking water taxis, all the way past here back into the city for the days when all them air-kissing, media darlings fancy a change from poncy Pontcanna.'

Morrissey nods up at all the old flats staring down at them.

'And you really think they're going to want all the shit from your city farm within wafting distance of their hooters, you must be totally fucking mad.'

Oz stares at a point behind Morrissey and Morrissey's going to realise why in a moment, but not yet because for now Morrissey's still flying.

'Give it another year, less than a year, about as long as it takes to say, do we get a free Chablis with our ticket, Captain, and this place'll be razed to the ground. Just another extension to Legoland.'

Morrissey pauses, makes one last appeal.

'This is a chance Oz, a chance for a fresh start.'

Then Morrissey stops as Oz cuts across.

'You're not going nowhere, Morrissey.'

Morrissey stares back at him.

'Not while she's still here.'

Morrissey turns and looks, and there's something in the air now, something in the way it moves when Morrissey doesn't want it to, not to mention the way a tell-tale flush is now creeping into his cheeks when he actually wants to look as if he couldn't give a tinker's cuss whatever a tinker is and whatever a cuss sounds like.

Because he now sees Kim approaching Aidan as he dumps dung in the nearby basin.

Morrissey turns back, flushing even more as the wily old fucker looks at him with that killer combination, smile on the lips, pity in the eyes.

'Fuck off.'

'So I'm wrong?'

Morrissey gestures back at the city farm, the poster for the elephant still visible.

'Why break the habit of a lifetime?'

'You're actually telling me you don't want to get back with Kim?'

'About as much as I want a hand job from Captain fucking Hook.'

Oz's look says it all.

Nice try, Morrissey.

But no banana.

And the worst thing of all?

He's right.

25. PRAWN VINDALOO

Later that night and Morrissey's sitting in one of Looner's Shoguns, waiting to transport Tia down to an all-nighter with some Lebanese face who took a shine to her on his last pilgrimage to Tower Block Heaven.

The punter's going to pay twice her normal rate, which in Tia's case is just about anything you care to mention. Why Mr Moneybags is expressing a preference for the cheapest tart in or out of the docks, new or old, is another of those eternally inexplicable mysteries of the universe. Either that or he's mixed her up with someone else which is why Morrissey is packing his trusty baseball bat again in case the gentleman from one of the world's most turbulent trouble spots starts dishing out some of the same.

As he waits, Morrissey watches Oz, now fixing a hanging basket to the soffit of his ground floor flat a hundred or so metres down the road. Behind Oz, fifty more hanging baskets squat on the floor, all destined for other flats up and down the same estate. It's an annual initiative from the council, delivered at around the same time they mow the communal grass around the playground once they can get a requisition order put through for the petrol and arrange for a mechanic to try and tickle an ancient old mower into something approaching life. All part of the same effort to make the place look at least halfway habitable or, to put it less charitably, put a shine on the shit.

Angel's standing next to Oz, her hanging basket in hand, Aidan with her, both trying to find the hook fixed to the chains but they're going to be in for a long search because there aren't any. The flowers are there, the baskets are there, the chains are there but some bright spark's forgotten all about the one addition that will actually fix said basket in place. Not that it's a problem for the ever-obliging Oz who's bent the end link of one of his chains into a makeshift hook and has fixed it in place and now he's doing the same with Angel's.

But suddenly there's this creaking sound and now Oz is moving away from the front of his flat as if he's suddenly grown jet-propelled insteps. A second later and it's a good job too as the hanging basket, complete with modified chain and hook, crashes down into the space Oz inhabited not a second or so before closely followed by a three-foot section of rotten soffit.

Maybe, the watching Morrissey reflects, it's a Trojan Horse in the form of horticulture. Hand out what looks like home improvements, then sit back and watch the homes disintegrate. Or maybe it's just like everything else, a complete and total balls-up.

Then the back door opens and Tia gets in, and she's not a pretty sight right now although Tia's never a pretty sight unless you're into the larger figure with a misshapen nose. The size is nature's gift, although Tia's always blamed it on the fast-food chicken shops that have sprung up all over the manor. The misshapen nose is courtesy of Tia's latest ruck. Add to that a cauliflower ear, courtesy of another ruck, the plate in the skull, courtesy of a ruck that turned into a kicking, and the limp, courtesy of Tia's stray kick during that kicking that connected with a concrete bollard rather than her adversary's soft calf tissue and you've got a walking, talking disaster zone begging the question, what the fuck is it about that Lebanese face?

'Fuck me, Morrissey.'

For one spine-chilling moment Morrissey thinks it's an instruction and his hand's on the door handle all ready to run, but then Tia emits a loud, headlining-rattling belch.

'I've had a fucking skinful.'

Only the belch contains the definite threat of something else and Morrissey's keeping his hand on that door handle just in case.

'Don't be sick, Tia.'

Now she's turning green, and that's some achievement given her virtually pure Nairobi ancestry.

'I'm not.'

But the way she's clutching her gut really isn't inspiring too much in the way of reassurance.

'I've got to pick up them Moroccans later, take them down the Indian.'

'Don't mention Indian for fuck's sake Morrissey, that's where I've just been.'

Fuck.

'Think there must have been a dodgy prawn or something in the vindaloo.'

Double fuck.

'Cos I am telling you, my guts do not feel kosher.'

Morrissey stares at her.

Prawn.

Vindaloo.

Tia's dodgy gut.

This could be one seriously expensive dry-cleaning bill.

Then the front passenger door opens and an even more unwelcome sight suddenly appears.

'You been avoiding me, Morrissey?'

Billy.

Billy as in Billy - fucking – no-mates.

Billy as in Billy - total – fucking – tosser.

Billy the Kid who should never have been allowed to become anything else, who should have been drowned at birth and who actually had been in some of Morrissey's more lurid prison fantasies.

Morrissey stares at the new arrival who's making even Tia, her misshapen nose, her dodgy left leg, and her even more dodgy gut, seem sweet company right now.

'Billy, fuck off!'

'Don't be like that.'

'Now!'

'I've only just got in.'

'So you're going to have no trouble finding your way back out again'

'I feel sick, Morrissey.'

From the back seat Tia cuts in, only Morrissey's not listening. Thirty seconds ago the contents of her guts were Priority Numero Uno, now he's all-but-forgotten her. Ample evidence if any more was needed that Billy's always been one distraction too many in Morrissey's world.

Billy turns his big, all-mates-together, hang-dog eyes on him, only Billy's not a mate, he's a walking, talking, living, breathing, complete and total balls-up of a human being, which coming from a man who's not unknown for his own walks on the unreliable side really is saying something.

Behind, Tia moans again, quieter this time, which is even more ominous, but still Morrissey's just staring at Billy.

'It wasn't my fault.'

'Not your -?'

Morrissey tails off, total disbelief shrivelling his vocal chords.

'It was a mistake, one little mistake, could have happened to anyone.'

'It didn't happen to anyone!'

'It had slipped my mind in all the excitement.'

'You worked there!'

From the back seat there's a rumbling sound but all Morrissey's hearing right now is blood pounding in his ears and it isn't helped by Billy strangling a smile as he tries to change the subject.

'So?'

Billy tries to smile wider.

'Anything going down?'

26. SANTA'S SLEIGH

Two years and more than seventy-eight days ago, Morrissey and Billy were stepping out from behind a JCB.

Bamford's finest had been digging the footings for a brand-new hutch that was about to go up next to four other hutches that had already gone up, joining about forty more that had already been snapped by just about every wannabe developer on the manor. Somewhere there must be a factory churning out twenty-somethings with white smiles, or there'd better be because all those wannabe developers were going to have one hell of a lot of empty rental stock on their hands if not.

But the demand's been pretty healthy so far and while the population may be on the itinerant side, most spend just a few months there before wafting off to a different hutch somewhere else, while they are there they want the best of everything to keep all those white smiles in place. So the local electrical stores have been doing as big a roaring trade as the developers, plasma TVs, stack systems, lightweight laptops, you name it.

Hence Morrissey and Billy and their close proximity to the JCB.

Billy nods up at a floor-to-ceiling window on the very top storey of the block in front of them with views up and down the docks, old and new.

'That's the one.'

Morrissey eyes the darkened windows, wary. Getting in is going to be the easy bit. Some total neanderthal employed Billy as a security watchman a few months ago so they're just going to use his pass. But getting out with a plasma TV tucked under your shirt and another one down your Y-front's was always going to prove that touch trickier hence Morrissey's unusually comprehensive preparations.

'The van?'

'It's by the fire door at the back.'

'Security cameras?'

'All pointing the other way.'

Billy grins.

'Bleeding kids, always mucking about.'

Morrissey looks up at the darkened hutch for a moment longer, which in retrospect really should have lasted just that little bit longer again, long enough for Morrissey to rediscover where his brain was hiding that night and hightail it the fuck out of there.

Then he nods.

'Let's do it.'

Three minutes later, using the JCB as cover to dodge the front security camera, because that one was too high for Billy to tamper with, Morrissey and Billy were inside the top floor flat. And the views really are shit-hot, as far as the eye can see everything stretching out like dreamland. Lights flicker like a mini-Vegas on the distant water and inside it's a magic carpet ride too with enough clobber, electrical or otherwise to fill Santa's sleigh a thousand times over.

And now Morrissey's looking at Billy with almost-new eyes. All Billy's scams in the past have come with something of a sting, if not a great big snakebite in the tail, although on second thoughts don't mention snakes. Billy tries, which is sort of his problem, he's always been very fucking trying. But not tonight, standing in the middle of this ticket to just about anywhere he and Morrissey want to go right now, and that's club class too, not cattle, once all this is fenced.

'Who the fuck's that?'

For a moment Morrissey thinks he's hearing things. The flat's been as quiet as the grave up to now. Ever since they'd let themselves in with Billy's pass, they'd been walking round, checking out this, hunting out that and they'd not heard a thing.

'Who the fuck's that?'

But there it is again. And it's coming from the next room. Morrissey stares wildly at the rooted Billy.

'Who the fuck's that?'

Which is Morrissey this time, not any sort of echo.

'I don't know.'

'You said they were away.'

'They are, I watched them pack up their Chelsea tractor first thing, I waved them off for fuck's sake.'

'So?'

'Who the fuck's that?'

Which isn't Morrissey this time, and it's not Billy, and it's no echo either, that's the third time that voice from beyond the door has asked precisely the same question and Morrissey for one isn't going to stick around while its owner investigates any further.

Morrissey makes for the door, Billy following close behind. The problem being that while the thinking's good the timing's not because as they exit the lift doors open, less than five metres away and two white smiles emerge from inside.

But that's not so bad. Billy's the security guard. A little bit of front and they'll breeze it. Only front's never been Billy's strong suit, that's always been in short supply, just like his brains and, true to form, Billy bolts back into the flat in a blind panic, Morrissey following, Mr and Mrs White Smile now staring after them, two very puzzled expressions on their faces right now, and Morrissey isn't going to hang around for enlightenment to dawn.

Back in the flat with two antsy intruders on one side of one door, a voice that's not going to content itself just with questions much longer on the other, Morrissey and Billy could be in some serious shit here.

'Back door.'

Morrissey stares.

'What do you mean back door, we're five fucking stories up.'

Billy shakes his head, breathless with tension and fear, only just managing to get it out.

'Fire escape.'

Which is something. It's not much but at least he's come up with something. Which is when they hear it again.

'Who the fuck's that?'

Along with a sound that sounds suspiciously like someone tiring of the strictly verbal approach, and that same someone making for the door that currently separates them.

Morrissey hisses at Billy again.

'Go.'

Billy quickly leads the way to what turns out to be a fully functioning fire escape, not a builders ladder Billy's confused for the real deal, a proper, watermarked, kitemarked, BS-standard fire escape, a good and faithful friend to low-level villains the world over, but definitely, as in very definitely, not the place for low-level villains to stop and have a chat.

Which Billy now does.

'Hang on a minute.'

Morrissey doesn't reply because he can't, something to do with him being inches behind the now-stationary Billy at the start of that short sentence, but no inches at all behind him at the end. Morrissey's head smacks up against Billy's shoulder and the laws of physics are about to exert their inexorable logic once more.

As Morrissey remembers it from his days at Vesuvius's knee, and he's going to have a fair old time to ponder it too, roughly two years, forty-eight days in fact. the laws of physics are something to do with irresistible force meeting immovable object and some sort of balls-up always ensuing. Morrissey had always been a bit hazy on the theory but he's never going to forget the practical, because his head now collides with Billy's shoulder closely followed by the rest of him, that irresistible force transferring Billy's frame into something less than an immovable object, tipping him right over the edge of the fully-functioning, watermarked, kitemarked fire escape which moments before had promised salvation, but now isn't promising any sort of salvation at all.

Billy grabs hold of Morrissey's jacket as he goes over the edge, an instinctive reaction and fair enough in a sense because he's falling and he doesn't want to. Morrissey digs his heels into the top step of the fully-functioning, watermarked, kitemarked etc etc because he doesn't want to either, but Billy's scrabbling fingers are now clinging onto Morrissey's lapel and he isn't about to let go, not with absolutely nothing now between him and a thirty-foot drop.

Morrissey follows the yelling Billy or maybe it's Morrissey who's yelling, things are beginning to get just that little bit confused. Halfway down Morrissey did wonder if he was going to see his life flash before his eyes or even get a chance to relive one or two moments from it, and, if so, could he drown Billy in that park pond they used to fish as kids? It might not change anything or lessen the moment of impact which could now only be a second or so away, but it would provide at least one image Morrissey could savour before he hits Mr Tarmac's finest.

But Morrissey doesn't hit the black stuff, he hits a bin. In fact he hits a whole pile of bins, all plastic, all black, and all full to the brim with the debris of various dinner parties from assorted upmarket flats. It's pretty disgusting stuff, to eat as well as to land in, but it does provide at least a half-soft landing. And Billy's also underneath Morrissey at the actual moment of impact which not only provides a makeshift cushion, but also goes to show that even if God wasn't exactly on Morrissey's side that night someone was looking out for him.

27. TIA'S HANDBAG

Morrissey stares back at Billy as a loud noise sounds and an evil stink begins to percolate from the back of the Shogun. Tia's finally giving up her struggle to hold onto her vindaloo although she must know Morrissey's really not in the mood for any extra aggravation tonight with Billy sitting next to him because she's opened her handbag and is now filling it full of undigested prawns.

But Morrissey is still just staring at Billy.

'You were the caretaker.'

Billy nods, miserable.

'I know.'

'You'd seen it, dozens of times.'

Billy nods, ever more miserable.

'You'd fed the fucking thing the week before.'

Billy tries to struggle a half-spirited defence but it's a painfully empty riposte in truth and he knows it.

'It had never actually said that before though. 'Who the fuck's that?'

'Of course it hadn't Billy, every time you walked in it saw you, so it knew who you were so it wouldn't need to ask who the fuck it was, it knew who the fuck it was because it could see'.

Billy nods, sage

'There is that.'

Morrissey just keeps staring at him.

'Is that it? I spend two years in stir because you get us running away from a talking fucking parrot and all you've got to say is –'

Words fail Morrissey again. Billy doesn't even attempt any, those hang-dog eyes of his now a picture of total misery.

'You're a twat, Billy.'

Billy nods again.

'I know.'

'A complete and total fuck-up.'

Billy just nods once more because there's nothing else to say. No defence. No point.

But now Morrissey's looking at Billy like he's always looked at him, like he looked at him as a toddler and then as a boy, like he looked at him as a teenager trotting around behind him in the alleys and rat runs of their old estate, because while he might be a sad fuck he's always been Morrissey's soft spot, was then, will be forever and for a good reason.

So now, and as ever, Morrissey struggles.

'You did one thing right I suppose.'

Billy looks up at him, the beginnings of light starting to shine once again in his eyes. Morrissey glances in the rear-view mirror at Tia who's looking as if she's just said goodbye to that stomach of hers forever

Then he looks back at Billy.

'There might be something.'

28. CHER

Lulu's fifty feet up in the air inside an iron cage, one hand on a lever, the other rifling through a fashion mag, acres of sequins on view, yearning in the big man's eyes. There'd always been yearning in truth, but now there's hope too and that's as in not just wishful thinking. And it's all courtesy of the large crate that's about to be lowered by Lulu's crane to the ground

The crate in question lands on the wharf around thirty seconds later with something of a bang, not delivered with Lulu's customary care and consideration given that his attention is more on a Julien Macdonald number, worn by Cher at some charity do years before, now up for auction, and which would fit Lulu a treat with a bit of judicious letting out around the back and the shoulders and the arms and the waist. If all goes well today he could actually afford it, and if Morrissey's calculations are right, maybe he could afford the Versace number on the next page too.

Which is when the voice breaks in from fifty feet below.

'You fat clumsy fucker!'

Looner's not exactly trim and fit himself, but maybe he has a point. After that debacle involving Angel, Mr Merc and assorted squashed coconuts, Looner really does not appreciate any more loud bangs and crashes so far as the rest of his specialist imports are concerned.

Looner bends over the crate to inspect for damage as Lulu puts his magazine back in his pocket, exits his cab and climbs onto the ladder to begin his descent. Down on the ground Morrissey's standing next to Looner, Billy next to them both hopping from toe to toe which is when Leanne breaks in from behind.

'I'm fucking freezing, Looner.'

Leanne's waiting for the docket from Lulu, all ready to file them when she gets back in the office and that's not a moment too soon because right now her tits are turning to concrete. Looner, still inspecting his crate, doesn't even look round, just snakes out a large paw, removes the fleece from the nearby Billy's back and drapes it over Leanne's shoulders. For a moment Morrissey's tempted to intervene on his soon-to-be-shivering pal's behalf, but he doesn't. It's cold, but it's not that cold.

Looner straightens up from the crate, contents undamaged, just as Lulu swings down from the bottom step of the ladder, and hands Leanne the dog-eared docket.

'All checked and accounted for.'

Leanne, still shivering despite Billy's fleece, misses the quick, half-glance exchanged between Lulu and Morrissey as, thankfully, does her boyfriend.

'Thank fuck for that, can I go in now?'

Lulu nods at the docket, trying to keep his voice level, his tone casual.

'Seventy-five this time.'

Leanne cuts across again.

'I'm sure standing out here's against Health and Safety, it's like the fucking Arctic.'

But Looner's looking behind her at two new arrivals, one looking as smug and stupid as ever, the other looking as if she wants to be anywhere on God's own earth than here right now.

Looner nods.

'Mac.'

Morrissey, Lulu, and Billy wheel round to see the man himself approaching from another unmarked police car with Carmel. Morrissey turns back to Looner, trying to look and sound as casual as Lulu that moment before, but it's not easy with a voice that's suddenly pitching the high side of castrato.

'What's going on, Looner?'

Looner shrugs, none too bothered about this in truth, but Mac seems to have a bit of a bee in his pork bonnet about it.

'There's a story going down a couple of out-of-town villains have sussed some action.'

Behind Mac, Carmel's urgently trying to communicate via her staring eyes, trying to tell them this is fuck-all to do with her. And Morrissey's trying to stay cool but he's not even beginning to manage it despite the chill, north-easter blowing in off the Bristol Channel. Billy and Lulu aren't noticing the temperature now either, their stomachs are churning as well, minds racing, blood pumping like porn stars overdosing on a bumper dose of Viagra which is all well and truly keeping the current cold snap at bay.

'Me and Billy can sort any bother.'

But Looner barely hears him, all he wants to do right now is get Leanne back inside that office because her tits really are jutting out now. She's so cold he might just get lucky. His rolls of flesh don't do much for the eye but as a human hot water bottle he sometimes cuts the mustard and he might just do again once he's got rid of the rabbiting Morrissey and his loser of a fucking sidekick.

'Mac's going to ride shotgun for the next few trips.'

And that's it. No debate, no further communication. A few seconds later the portacabin door bangs shut behind the departing Looner and Leanne.

'Well come on Morrissey, what the fuck are you waiting for?'

You to die a slow and painful death, somewhere miles away from here you stupid, useless fuck . . .

. . . was Morrissey's reply to the staring, belligerent Mac. But it was one of those silent ones again.

Morrissey just keeps a sicky smile pasted on his face instead as he moves towards the waiting Shogun.

29. BILLY'S FOOT

A couple of minutes later, Morrissey and Billy are pulling away, Mac's hurry-up wagon following, Lulu back on the dockside, tears in his eyes as he looks at all those dresses in his magazine, wondering if dreams have already turned to dust.

By Mac's side, Carmel's mind's racing on just one problem but it's a big one. How the fuck to get Mac out of that motor and out of the way for the ten minutes it's going to take for Morrissey to meet Fomo and make their drop? For a moment she contemplates the ultimate sacrifice, extracting Mac's shrivelled dick from his capacious pants and blowing him, literally, to distraction. This is going to be a fair old payday after all. Then Carmel looks at him, hunched behind the wheel like some reject mould in a plastics factory and decides that however big the payday it isn't enough.

Which is when out it comes.

'Fuck.'

Mac looks at her.

'What?'

Carmel hesitates.

'Nothing.'

Mac stares at her some more.

'You just felt like saying, fuck?'

'Yeah.'

Mac turns back to the road, shaking his head.

'Twat.'

Meanwhile, a few metres ahead but tied to the car behind as if it's on some sort of umbilical, Billy's panicking too.

'What are we going to do?'

Although it might be better if he just follows Carmel's lead and says, fuck.

'The multi-storey's coming up.'

And it is, a pressured Morrissey can see it just a few hundred metres away now, salvation.

'We miss that, we miss the drop.'

'Billy, shut up, I'm trying to think.'

'It's just there, look.'

'I said, shut the fuck up!'

Billy turns those big puppy-dog eyes on him again.

'Only trying to help, Morrissey.'

'By asking stupid fucking questions?'

But actually they're not stupid questions, they're very good questions because they're exactly the same questions tormenting Morrissey right now too.

Billy lapses into silence as Mac's unmarked car maintains the same even distance behind. Only Billy's not lapsing into silence because he's being cowed into silent submission by lashes from Morrissey's tongue. Billy's lapsing into silence because Billy's actually thinking right now too and that's not thinking as in Morrissey's thinking which is actually just mental meltdown, this is proper thinking as in coming up with some sort of plan.

It's not a great plan. It's not the sort of plan that's going to stop the world revolving on its axis, but it might just stop Mac following them and in Billy's book that's something at least.

'Slow down.'

Morrissey stares at the suddenly animated Billy.

'What?'

'Slow down.'

'What for?'

'Just fucking do it will you!'

And Morrissey's so stunned for a moment at the new and more forceful Billy seemingly being born before his eyes, butterfly from a chrysalis, and a voice that's actually issuing a command rather than pleading the usual whining entreaties, that he does just that.

Morrissey lifts his foot off the accelerator and the rear wheels of the Shogun start to drag on the tarmac. Then Morrissey recovers what's left of his senses and makes to stamp on the loud pedal again because the last thing he needs on a fucked-up day like this is to listen to a fuck-up.

'Just shut up and let me think will you, Billy?'

But suddenly Morrissey's talking to thin air, an empty space beside him that was once occupied, a passenger door that was once slammed tight shut now flapping backwards and forwards, and now he hears an agonised yell from nearby but far away at the same time.

Morrissey stares into the rear-view mirror.

Billy's just jumped out into the road.

For a moment Morrissey's thinking, OK, he's more than a bit agitated himself, but this has got to be a bit of an overreaction. Yes, if they miss this drop it's a blow, but given the amount of coconuts Looner's shifting right now there have to be plenty more chances, so why try and top yourself after one little setback?

Then Morrissey starts looking at the traffic already beginning to bunch behind, and twigs.

Back in the motor with the in-built ice cream siren, the female from the blues and twos is also staring ahead at Billy now writhing around on the road.

'What the fuck?'

But Carmel's already got her hand on the door handle. It's taken her a couple of seconds but, like Morrissey before her, she's beginning to suss Billy's not-so-stupid little plan here too.

'I'll check it out.'

'What the fuck's he done?'

'Just wait there.'

'I haven't got any fucking choice have I?'

Mac gestures at the prone figure of Billy lying in the road ahead of them, the traffic now bunching even more.

'Just get that useless fucker out of the way and give him a ticket for obstruction.'

Carmel dashes out of the car, races up towards Morrissey's Shogun, passing Billy whose face is now contorted in pain, and while everything else about this little charade might be play-acting this is the one hundred per cent genuine article because Billy's leg is now giving him serious jip.

'My fucking foot.'

But Carmel's mind is well and truly on the bigger picture right now and that doesn't include Billy's toes. A breathless Carmel nods in at Morrissey, still staring in his mirror at Billy who's now sitting up but making no attempt to stand, not only on account of the fact it's charade time but also because of his foot.

'Is Billy OK?'

'Never mind Billy, just drive on.'

'He just jumped out.'

Carmel hisses at him.

'Now, Morrissey, before Mac commandeers a convoy of flying fucking motorbikes or something.'

Carmel turns back towards the still staring and ever-more-puzzled Mac, Billy moaning up at her again as she passes.

'My fucking foot.'

'Don't pile it on.'

Which is a pretty poor mark of appreciation in Billy's book, given all his efforts to help the common cause.

'I'm fucking not.'

'And he isn't. Because of -

'My fucking, fucking foot.'

Other motorists are now leaving their stationary cars and coming over to investigate, an ever-larger crowd beginning to mill between Mac and Morrissey's Shogun, meaning Billy really has been double if not treble clever here. But there's no time for grateful thanks, not with a fat slug staring out from behind the windscreen of a now-landlocked police car.

Mac puts his head outside the window as Carmel re-joins him.

'What's the stupid fuck-wit done?'

'He fell out.'

'What do you mean, fell out?'

'Door must have been dodgy or something.'

A pop-eyed Mac stares as he sees Morrissey, on the far side of the fast-bunching crowd, now pulling away in the Shogun.

'And where's that fucker going?'

Carmel stares back at Mac, something approaching pity in her eyes and she's only half-acting now too because there's always been something lacking in Mac despite his forty-six-inch gut. And it's not just his two-inch cock, flashed one day during a stake-out that turned out to be a bust, although not as much of a bust as Carmel's response to his not-so-subtle invitation to get down and dirty in the back of the squad car. It's the grey matter department too.

'Any minute now this place is going to be crawling with Black Rats.'

Carmel gestures at the crowd beginning to mill around Billy.

'At least two of these upright and upstanding Good Samaritans have already hit the treble 9s.'

Carmel nods back at the still-staring Mac.

'So what happens when one of the seagull squad begins wondering if maybe Billy's accident wasn't an accident at all, starts wondering if maybe him and Morrissey had some sort of argument about something, if maybe Morrissey had kicked him out or something and then starts poking round in the back of the Shogun to see if there's any reason why?'

Mac shrugs.

'I flash my warrant card and tell him to fuck off.'

'Why complicate things? Why risk some fresh-faced rookie straight out of Police School doing his impersonation of Serpico?'

Mac's staring eyes are beginning to return to something approaching normal size, Carmel actually having some sort of point here.

'And that's leaving out the paramedics, what happens if they decide to do a bit of digging, some of them'd do anything to relieve the boredom of a graveyard shift, and if they can drop the boys in blue in it at the same time that really is going to spice the day up.'

Carmel shakes her head, the smallest of smiles playing on her lips at the same time, which isn't any sort of promise but it still makes a connection, just like it's meant to.

'No one's staking us out, we've been following them for the last fifteen minutes, we'd have spotted any trouble by now.'

Carmel nods towards a fast-disappearing Shogun.

'I've sent Morrissey on.'

30.   A SERIOUS CASE OF RABBIT

Three minutes later and Morrissey's swinging into the multi-storey but he's agitated, driving way too fast, and nearly hits one of the concrete supports and Fomo who's hiding behind it

What is it about multi-storeys? Morrissey's always wondered. More pillars than the fucking Athenaeum. But Fomo has other matters in mind.

'Why are you so fucking late?'

And.

'Where the fuck's Billy?'

Two questions connected in ways he can't possibly imagine right now but Fomo's not going to get an answer to either, because Morrissey's now breathing like a man in serious need of an iron lung, the reversals and counter-reversals of the last few minutes having very definitely had their effect.

Morrissey just gasps instead

'Jam.'

Fomo stares at him.

'Billy stopped off for jam?'

Morrissey gasps again.

'Traffic.'

From outside the multi-storey a siren sounds as an ambulance passes, and Morrissey tries again.

'Billy.'

But that's as far as Morrissey gets, a coughing fit now claiming him and Fomo's still totally confused.

'OK, that's why you're late, you got stuck in traffic, but what happened to Billy, did you forget him or something?'

'Does it fucking matter?'

Morrissey finally gets his breathing back under control and his brain back into gear and the one thing he does not want to talk about with a Shogun full of coconuts is Billy. It doesn't matter that he's actually the hero of the hour right now, none of them are going to be anything other than dead men (or woman in Carmel's case) if they don't start shifting four of those coconuts and pronto.

'Get the back of that motor open and get them coconuts into your boot.'

'And that's another thing.'

Morrissey stares at him. Normally, you can't get more than a few words out of Fomo unless it's something to do with kittens, now he's got a serious case of rabbit.

'Do we have to stop at four? There's dozens in there.'

Then Fomo stops. And he stops because he can't say any more, not with Morrissey's hand wrapped around his windpipe.

'We agreed. Four.'

'Uuurgh.'

Which could be Fomo's fulsome agreement or his violent protest, it's difficult to say.

'Now open the back of this motor. Take out four coconuts, put them in the boot of your motor and then get the fuck out of here while I do the same.'

Fomo now released, massages his throat, sulky.

'Only a thought.'

'A stupid fucking thought.'

'I was only saying.'

'Fuck off.'

And Fomo does. With four coconuts. No more, no less. Morrissey watches Fomo get back into his car with the cargo and he keeps watching as he swings down the first of the ramps that'll take him back onto the street if he doesn't get a serious attack of the bends by then.

And then, suddenly, Morrissey starts to smile.

Because this is the first thing that's actually worked out roughly as it should in two years, seventy-eight days and more minutes than Morrissey cares to remember and something unaccustomed is beginning to bleed through his veins right now, a feeling of well-being, of satisfaction, a feeling that maybe, just maybe, things are starting to go his way at last.

31. LULU'S DOILIES

Six hours later, Morrissey, Carmel, Lulu, Fomo and Billy are in Lulu's flat on the fifteenth floor of the southernmost tower block, an uninterrupted view across the barrage to Penarth.

T-Bone, is pouring tea from a china pot into china cups, Lulu's handing round slices of cake, Battenberg, each one with its own doily underneath on small Wedgewood plates.

And Morrissey's bewildered.

'Where the fuck do you get them?'

Lulu, his mouth full of Battenburg, eyes the Wedgewood.

'Any decent china shop.'

'The doilies, not the cups and saucers.'

Carmel cuts in

'More to the point, why the fuck would you want to?'

Morrissey nods in total agreement here.

'They stick to the cake for one thing.'

Morrissey excavates bits of paper as Fomo stares.

'Fucking philistines.'

Lulu cuts across, firm, putting the kybosh on all this before an upset T-Bone runs out of the room, the cake going with him, because his diminutive lover has gone to a lot of trouble here and some people just don't have the grace they were fucking born with.

But Fomo's still staring at them.

'You mean you're not supposed to eat them?'

Fomo stares back at his plate, having just worked out why the bottom of this cake tastes like paper as Lulu eyes him back, caustic.

'Whoever's heard of edible fucking doilies?'

'No one in Nakhon-fucking-Sawan has ever heard of fucking doilies at all.'

'More fucking fool them then.'

Fomo looks at his half-eaten cake, unhappy.

'They're not poisonous are they? You can get all sorts of newsprint.'

'Doilies aren't newsprint.'

Fomo gestures down at it.

'It's got lines on it.'

Across the room, Billy cuts in, has been silent up to now but he's got something else very much on his mind and it's not doilies.

'Can I say something?'

But Fomo's still pointing.

'There.'

'That's a watermark.'

Billy tries again.

'Can I?'

'A what?'

'Look, will you all just shut the fuck up!'

And everyone does because Billy's now getting mega-agitated at being ignored like this, especially as it really shouldn't be that easy to ignore a man with one leg spread over two chairs when there's only three chairs in the room anyway but everyone's been managing it up to now.

'Stop talking about fucking dollies.'

'Doilies.'

Billy nods at a cold sponge in a nearby bucket.

'And put that on my fucking foot.'

Morrissey leans forward, slapping it on, Billy howling in protest as he does so.

'It's cold.'

Morrissey nods back, sage.

'It's a cold compress. There's a clue in there somewhere.'

'Fucking cold.'

Carmel grins.

'Put a doily on it instead then.'

Lulu, one eye on the temperamental T-Bone, isn't grinning.

'Not one of our fucking doilies you won't.'

But then Morrissey cuts across.

'I didn't know you were a Sunderland fan, Billy.'

Morrissey stares at Billy's foot and a tattoo he's never seen before, but then again Billy's unclothed left foot has never exactly been high on the list of sights Morrissey really has to see before he shuffles off earth's mortal.

Everyone else stops and stares now too, Billy growing more and more uncomfortable as they all take in the tattoo just above his ankle which looks like it's spelling Sun from one angle, land from another, meaning you've got to circle all the way round, which everyone is also doing right now, to get the complete picture.

Morrissey stares up at him.

'I thought you were a Bluebird.'

'I am.'

Lulu takes it up.

'Born and bred. Always have been, always will be, least that's what you've always told us.'

'I fucking am.'

'So why have you got Sunderland tattooed on your ankle?'

'Are you some kind of Fifth Columnist, Billy? All that time spent up on them terraces, yelling, cursing, celebrating every now and again.'

Carmel cuts in, smug.

'Very every now and again.'

Carmel's an Arsenal supporter, always did know which side her bread was buttered, because you don't see too many coppers or Masons which is roughly the same thing in Cardiff nick watching the Bluebirds, not with all that corporate hospitality swilling around all things Emirates.

'When all the time your heart was pounding for some other team instead.'

'Well if it was it wouldn't be fucking Sunderland! The Stadium of Shite? Fuck off Morrissey.'

'So why's it tattooed on your ankle?'

Billy struggles for a moment, but everyone's now well intrigued and he knows he's not going to get his leg off any of those chairs without offering up some sort of explanation.

'I got pissed up on Tyneside a few years back. Before that cup match, you remember Morrissey, we took Aidan, it was his first away game.'

'That still doesn't explain Sunderland.'

'Like I said, I got pissed, now can we leave it at that?'

'And decided to get a tattoo?'

Morrissey shakes his head.

'Fucking hell Billy, get a rose or a dragon or I've got a nine-inch knob, do not go to Geordie land and come back indelibly dyed with fucking Sunderland.'

'I met this bird.'

Billy struggles some more.

'We got on. Well, I thought we got on. I told her I was from Cardiff, up for the match and she didn't seem to hold it against me neither.'

'So who was she, Alan Shearer in drag?'

'Shearer was Newcastle wasn't he?

'I never found out who she was! We went back to her place with all her mates and after about seventy Sambucas, I passed out. Woke up to find my keks missing. For a minute I thought it was the ultimate choker, I'd had my end away, couldn't remember a fucking thing. Then I looked down, saw my ankle.'

And Morrissey, Carmel, Lulu, and Fomo all say it together, all grinning at the same time now too.

'Sunderland.'

'It's not fucking funny.'

'You're not standing where we're standing.'

'I'm not fucking standing at all, I can't! So let's get back to the matter of the fucking moment shall we, like the reason you're all looking at this fucking tattoo in the first place!'

Billy nods across at Lulu's table, the coconuts in pride of place although not on any doilies.

'There's only four.'

Billy nods back at them.

'Four coconuts.'

And everyone's now forgetting about tattoos, anything to do with Sunderland, wayward footie fans or Geordie tarts, everyone's just staring back at him, blank.

'Count them. I fucking have.'

'So?'

'So there's five of us.'

'Us?'

'Count again if you don't fucking believe me.'

Billy counts on his fingers, pointing at Morrissey, Fomo, Carmel and Lulu at the same time.

'One, two, three, four -'

Then he pauses, maybe for dramatic effect or maybe because his powers of addition have just momentarily failed him, Billy never being all that blessed when it comes to mental arithmetic or anything mental in truth.

But then he completes the count, indicating himself at the same time.

'Five.'

Morrissey eyes Fomo, sour recent memories returning.

'Don't you start, I had all this from Fomo.'

Billy eyes him, eager.

'So you think there should have been five as well, nice to know someone's been thinking of me.'

But Fomo shakes his head.

'No, I thought there should be forty, never mind four and it was fuck all to do with you.'

Carmel cuts in.

'Anyway, you only came in right at the end.'

Lulu nods.

'And why the fuck Morrissey agreed to that I'll never know.'

'It's not even as if you've any special skills.'

'How about free-falling out of a fucking Shogun?'

But Lulu's still not impressed.

'You call falling down a skill?'

Neither's Carmel.

'My son falls down all the time, no one says well done Jamal to him.'

'I don't fucking believe this.'

'Most times he just yells his head off and gets back up.'

'I fell in front of a fucking artic! I could have been mashed.'

'You will be, any minute, if you don't shut the fuck up.'

Now Morrissey cuts across again, Billy now actually in danger of popping.

'You'll get a cut, stop moaning.'

It had always been his problem, easier to wind up than a retractable tape measure. The trouble being that a raving Billy's well and truly past the point of reason now.

'I've already got a cut.'

Billy indicates his leg, the bruise turning mauve together with a multitude of surrounding lacerations and scratches, ample evidence if any more were needed that any contest between human flesh and the non-human black stuff is always going to end up with just the one victor. Billy nods over at the four coconuts again.

'It's a slice of that lot I'm talking about.'

'Coconuts don't slice.'

'Yes they do.'

'Do they?'

'I've had sliced coconut.'

'No, you fucking haven't.'

'Or was that pineapple?'

'Coconut's all runny.'

'Maybe it was lychee.'

Billy's now in real danger of having some sort of fit, and Morrissey steps in again.

'You'll get a cut, a slice, a portion, a segment, a share, whatever the fuck you want to call it OK, now can we all shut the fuck up, stop winding up Billy and divvy up our fucking mojo.'

Morrissey picks up a cleaver, hands it to the man with the doilies.

'It's his gaff. Lulu can go first.'

32. FRONTAL SCOOPS

How did it happen? Lulu was born a brick shit-house, his Mum said it herself when he first popped out, that is a fucking rugby player or a fucking lumberjack or a future heavyweight champion of the whole fucking world.

Lulu's Mum was still suffering the after-effects of too much gas and air and swearing like a docker, even though she'd promised herself she'd act like a lady around all those doctors and nurses. She knew they'd take one look at the address on her admissions form and think she was lowlife and she really wanted to prove she wasn't.

But if they'd told her then that she'd given birth to a lady, she really would have blamed all that gas and air. Lulu had muscles at ten minutes old. He could have bench-pressed before they left the hospital. He was already a man mountain by the time he was out of nappies. So why did the Good Lord give him that body and everything different inside?

It had tormented Lulu for years. At school, poring over the sort of mags you'd find discarded in dockside boozers, eyeing the sort of women you'd find waiting around inside, he made all the right noises and said all the right things, but he was just going through the motions. Nothing he ever said sounded or felt even remotely real.

Until one day when he went shopping on Albany Road, dragged there by his Mum who wanted an outfit for a night out in the old North Star, a cabaret event to celebrate the return of a local girl who'd made it big on some TV talent show that was running at the time. Everyone was turning up for the homecoming because everyone wanted to rub shoulders with the new, albeit short-lived, star and everyone wanted to look a bit like her too, all big hair and sparkly dresses.

Lulu's Mum picked out this sequinned number, low cut, slashed high, pink and white, bows and curls to the arms and sleeves and it was like someone had kicked Lulu in the guts. None of the naked women in the mags had done it for him, none of the half-naked tarts in the boozers had done it for him, none of the girls in school had even remotely done it or would despite him getting more than his fair share of offers, a fair few of them looking at his massive frame and wondering if everything else might be in proportion.

But that did it. That sequinned vision reached out across that small, cramped ladies' outfitter with dresses piled high in every nook and cranny and grabbed him by the heartstrings and turned his whole world upside down.

Catalogues were his salvation. A couple of the other lads would pore over the underwear section every now and again, but Lulu, alone at night, would snuggle under his bedcovers and turn to evening wear. He'd spend hours fantasising about that shade of lavender or that frontal scoop and not the women inside them either, just the dresses. And each morning he'd wake up, look at the giant staring back at him from the bathroom mirror, the night's new stubble already turning his face half-black and weep at the disconnect between the man who huddled down at night dreaming of ballgowns, and the outsized gorilla who got up in the morning and put on his XXL jeans and top.

Only Lulu's not dreaming now. OK, he's still not going to be touring the superhighway of his imagination, the chic little shops of far away South Moulton and New Bond Street, but with the windfall from this little pay-out he's definitely aiming a bit higher than Primark.

And Lulu brings the cleaver down on his coconut to reveal his little stash from heaven and lets out a most unladylike roar.

33. ROGUE CARDS

Pussies are Fomo's thing although not the kind barely covered in skimpy thongs. He never understood the skimpy thong bit anyway, in his practical book the more you pay the more you get, not less. So far as the exile from the South China Sea was concerned you really had to be a woman or Lulu to even begin to get your head round that sort of logic.

It was the feline kind that did it for him, and all makes, varieties, shapes and sizes too. From Persian to Egyptian, from polka dot to jet black, from ginger to any shade in between. Fomo just loved his little pussies.

What was the psychology? Why the attraction? Why do some men like trains? Why do some people collect stamps? Fomo doesn't know and doesn't care, all he knows is he does, and he's already amassed a fair old collection of the mewing miracles. Sixteen at the last count, all strays at one time, none of them strays anymore, all loved and cared for in a succession of flats that are usually closed to him the minute the landlord finds out about the additional items on the inventory.

So Fomo dreams. About a place in the country with the grounds full of purpose-built hiding places for his feline friends, a sanctuary for every lost and stray pussy soul on that and every other manor, Fomo walking through his specially created wonderland each morning greeting his adoring charges.

His little stash won't do it, not by itself. But it'd be a start, a stepping-stone to muscle in on some of the poker games organised late at night by a few of his fellow exiles who also work in Chang's and with a stake that won't now be laughed at.

And if he helps matters along a bit courtesy of a very special pack of rogue cards he's been keeping back for just such an occasion, then maybe, just maybe.

So now Fomo raises his cleaver and splits his coconut, revealing his very own passport to dreamland inside.

34. LITTLE JACK HORNER

Carmel's not dreaming of adornments like Lulu or cute little kitties like Fomo. Carmel's mind's running on more much temporal matters, flesh and blood in fact and not of the animal kind either, this is human and precious although try telling Fomo his prized pussies aren't.

Carmel's son, Jamal, is now four years old. Five years before, Carmel was a wild child, frequenting all the local clubs, imbibing all she could each and every night, Blow, Smack, Ket, you name it, although in truth she wasn't too bothered if it even had a name, she just did it.

But one chance meeting, one incautious shag, and she had an encumbrance, an unwanted complication, or at least that's how she saw it at the time. Then came the birth and it was like a shaft of light breaking through, a stake in the future where before hers was a life lived exclusively in the present with no thought of what was to come, maybe because what was to come was looking pretty bleak back then, no proper home, no prospects, no job.

Not that Social Services saw it that way. They saw an unstable young woman with a child and she was monitored from day one., She was already on the local risk register and when she accidentally overdosed on the one night she'd been out in more than two years, the Social swooped. Carmel came round in her hospital bed to find Jamal had been taken into care.

She could have done what she'd done before. Destroyed everything around her in a murderous fit of frustration and rage. But she didn't. She buckled down to prove herself a worthy mother to her son and she got a job, and not just any old job either.

The Bizzies, the Bill. How many variations of the one job description are there? Every variation and combination had been uttered by her mates over the years, all of whom now very quickly became former mates once she signed on the thin blue line.

She didn't get much in the way of fraternal support from her new bluebottle family either. Positive discrimination turned out to be almost as dirty a couple of words on that side of the fence as the fucking filth was on the other. And so it's remained, a no-man's land of distrust and suspicion everywhere she looks.

But given her now-consistent employment record and no more falls from grace she's one court hearing away from having Jamal restored to her full time. And if she could cop some sort of break at the same time, a leg up of some kind, a fresh start of some description, they could both start over somewhere far away from her old home turf and its even older temptations and pitfalls. She just needs the one chance. The one opportunity.

The scratch cards and the lotto tickets haven't provided it, a single win of ten quid over the last twelve months being pretty scant recompense for an investment of at least fifty times that. Which leaves some non-legit means, but that's not too promising either. There are so many fingers in so many pies down in her local nick they should adopt Little Jack Horner as divisional mascot, but she's frozen out of all that too given all that distrust and suspicion.

But maybe this is it. One single stash in a coconut. Like Fomo, she knows it's not enough for a brand-new life, but it's enough to make a start on one. Maybe she can invest the proceeds in some little business.

Carmel lifts her cleaver and splits her coconut, her small stash of hope now winking back at her too.

35. WHITE SAND

It's typical isn't it?

The story of Morrissey's life.

Carmel, Fomo and Lulu all have aims and goals, something to strive for. It doesn't matter how weird or wacko they might occasionally be, they've all got dreams.

But Morrissey's less focused, not so structured in his outlook and ambitions immediate or otherwise, or at least that's what he tells himself. In fact he hasn't got a clue. He just wants to get away somewhere as in anywhere, do something as in whatever, he just doesn't know. All he does know is that whatever he does it's got to be better than this. And if it isn't, then he'll move on again until he finds what he's looking for even if he hasn't the fuck of a clue what that might actually be in the first place.

Images swim before his eyes as he raises his cleaver, nice cars, expensive hols, a lovely little apartment somewhere.

And girls, lots of girls, all sitting on a beach, all with their backs to him right now, but all turning towards him as he walks out onto those acres of white sand.

And now Morrissey's stopping dead, even as the cleaver hits his coconut, because as all those girls turn towards him, every face is Kim's.

36. DEMENTED KANGAROO

One second before, Morrissey was wondering why his mind just played that sneaky trick on him.

But now, and more immediately pressing, his main preoccupation is why the fuck his right-hand feels like it's just gone eight rounds with a fucking jackhammer?

A yelling Morrissey's hopping round the room clutching his wrist and Billy's yelling too because that cleaver's just ricocheted away from his grasp and has very nearly added Billy's neck to his current list of serious injuries and if it had then he wouldn't be yelling because it would actually have separated his neck from his shoulders which is why he's yelling his head off.

'Fuck.'

That's Morrissey, still clutching a hand which feels like it's ringing.

'You stupid - fucking–'

That's Billy.

'Fuck.'

And that's Morrissey again, still hopping, still holding his hand with Carmel, Fomo and Lulu staring at him in total bewilderment. What's he doing, auditioning for Riverdance?

'What the fuck's wrong with you, Morrissey?'

But Morrissey's still feverishly rubbing anything remotely connected to his fingers as the shock of what's happened works its way through his body from tip to toe meaning Morrissey's going to be hopping like Skippy the demented bush kangaroo for some time yet.

'What the fuck's that?'

Morrissey just manages to spit out three words which is some sort of advance on just the one he's been spitting out so far, although Lulu, Fomo and Carmel are still staring at him in blank bewilderment and Billy's still shaking because he can still see that cleaver flashing through the air towards him as it flew out of Morrissey's hand and he's going to for at least as long as it's going to take that sudden shock to work through Morrissey's slim frame and leave him more or less shake-free.

'What?'

'That! Fucking that!'

Morrissey gestures towards the table, and Carmel, Fomo and Lulu are now even more bewildered because it's a coconut, just like the previous three, hairy on the outside, white and milky on the inside apart from the hollowed-out bit that houses the stash.

Which is when they all fall silent, although Billy's now yelling even louder. He's just seen the cleaver embedded in the wall behind him, at neck height, which has done a fair bit of damage to Lulu's antique flock, but not half as much damage as it would have done to Billy's windpipe.

'What is it?'

Lulu, Carmel and Fomo all now stare at the hollowed-out bit of Morrissey's coconut that houses the stash, only it doesn't house the stash, because there's no stash to be seen.

In its place is a rock, which clears up the mystery of why Morrissey's still hopping like that as the after-effect of the shock of hitting it works through. It also clears up the mystery of that cleaver turning into a deadly projectile because it looks like one fuck of a hard rock as well.

The only remaining mystery is what's it doing in one of Looner's coconuts?

37. A FUCK OF A BIG ONE

Half an hour later, Morrissey, Carmel, Lulu, Fomo, a hopping Billy and Aidan are crowded in Aidan's small bedroom, the young boy himself hunched over an old tablet, all coloured lights and asthmatic wheezes because it's not exactly state of the art, but it works and it's got an internet connection, and that's the main matter of the moment right now so far as Morrissey, Carmel, Lulu, Fomo and the still-hopping Billy are concerned.

It's also a tablet with an internet connection that isn't in Looner's office, because it wouldn't be the best career move right now, checking out one weird-looking rock courtesy of the maniac you've just lifted it from.

And it's a tablet and an internet connection that's not in the local nick, which wouldn't have been the most sensible notion under the sun either, checking out a hot rock under the eyes of the outfit probably deputed to look for it sometime in the not-too-distant.

It's also a tablet with an internet connection that isn't taking up any room in Chang's which is another big plus, Chang himself being likely to take more than a passing interest in all matters rock-shaped once he's alerted to his business partner's latest loss.

Morrissey's not in possession of any sort of tablet and neither's Fomo or Carmel, at home anyway. Lulu wouldn't know how to turn one on and nobody for reasons anyone needs to go into even thinks of Billy. Billy's not even thought of Billy. But tablets and internet connections are the sort of things every eight-year-old boy would have mastered from birth so the next logical step was to find one.

And this one's on his own right now too, Kim being out at yoga and Angel out at bingo so now it's Morrissey, Carmel, Lulu, Fomo's and a still-hopping Billy's turn to try to secure their very own full house.

But Carmel's dubious.

'This is stupid.'

Morrissey gestures at the intent, concentrating, eight-year-old.

'You got any better ideas?'
'Not this'
'What?'
'Not Aidan.'
'What then?'
'This.'
Carmel gestures at the strange-looking rock squatting by Aidan's tablet, which is looking stranger by the moment.
'It can't be.'
'What else can it be?'
'Looks like one.'
'If it is it's a fuck of a big one.'
'Lulu, do you mind?'
Morrissey gestures across again at Aidan, still hunched over the screen, fingers jabbing away at the keys.
Have some consideration for the innocence of youth, for fuck's sake.
'It explains Big Mac and Chang getting involved.'
Morrissey nods back at Fomo.
'Yeah, that's a lot of money for us, but it's probably just pocket money for them.'
Fomo nods at the rock.
'But if that's just an entrée and this is the main course.'
'How are you doing, Aidan?'
Morrissey nods across at the young boy.
'I'm still logging on.'
'What's that mean?'
'He's getting it going you fucking Neanderthal.'
'Fomo!'
'Sorry Aidan.'
Aidan himself nods at the screen, now filled with strange-looking rocks, all shapes and sizes, none of them exactly matching the rock still squatting by the tablet, but none of them that far off either. It could definitely be from the same sort of family as five souls currently crossing their fingers are hoping, well, four souls and one who'd like to cross his fingers because Morrissey's still suffering the after-effects of that close encounter with the coconut, or more accurately that rock in the coconut and can't cross anything.
'Here we go.'
The tablet's wheezing some more.

'What's it say?'
'Give me a chance.'
Aidan scrolls down the screen.
'This is all about where they come from.'
'That one came from Looner's coconut.'
'Where they come from as in what country.'
'Does it say anything else?'
Aidan checks, reading all the while.
'How they're bought and sold, how the prices are fixed.'
'Is there any way of telling if they're kosher or not?'
'Fake or real?'
'Short of going to some shop or something?'
'Is there some simple test?'
'Like dropping them in a glass of coke.'
Four pairs of eyes swivel back towards Billy as Aidan continues to scroll down the screen.
'Why would you want to do that?'
'What?'
'Drop that in a glass of coke.'
Lulu, nods at the rock, and is it Morrissey's imagination or is it changing colour a little, changing shape, or are his eyes finally settling like the rest of his body to something approximating normal operating speed?
'I didn't say you would.'
'Yes you did.'
'We just fucking heard you.'
Lulu stops again.
'Sorry Aidan.'
Morrissey cuts across.
'For Christ's sake, does this matter?'
'It's a test, I read about it somewhere.'
'All that'd do is make it sticky.'
'There's something in the chemicals or something.'
'You're on some kind of chemical, you must be.'
'Fake ones do something and real ones don't.'
'Do what?'
'I can't remember that bit.'
'Twat.'
'Lulu!'
'I said twat, not fuck.'

'Cleans ten-pence pieces, mind you.'

Four pairs of eyes now swivel towards Carmel who begins to grow defensive.

'Jamal did it in school with Vesuvius.'

'That's not a ten-pence piece.'

'In one of his science experiments.'

'For fuck's sake!'

Now it's Morrissey who stops, glancing over at Aidan again who's still staring at the screen, but before he can apologise too Aidan cuts across.

'There's nothing about how to test them on here.'

'Bet there's nothing about glasses of coke neither.'

'For fuck's sake!'

'Or ten-pence pieces.'

Morrissey pauses, head now pounding as Aidan grimaces at the computer screen, stumped, Fomo, Carmel, Lulu and Billy just shoot dark glances at the other, no one exactly sure what to do next.

Then Morrissey takes a deep breath.

'Let's go and talk to Slippery.'

38. A FUCK OF A STATE

Half a mile away, Looner, Mac and Chang are in one of Looner's lockups, the latest delivery laid out on the floor, an irate Looner about to go into orbit, boosters well and truly engaged, Looner, in short, in one fuck of a state.

'You must have missed one.'

Looner eyes Chang, not the most sensible thing to say if you're even remotely attached to the idea of your head remaining attached to the rest of your body.

'Say that again?'

Chang, sensibly, does not.

'Missed one? Fucking –'

Words momentarily fail the incandescent Looner.

'Think I can't fucking count? Seventy-five fucking coconuts. That's what it says on the docket.'

Looner advances into a graveyard of split coconuts, stashes dotted all around on the floor as well but Looner's not looking at them, exotic foodstuffs being way down his list of priorities right now.

'That's a hundred and fifty split coconuts. And I've split every fucking one of them just like I'm going to split your fucking head open if you say one more stupid fucking thing like I can't fucking count.'

'I didn't say you couldn't count.'

Chang stops as Looner moves among the coconuts, kicking out at any that get in his way, sending plumes of white milky liquid up into the air.

'Seventy-five coconuts. That's a hundred and fifty half coconuts just like it says on the docket. Every single one present and correct and accounted for and it's not in any – fucking –'

A huge splat sounds as a virtual monsoon of coconuts head skyward courtesy of Looner's outsize boot.

'- one of them!'

'So where is it then?'

Which is Mac's only contribution to the debate so far but a second later he regrets saying even that because Looner now pushes his face close to Mac's, spittle flying from his gob.

'That is what you –'

Looner jabs his fingers into Mac's chest like a jackhammer.

'- are going to fucking find out!'

A helpless Mac looks back at Chang as Looner stamps away out of the door, kicking more coconuts out of his way as he does so, Mac's face saying it all.

How?

39. ICE

Slippery's out when the makeshift posse and Aidan call, which is out as in out of it, not out as in down the bookies or out as in some pub somewhere and he's out of it because he's got fuck all else to do and hasn't for a long time.

Like Fatman, Slippery's trade is now a dying art, assorted high street chains well and truly having done for it over the last few years but it was probably only a matter of time anyway in his case. Forty years ago Slippery discovered the wonderful world of the single malt and even though blended is now all his impecunious pocket can run to, his heart well and truly remains with all things golden.

Five pairs of eyes belonging to five hugely sceptical souls are now staring at him as he struggles to fix a jeweller's loupe to first one eye and then the other and then back to the first one again, as if somehow in the minute or so that's passed since that first manoeuvre he's suddenly regained something resembling coherent vision.

But one pair of eyes in amongst all those others is silently pleading with Slippery to work his magic because Morrissey's well and truly out of options if he doesn't come through for them.

Now Slippery's dropped the loupe onto the cigarette-stained rug that's struggling to cover the chipped and stained linoleum running through his one-bedroomed shithole of a flat.

'Are you sure about this?'

That's Carmel and she's not alone in the deeply sceptical stakes.

'I'm fucking not.'

Lulu eyes the scrabbling Slippery in turn, still searching for his loupe on the floor, the big man having made way beyond apologies for bad language to Aidan now.

Morrissey has a stab at sounding convincing as Slippery gets to his feet having finally retrieved it.

'He's a jeweller isn't he?'

'He used to be.'

Then Slippery drops it again.

'So once a jeweller always a jeweller, it's like riding a bike, you never forget.'

Morrissey stops. Having retrieved it for the third time, Slipper's now trying to fix it to his ear. Morrissey takes the loupe from Slippery's shaking fingers, fixes it, right way up into his left eye, praying that memory, instinct, something, anything, will do the rest.

'Looks like a washed-up old fuck to me.'

Slippery, the loupe in place, fixes a hopeful hazy eye on his companions.

'Anyone fancy a drink?'

A hope that is definitely going to prove just that little bit too hopeful.

'Later, Slippery.'

'Things always look so much clearer when I've had a bevvy.'

Morrissey hisses at him.

'We'll fill your boots for you, just look through that thing that's clamped to your eyeball right now and tell us if that.'

Morrissey gestures at the strange-shaped rock now just inches from Slippery's shaky stare.

'Is what we think it is.'

'A wotsit.'

'A thingy.'

Slippery stares at the incoherent foursome before him, growing ever more puzzled now by the moment.

'What's a wotsit?'

'For fuck's sake, isn't it obvious?'

'Ice.'

'Ice?'

Five pairs of eyes and Slipper's one loupe-less eye stare at Billy as he translates.

'A diamond.'

Slippery looks at it, then looks back at them

'Is it fuck.'

Six pairs of eyes now stare back at Slippery. They've finally got a straight answer to a straight question and it's clear and it's concise and it's absolutely not what any of them want to hear.

'It's not?'

'No fucking way.'

'So what the fuck is it then?'

135

But Slippery's mind returns to the main matter of the moment. 'You sure none of you fancy a drink?'

40. SHIMMERING WITH DARK INDENTATIONS

Looner's specially constructed roof juts out over the largest office on his site.

It boasts a totally level pitch with a non-slip surface. Large bolts anchor the structure at all corners to concrete footings dug extra deep into the earth, because no way does Looner want this lifting off in the wind, not with his state-of-the-art telescope squatting proudly up there staring at the heavens, or to be strictly accurate the only piece of heaven Looner's ever been interested in although maybe obsessed is a better way to put it.

And right now Looner's doing what he does every night. He's staring through the lens at the moon above, all white and shimmering with dark indentations.

And like on every one of those other nights, Looner's hardly breathing.

41. BETTER THAN SEX

Back in his one-bedroomed flat with the peeling linoleum, Slippery concedes defeat on the bevvy front for now anyway, as those different pairs of eyes keep staring at him.

'He's been after one for years.'

Those same eyes swivel back to the strange-shaped rock, disbelief mixing in with an all-too-familiar feeling of let-down.

'He kept on and on about it as if I'd know where to get one, it's a rock he said, a stone, what's a pearl or a sapphire, same fucking thing, there's a trade in them so there has to be a trade in these as well.'

Slippery shakes his head as he relives the delusions of the deranged and dangerous loon.

'I didn't have a fucking clue, but he kept on, find one, ask around, I told him time and again I couldn't, but would he listen?'

Slippery stares back at the rock.

'Looks like someone has though.'

Meanwhile, at that very moment and back on his roof, Looner's mouth's opening and closing, his heart pounding ever faster as he keeps staring up at the glowing orb above, a man and his telescope, Looner and his moon, this better than sex in his book although in Leanne's book most things would be better than sex so far as the fat useless fucker's concerned.

'So it's just a rock?'

Lulu picks it up, the look on his face saying it all. If this really did come down from the heavens, it might just be going back up there in roughly thirty seconds if Lulu has anything to do with it.

'Pretty special sort of rock.'

Not to Lulu or to Carmel or Morrissey or Fomo or Billy or even Aidan right now, not when they had in mind something really they'd normally only see in films or on the fashion pages of glossy mags or red carpets worn by movie stars.

'Actually, a very special sort of rock.'

Which is still not doing it and never is going to from the look on all those faces right now

'A fucking moon rock.'

Half a mile and an unbridgeable divide away, Looner's staring at the complete article, the whole moon, not just a tiny-chiselled fragment, dreaming, imagining how would it feel to hold part of it one day, little knowing that Lulu doesn't have to imagine, that he's holding it right there and then and it doesn't mean a fucking thing.

'Does it honk?'

'What of?'

'Cheese?'

'Ha, fucking, ha.'

'So it's not true then?'

Lulu eyes Billy who really thinks he's being funny.

'It doesn't honk, no. But it's hard, very hard and it'd make a fair old dent in a bone head like yours, want a demonstration?'

Tempers are starting to fray now, Lulu waving the rock around like it's some sort of deadly weapon which, if there's any more disappointments tonight, it might just turn into.

Meanwhile Slippery's rolling on.

'The first lot of astronauts, the Apollo lot, they started it off, bringing bits of it back and you know how potty he is about that sort of thing.'

'A lump of the fucking moon.'

'Over the years it's built up into a tidy little business.'

An incredulous Carmel stares at him. She's seen some sights in even the short time she's been maintaining the thin blue line and she's come across more than her fill of life's saddos and sickos, but even she's finding it difficult to square this oddly shaped piece of stone with an object, however obscure, of actual desire.

'You mean people actually pay for things like this? As in actual dosh, not Monopoly Money?'

'They're highly prized by collectors.'

'By fat fuckers with nothing else to think about.'

But Fomo's now looking at him, a faint, very faint, gleam of distant hope starting in his eyes.

'You mean it's really worth something?'

'Oh, it's worth something.'

'How much?'

'Well, I can only hazard a guess.'

'Hazard.'

Lulu tosses the rock to Morrissey, still finding it impossible to really believe something like this can actually be worth anything at all.

Slippery muses.

'Something that size?'

He ponders some more.

'Let me have another look.'

Billy collects the rock from Lulu who tosses it onto Slippery.

'Two –'

Slippery stares up towards space, or at least his ceiling for a moment, mouth opening and closing like a guppy.

'No, that size –'

When Slippery's thinking out loud like this you can almost hear the wheels grinding into motion.

'Nearer three –'

Morrissey looks at Carmel who looks at Fomo who's looking at Lulu with Billy looking at them all and Aidan looking on, because all of a sudden there's just a chance this may not be quite such a busted flush after all.

But then Slippery shakes his head again as he palms it back to Lulu.

'No, it has to be two.'

Which isn't as good as three and it's still not anything that can be called a result, but it's enough for a drink which for five souls in that room right now is partial compensation at least.

Slippery cuts in again as Lulu tosses it up towards the ceiling.

'Actually now you really look at it, from all angles and that.'

The moonrock spins, slowly, back to the ground.

'It might be three.'

Morrissey looks at his partners in what's turned out to be not-so-lucrative crime and shrugs.

'Three grand ain't bad for a day's work.'

Slippery cuts in again, correcting Morrissey a milli-second before the rock crashes back down to earth.

'Million.'

Six pairs of eyes stare at Slippery, but the ones closest to floor level are the first to react. Aidan snakes out a hand, catching the rock just before the moment of impact, which is no mean feat seeing how, and like the rest of them, he's staring at Slippery at the same time.

And a stunned Aidan is the first to recover his voice too.

'Fucking hell.'

42. BEST BIT OF BLOW

One hour later and Morrissey's walking by the river in the moonlight and it's like no moonlight he's ever seen before, and the river's like no river he's ever walked beside either, how can it be when the sky's dripping white honey and the walkway his feet are floating on right now is made of the most perfect down.

And the skies are playing more tricks now too because new stars are appearing all over the constellations and they're multiplying all the while, each one shining brighter than the one before and the ones before were blazing with all the force of a billion candles.

It's like the best bit of blow you've ever scored. The most potent joint. The very best shag only they end, and this isn't going to end or at least it's not going to end for a fuck of a long time, not with three million smackeroos turbo-charging it even if Morrissey does have to split that a bit.

And then he sees the angels and he's not talking Kim's sister. And he's not talking Christmas tree angels with billowing frocks and wands in their hands, but real-life angels, not that Morrissey's ever seen a real-life angel but they're just how he imagines angels would look. Morrissey would be the first to concede he's floating somewhere above Cloud Nine right now and at that sort of altitude the head might be pardoned if it plays the odd mischievous little jape, but they're floating, twisting and turning, doing all the things you imagine angels might do and there's no singing or chiming of bells but who needs sound when you've got the pictures as Buster Keaton used to say. or would have said if he'd had sound. And Morrissey knows he's spinning round in circles himself, but he doesn't give a monkeys, in fact he wouldn't even give Oz's elephant because right now he doesn't care.

Morrissey is a little more exercised when the face of the angels are actually revealed to him, because if the Good Lord is going to send congratulatory visitations to a soul he's more or less ignored up to now, he might have expected their faces not to be the unattainable Kim, that

Good Lord above having already played that trick on him just before he split his coconut.

But it's a minor quibble on an otherwise perfect night, although maybe it's also a reminder from the big man beyond the moon and the stars and all the constellations that his angels may be fab to look at but don't touch, because Kim is pretty shit-hot to look at and to touch too from what Morrissey remembers, but he certainly won't be going there again now.

Later, and in a rare moment of reflection, Morrissey's going to wonder if there's something else going on here, some other message being sent along the celestial hotwire. Whether he was ever-so-slightly accessing the future which isn't actually that far away in fact, trying to prepare himself for a test ahead. Or maybe all that's bullshit, just like the white honeymoon and the angels and the stars burning like supernovas in their final eclipse.

Maybe the simple truth is that Morrissey for the first time in as long as he can remember is high on life.

And so is Carmel, but she's also feeling horny.

43. ONE OUT OF FOUR

It's like being drenched by the biggest bucket of the coldest water.

Not that it's unpleasant, far from it, the sight of a naked Carmel rising from Morrissey's sofa being very definitely one for the scrapbook.

The question being, whose scrapbook?

Maybe not Morrissey's.

'Shit.'

Morrissey once caught a flash of Carmel's long legs as she ran, gazelle-like, across the sports field in school one summers day way back when there were summer days, and he remembered thinking then that she was a fuck of a lot different from any of his other pals in the playground which might sound obvious, but he was only four at the time.

Morrissey celebrated his new youthful insight by beating fifty pieces of shit out of her when she beat him in the thirty-yard dash a few moments later, but as she beat fifty-one pieces of shit out of him by way of payback straight after, the day ended more or less honours even with no lasting damage done to a friendship that had more or less survived ever since.

But now Morrissey knows all his childhood instincts were correct. Carmel is a fuck of a lot different from any of his pals in the playground. She's a fuck of a lot different from any of his pals outside the playground too, she is absolutely fucking gorgeous in fact which makes his first reaction to the sight of her naked body even more curious and it's not just his first reaction but the second too because now Morrissey repeats himself, after a fashion anyway.

'Fuck.'

Carmel eyes him, clearly none too impressed by either of those reactions, and all Morrissey can think is what's wrong with me, beautiful woman, more or less normal bloke, both single, an empty flat.

'No – I don't mean – I mean – wow –'

Carmel stares back at him, a hand on one of her hips, one leg bent slightly forward, back arched slightly now too and Morrissey's not going to be able to get that image out of his head for weeks to come and why is he doing everything but acting on it?

'Double-wow.'

Carmel stares at him some more.

Morrissey hesitates some more, knows he's offending the lady, in fact he's even offending himself.

'It's not you.'

Carmel's face now freezes, hand tightening on her hip, back straightening at the same time, turning ram-rod stiff in fact which is about the only thing that is ramrod stiff in that room right now which is sort of the problem.

'It's not that I don't fancy you or nothing – I mean, who wouldn't, just look at you, I mean - wow – double – '

Carmel's hand moves away from her hip as Morrissey tails off, Carmel turning back now to Morrissey's sofa and her discarded clothes.

'I do fancy you, 'course I do, anyone would, you'd have to be fucking dead not to, it's just – '

Carmel, still naked, looks back at Morrissey, his mouth in search of air.

'And it's not 'cos you're a copper neither.'

Carmel steps back into those discarded clothes, long black legs disappearing inside skin-tight denim.

'Aren't you ever going to get over her, Morrissey?'

Later that night and Morrissey's alone again. Carmel now a distant whiff of regret. Someone else is there instead and it's that ever-present stranger at the banquet, that constant ghost at the feast, that spectre always on the edge of his vision.

Morrissey deals with it, he lives with it, he gets on with it, but will he ever get over it? He knows the answer. It's yes to three, no to one.

But maybe one out of four isn't bad.

44. OZ'S ELEPHANT

In the old community hall paint peels from the ceiling and the wooden floor's scuffed with a rotten piece just by the door to trap the unwary stumbler on their way home with too much warm beer and cold lager inside them, and right now a couple of hundred of those potentially unwary stumblers are packed inside.

Oz is on a makeshift stage, Aidan with him, a state-of-the-art DVD player on stage too, but this is no illicit auction of dodgy clobber which is not entirely unknown in these surroundings. But what actually this is, that's proving a bit more bewildering.

But then the DVD player powers into life and pictures fill an outsize screen and the pictures are pin sharp too so there's no mistaking what everyone's seeing right now which is an elephant.

But then it starts jerking around all over the place and that's nothing to do with the warm beer and cold lager sloshing around inside most of the onlookers, or the illegal substances being imbibed by others. This isn't down to some bad trip, Oz has hit the fast forward button instead of play and now he's hitting rewind instead and the screen's fast filling with flickering images of an elephant seemingly on speed.

'We're in the shit.'

Lulu, just arrived, approaches Morrissey, Fomo and Billy, a cold dose of reality having now well and truly kicked in. Then Lulu pauses as Kim comes in behind, this very much not for anyone else's ears but theirs, which is when he spots the elephant.

'What the fuck?'

Then Lulu stops again as Aidan appears at their side, flyers in hand.

'You're all going to be in a football match.'

Billy stares up at the screen.

'I'm not playing no elephant.'

By Billy's side, Morrissey's suddenly finding the flyer of intense if not enormous interest, partly because Aidan's so obviously up for this and anything Aidan wants to do is forever OK in Morrissey's book, but mainly because Carmel's just walked in too and Morrissey really isn't sure how to play this in the light of recent events.

Or as it turned out, one great big non-event.

A cool Carmel cuts in.

'It's Oz's latest fund-raising stunt.'

She knows exactly how to play this, pretend it never happened which as nothing actually did happen makes sense, even if Morrissey now can't quite help looking at her and wondering, knowing only too well that wondering is all he's ever going to do from now on because that door opens once and is now slammed shut forever.

'There's flyers all over the place, have you lot been hibernating or something?'

'No, we've been keeping our fucking heads down.'

Then Fomo's hissed retort is cut short by a warning kick on the shin from Morrissey or, more accurately, by an agonised yell from Billy as the warning kick connects with his injured shin by mistake.

Aidan nods back at them as evermore pissed onlookers mill all around.

'A big match, out on the rec like Oz says you used to have.

Billy is now rubbing his leg, mortal injury the matter of the moment and not just his damaged and now-aggravated shin.

'Jesus, I remember them matches.'

Morrissey nods.

He does too.

'Like war minus the shooting.'

'Sometimes with the shooting.'

Then Oz yells across from the stage. He's hit the wrong button again and now the elephant's starting to jiggy-jig.

'Aidan!'

Aidan exits with the rest of his flyers, Carmel regarding Morrissey coolly for half a second as he does, but then Lulu cuts in again, getting back to the real matter of the moment, never mind Billy's throbbing shin and Carmel's non-existent shag.

'And that is as in the complete and total fucking shit, up to our fucking earlobes.'

Fomo, as jittery now as Lulu, nods.

'It was OK when it was rhino horn and scorpion shit, like you said he wouldn't have missed any of that for ages, probably wouldn't have missed it at all.'

Billy cuts in, still massaging his shin.

'But he's missing that all right.'

Billy gestures to the skies, four pairs of eyes following in an involuntary reflex.

'He's going fucking bananas, I heard him on the dog to Mac back in the yard.'

Lulu, Fomo, Carmel and Billy look at each other. And if four pairs of eyes, legs and arms were nervous before that's nothing compared to the mass hysteria that's about to break out.

'He's trashed three warehouses looking for it already, now he's starting on the boat that brought it in, if he doesn't find it on that it'll be scrap by the weekend and the Harbour Master's going to have to walk the plank.'

Which is when a panicked Billy stands, dodgy leg and all, getting ready to run. Everyone knows that Looner's a vicious fuck who'd run you through with a cleaver as soon as look at you, and that's just for you looking at him, so what he'd do about something like this is really giving Billy wind beneath his wings.

'What are we going to do?'

And from the look on Fomo's face he'll be following Billy any minute now on that high road to Scotland or that slow boat to China, the destination's unimportant, just anywhere away from lunar-obsessed lunatics.

Lulu, looking as panicky as Fomo and Billy, cuts in.

'What do you mean, what do we do, it's fucking obvious, we stop sitting in shitholes like this looking at dancing fucking elephants and get the fuck out of here.'

Lulu nods at them, Billy and Fomo nodding back, which is when Morrissey cuts across.

'We don't do nothing.'

And whatever else his staring companions might think about that particular contribution to the proceedings, Morrissey has at least stopped them nodding.

'As in fuck all. Zilch. Absolutely nada.'

'Have you fallen out of your tree, Morrissey?'

'Fuck his tree, it's falling off his perch he should be worried about and that's what we're all going to be doing any minute.'

'Think about it.'

'There's a time for thinking and a time for doing Morrissey and no cigar for working out what this fucking time is.'

'We just wait.'

'For the fucking axe to fall?'

'Onto each of our fucking heads?'

'If we're lucky, very lucky and Looner doesn't start with any other bits of us first.'

'And the one thing we're not is fucking lucky, this has well and truly proved it, even when we do get a stroke of luck it turns out fucking awful.'

But Carmel is eyeing Morrissey.

'Wait for what?'

'We just sit tight.'

'There he fucking goes again.'

'Do what we were always going to do. What we agreed to do for fuck's sake. Wait for Looner to waste half the villains in Euroland looking for his little piece of heaven.'

Morrissey hunches forward.

'Wait till he works through the people who sent it over, the people who packed it in the coconut, the little piece of balsa wood that brought it across that not-so-sparkly sea, wait until he's wasted that lot and, with a bit of luck, gets wasted himself along the way.'

Fomo, Billy and Lulu begin to quieten as Carmel eyes him, remembering again, and with more than a pang of regret, why she always found this fucker so attractive.

'And while he's doing that and while we're still keeping our heads down we fence his –'

Morrissey gestures up towards the sky, not putting it into words, four pairs of eyes almost involuntarily ascribing the arc.

'And then one by one, very slowly, still keeping our heads down, still not doing anything to draw attention to ourselves, we each take our cut, and one by one again and even more slowly we slip away into the night.'

Morrissey nods around his now-hushed congregation.

'Yeah?'

And one by one, eyes begin to lighten. One by one, brows begin to clear and tight-lipped mouths begin to loosen into something approaching cautious smiles.

By the bar, Kim's thinking that whatever Morrissey's got they should definitely bottle it because he really is at the hub of a little ray of spreading sunshine with Fomo, Billy, Carmel, and Lulu right now.

Then again, she's never had any complaints on the sunshine front where Morrissey's concerned, he always had burnt brighter than a thousand-watt bulb, the only problem being the night that follows those days.

But he's definitely still got something because as she keeps watching, Lulu starts to giggle and Billy starts to splutter so this really must be good because his leg's still up like a balloon from when he fell out of Morrissey's moving motor which is a mystery in itself, brand new Shogun's not usually being prone to developing faults with their doors.

And Carmel's beginning to smile now too which is another turn-up because she's turned into a serious old cow since she's started pounding the beat, but here she is, Little Miss Personality Bypass, grinning as if Morrissey's just cracked the best joke she's ever heard and Fomo's getting in on the act as well, the diminutive Chinaman actually getting a fit of the giggles right now.

Back on the stage and courtesy of Aidan, Oz's video has finally slowed to normal speed and the city farm's latest attraction is unveiled at last. Now they just need the dosh to arrange transportation from its present home in some religious retreat somewhere in the wilds of deepest west Wales and this little bit of the docks is going to be turned into a piece of land that is forever Africa or India or wherever that thing's actually from in the first place.

Not that anyone cares where it's from, it's where it's heading that matters as Oz's valedictory speech now makes clear and that's one abandoned patch of a fast-developing city that's being fast left behind and will soon be cleared completely, so dig deep and contribute and if you can't dig deep and contribute then come along to the football match in a couple of days and turn it the sort of spectacle that's going to attract a record crowd all of whom will be digging very deep if Oz, not to mention Aidan, not to mention the strangest collection of animals this side of a two thousand-year-old ark have anything to do with it.

45. BURLY CHASSIS

It's party time.

One hour earlier and no way was Lulu going to do it, no way was he going to be standing up on stage, belting out the usual when all the time he was waiting for Looner's cleaver to slice through the bits he never much cared for, but really does not want surgically removing by Looner's not-so-gentle hands. That prospect was shrinking his larynx, not to mention those bits he'd never much cared for, and he knew that if he got up on that stage then all that was going to come out of his gob was a strangled croak.

But that was before Morrissey and his little reminder of a pep talk. That was before that mass attack of the giggles. And now Lulu's feeling like he can do anything, and he's going to do it, right now in fact. Lulu's going to don the Julien Macdonald and Lulu is going to give it mega.

Actually, Lulu calls it a Julien Macdonald, but the boy from the neighbouring valley would probably vault several mountains in disgust if he could see it now. It's still got the same lines and cuts, still the same swooping neckline and it's still slashed to the thigh, but now there's sequins hand-stitched by an adoring Lulu and T-Bone, as many as could be fitted without the whole thing collapsing under its own massively increased weight, all different colours and designs and all a hymn to excess which so far as Lulu's concerned is the only thing he can never get enough of. the

The lights dim, and then the music begins, faint at the start, then louder, a spotlight picking out the stage. Faint white spirals appear as an unseen Lulu blows a plume of ciggy smoke, floating wing to wing, building the moment, milking the anticipation, whipping the audience up to fever pitch before he finally delivers. Then with three strides, he's on stage, music crashing in at exactly the right moment because T-Bone's manning the sound system and there's no Oz-type cock-up here, the only cock-up T-Bone's interested in is going to take place later, for now this is slick professionalism as Lulu pays homage to the only singer that can still move him to tears.

Even his choice of dress is a not-so-subtle tribute and if anyone as in anyone ever, as in ever at all, dares call Lulu's beloved Shirl by the bastardised moniker she's sometimes known of Burly Chassis, then they've got a date with the sharp end of Lulu's crane and a terrifying descent from sixty feet up all-the-way-down fifty-eight of that sixty if Lulu's feeling generous, sixty-one if not.

And then he starts. And Morrissey and the boys, not to mention the girl, join the rest of the hall in belting out the first in the song sheet, one of their much-loved local girl's finest.

Square cut –

The words echo round the hall.

Or pear shape –

Getting louder and louder all the while.

These rocks don't lose their shape –

And by the time Lulu gets into the second verse everyone's on the dance floor and everyone's joining in, and if only Morrissey could now get his rocks off with Kim, then this is going to be one fuck of a fuck-off night.

Which he attempts to do just thirty minutes later.

46. THE NIGHT OF THE HUNTER

Across the hall, two strippers are talking to the local Vicar who used to be the local bookie before he lost his shirt in Cheltenham a year or so back and decided to give the dog collar a shot. He may not be too hot on God and all the saints and the apostles, but he knows a lot about fallen souls in need of helping hands.

Kim's with them, she's not a stripper and she's none too religious either but she is enjoying the crack and it keeps her away from Morrissey who's circling like a shark waiting to move in for a bite he's never going to have, but she knows he's never going to give up trying and Kim can't decide whether she'd be disappointed or relieved if he did. Which is why right now she's sticking to the company of strippers and the strangest clergyman this side of *The Night of the Hunter.*

But even she's got to obey calls of nature and even though all logic told her she'd be safe in there at least, hearing Morrissey's voice from the next cubicle really isn't that much of a surprise either seeing as how he always was a resourceful little fucker.

'Can't we at least talk about things?'

'For fuck's sake, Morrissey!'

'Five minutes, that's all I'm asking'

'I'm having a slash.'

'I'm not stopping you.'

'And I'd appreciate a bit of privacy.'

'I'm not looking either.'

'Morrissey!'

'I'll have one myself. Just to keep you company.'

Kim sits on the seat having her slash, listening to Morrissey having his and wondering, who else, who fucking else? Testing herself all the time, checking, waiting for that quick, secret smile to start, ready to choke it, stillborn, because she knows where that leads, where it's always led, give in to that and in six months time she'll be held back from her own personal madness by a thread so gossamer-thin she wouldn't dare breathe in case everything collapses.

So there's nothing. Because she still doesn't trust herself one single solitary inch.

'Just a simple conversation, that's all I'm asking. I'll stay in this cubicle, you stay in yours, you won't even have to look at me, where's the harm in that?'

Kim hasn't looked properly at Morrissey for two years and forty-odd days and the fact she knows how long says it all. One fuck of a lot of harm is the answer, but Kim just keeps quiet, praying he'll take the hint and go away.

'If you fancy a crap, just say so.'

For fuck's sake!

'That deserves a bit of privacy, fair enough.'

And now she does need to do it, now she does kill that quick, secret smile.

'I'll tell you if I do too, 'cos you never know do you, sitting on the throne, it's like a reflex action or something.'

Kim cuts across.

'Talk about what?'

'Me and you.'

'There isn't a me and you, so that's going to make this a very short conversation, in fact, that's it.'

'You've never wondered, what if?'

'I don't need to. We had what if, and a fuck-load of shit it landed me in so why would I need to imagine anything?'

'I do.'

'You've spent too much time on your own.'

'I've been banged up twenty-four seven with about two thousand lowlifes for the last two years.'

'Then you haven't even got that excuse, you must just be a saddo, get over it.'

Morrissey pauses, struggling now.

'Everything that happened, what I did, that was for us, Kim, that's all it was about.'

'And I told you, time and again, I can't live like that, nothing one day, a flat full of knock-off the next, your trouble is you can't live any other way.'

And now Morrissey's really struggling.

'This is just like last time isn't it?'

'Last time, the time before, take your pick Morrissey, times change, the scenery changes, sometimes we manage something a little more upmarket than a fucking toilet, but me and you, that never changes.'

'We split up for no good reason.'

'For no what?'

A disbelieving Kim tails off, speechless for once and now there is warmth deep inside, but it's not the glow of icebergs melting, this is white heat and instant too.

'I come back, try and sort things out.'

'You can't sort out what wasn't there in the first place.'

'You don't even listen, you didn't the last time, you're not now.'

'The time you went away for three years and I had a kid, just a few months old when you came back, didn't that give you just the slightest little clue that things had changed in my world and you weren't part of it no more?'

'Everyone knew what that was.'

'It was a baby. It was Aidan.'

'I don't mean Aidan, I'm talking about what you did.'

'One sort of led to the other, Morrissey.'

'It was boomerang time, you were on the rebound. Angel told me what you were like back then, latching onto every face you could find, ditching them two minutes later, I'll bet the poor sod who got you up the duff didn't even know about it, still fucking doesn't probably.'

Kim cuts across again.

'And I did all that, signed myself up for a lifetime's care and concern for another human being just because I was obsessed with forgetting you? Bet there's lots of mirrors in your gaff, Morrissey, talk about thinking one fuck of a lot of yourself.'

'I made a mistake, Kim.'

And there it is again, that sideways lurch in the stomach, and all down to that little boy lost note in the voice that always, momentarily anyway, gets through.

But not this time.

'No Morrissey.'

Kim stands, pulling her knickers back up over her bum

'I did.'

Kim flushes the pan.

'And I'm not doing it again.'

Then she walks out, Morrissey still sitting in the adjacent, still-open cubicle, toms and strippers walking in, not even giving him a second glance, it's just Morrissey and Kim, situation normal, all fucked-up.

Three hours later and with Morrissey finally in kip there's a huge banging on the door.

For one deranged moment Morrissey's thinking maybe Kim's changed her mind, has suddenly decided she's got a massive dose of the hots for her long-time and often-absent lover after all and has charged round pronto to tell him.

But she hasn't and he knows it and that's not just because an eager Morrissey's opened the door and is now looking out on his actual caller, it's because he's still got half a functioning brain cell.

Morrissey blinks in the open doorway, the light from outside momentarily blinding him, but it's not his eyes that are bothering him, it's the iron fist that's grabbed him around the throat, the fingers that are that's choking off his oxygen supply, that are knocking his knees together and blowing out his cheeks and making him thank the Gods of Good fortune that Carmel never took real offence just those few hours before.

Carmel stares at the gasping Morrissey, one question and one only on her lips.

'Where is it?'

PART THREE

'The Sun and the Moon Stand Still'

Joshua, 10

48. DOWN THE PAN

A second or so later and Morrissey's still gasping, his legs still knocking, his cheeks still fully distended, so all in all it's really not surprising he's not able to muster too much by way of a reply.

'I said, where is it?'

A strangled cry is all Morrissey's managing which should be coming out as, what the fuck are you talking about? But he's not even managing that at the moment as Carmel's eyes flash ever more dangerously.

'Talk to me, Morrissey.'

What Morrissey tries to say next is, how the fucking hell can I? But it actually comes out as a cross between Urdu and Sanskrit if you tried writing it down, but something in his eyes must be getting Morrissey's bewildered message across because Carmel starts to loosen her grip, beginning to get herself back under some sort of control although it's a pretty fragile sort of control because that hand snakes right back out again just three seconds later, which is about as long as it takes a very croaky Morrissey to try and lighten the situation with a little levity.

'Don't you ever take no for a fucking answer.'

Which is clearly a bad move, because this, equally clearly, is not a situation that's going to be remotely alleviated with any sort of levity.

Carmel shakes her head, her grip tightening all the while.

'Two mill, maybe three, split five ways, just disappeared down the pan and all Morrissey can do is crack fucking jokes.'

Only suddenly he isn't. And he's also forgetting there's no oxygen flooding his lungs and his knees are still knocking and his cheeks are now roughly treble the size they should be.

Now he's just staring at her.

'I'm going off my fucking trolley and you think it's cabaret time.'

Morrissey cuts across.

'What's disappeared down the fucking pan?'

And now Carmel's eyes are growing troubled. They've known each other virtually all their lives and would have got to know each other a fuck of a sight better if Carmel had her way, but she's still witnessed most of Morrissey's scams from the cradle to what's promised to be the grave on more than one occasion.

And the one thing Morrissey's staring eyes are telling her right now is that something may well be very wrong here and it is, but it's nothing that's going to be laid at his door.

49. ONE HAPPY ENDING AT LEAST

Ten minutes later, Morrissey and Carmel are in Carmel's kitchen, a large and well stocked chest freezer open in front of them but neither are exactly in the mood for the selection of ready meals on offer inside.

Morrissey and Carmel are staring at a space to the side of a bumper packs of fish fingers, her little boy being particularly partial to that part of a marine creature's anatomy.

A large, two to three million quid, sort of space.

'It's my weekend to have Jamal.'

That's Carmel although Morrissey's having trouble hearing with her voice seeming to be coming from somewhere out in space which is maybe where Looner's moon rock has returned to. Because the one thing for sure is that it's not in Carmel's freezer anymore.

'I took him out to the park. Half an hour, a quick kick-about then back for his tea before I take him to see his Nan, then deliver him back to the Social.'

Morrissey stays silent because if he didn't he'd be letting out the silent scream that's been building up inside ever since he first realised just why Carmel's hand was wrapped round his windpipe.

'Nothing else is missing, no money, no credit cards.'

Carmel keeps staring at the freezer.

'Now call it my police training, but that seems to rule out any sort of opportunist thief. And my knickers are still hanging up on the washing line so that seems to be the pervert angle knocked on the head as well'

Carmel's beginning to rant now, and she knows it, and she can't help it.

'This is not me doing my impersonation of Sherlock by the way, this is plain, simple, common, fucking sense. Someone got in here, that same someone went to one place and one place only and took one thing and one thing only, that rock and the stash of stuff we collected from the rest of those coconuts.'

A reeling Morrissey finally gasps it out.

'Who?'

Carmel looks at him, a grudging admission.

'OK, you're a sly, conniving piece of shit, capable of any sort of sneaky little scam but I suppose this would be beyond the pale even for a wanker of a chancer like you.'

'Cheers.'

'And it's not Jamal, I kept my eye on him all the time in that park, you tend to where four-year old's are concerned, no way could he have given me the slip, hightailed it back here and lifted his mum's very own personal pension plan.'

Morrissey cuts across again.

'Which leaves?'

'Which leaves the only other people who knew that rock and that stuff was here in the first fucking place.'

'I don't believe this.'

'Ten out of ten Morrissey, you've caught me out, I'm making it up.'

'This isn't happening.'

'Got me again Morrissey, it's all a dream, a figment of my over-active imagination and so's this dirty great space where our dosh in waiting used to be.'

She doesn't get any further. And she doesn't get any further because Morrissey is now heading for the door, Carmel following, her last burst of venom wasted on the wind, the open lid of the freezer mocking them as they go, Jamal's grub inside already beginning to lose go off, the little boy destined to return from his Nan's to bitter disappointment in the fish and finger stake.

But then, as the front door slams behind the exiting Morrissey and Carmel, the lid of the freezer slams down too making for one happy ending at least.

50. PATIO WINDOW

Five minutes later and Morrissey and Carmel are striding up the small garden that leads to the rear patio window of Lulu and T-Bone's immaculately maintained brand new townhouse.

It's two or three clicks down the property ladder from Mac's gaff according to any one of the local estate agents you might care to consult, but Lulu's done his best. Patio furniture is dotted around a small concrete paved area, an in-built barbecue in pride of place, gas powered, meaning no messy charcoal, everything neat and tidy, a place for everything and everything in its place.

The question on Morrissey and Carmel's minds being, does that include a small piece of rock and a large amount of stuff and if it is in some place in or around here then where the fuck is that?

Morrissey decides to announce their arrival in a more immediate way than just banging on the window, giving anyone inside time to shoot out of the front while they're hammering away at the back. He picks up a patio chair, hurls it at the large expanse of glass before them. That way they'll walk straight in through that smashed window and seize the initiative from the off.

The patio chair bounces back off the double-glazing, Carmel and Morrissey diving out of the way as a simple chair, transformed into a sudden lethal projectile threatens to put them both in A&E.

Carmel stares at Morrissey in disbelief.

'What the fuck did you do that for?'

'It's what Looner did.'

'What?'

'At that barbecue at Mac's, that chair went clean through.'

'Because that chair was cast iron best quality Sheffield steel, not –'

Carmel picks up Lulu's sad alternative.

'– fucking plastic.'

Then Carmel stops and Morrissey's spared any more blushes by the patio window opening, cautiously, an equally cautious Lulu poking his head out, alerted by the crash, not wanting to cop any more stray missiles or pigeons or whatever the fuck just hit his window like that.

Lulu stares at Carmel and Morrissey, a weird weapon of evil intent in his hands or at least what looks like a weird weapon of evil intent but which will turn out to be a tile cutter.

'What the fuck was that?'

Carmel nods at her companion to her side.

'Ask fucking Mastermind.'

Lulu looks at him.

'Morrissey?'

'I thought it'd go straight through.'

'What would?'

'The chair.'

'My chair?'

'Well I didn't bring my fucking own.'

'Why did you throw my chair at the fucking window?'

Then Lulu, beginning to grow irate as well as bewildered, stops as Carmel frogmarches him back inside his immaculate townhouse just as Looner did with Mac, although he did smash his patio window first which just goes to show that where everything seems to go OK for other people, everything just goes tits-up for Morrissey.

51. GROUTING A GODDESS

Lulu's bathroom is much like his doilies, all frills and swirls with the addition of a large mural of some sort of sea creature on one of the walls, and it says something for Lulu's pride in his domestic surroundings that even as he's flung back against his pink bath by a vengeful Carmel he reaches out to stop a stacked display of ornamental soaps toppling to the floor.

'So was this the idea right from the off?'

'What?'

'Sitting up in that ivory tower fucking crane of yours, is that where you dreamt it up?'

'What the fuck are you talking about?'

Morrissey takes it up, all thoughts of patio furniture now well and truly wiped.

'You thought, I'll come in.'

Morrissey picks up one of the ornamental soaps, flings it at Lulu. As lethal weapons go it's none too impressive, but as a statement of general intent the message gets through.

'And shaft us.'

Fruits of the Forest flies past Lulu's ear closely followed by Scent of the Valley, but that's actually flying way past Lulu's ear because Morrissey really is one shit shot. Carmel watches, despairing. As intimidation goes, assault by scented fragrance is never exactly going to be up there anyway, but assault by scented fragrance that doesn't even get to within five feet of its target is going to start losing them all serious credibility.

'Fucking hell Morrissey.'

'Then get the fuck out?'

Lulu's not even trying to dodge out of the way now seeing as how it's quickly dawned on him that all he's got to do is stand stock still and Morrissey isn't going to get within a barn door of him.

Morrissey collects another of the exotic collection of sweet smellies only to stop as his hand's held in another vice-like grip by Carmel, and even in his manic desperation to recover his small piece of the heavens Morrissey still can't avoid a quick pang of regret. If her wrists grip like that, just imagine the thighs.

'Don't ever take up fucking baseball will you?'

Then overhead lights suddenly flash on, what feels like a million sunbeams immediately dazzling Morrissey and Carmel as a strobe effect display in the ceiling plays over the stand-alone shower and the pink bath with its clawed feet, another stream of light picking out the mural, now revealed to be a sea urchin, a diminutive Somali now standing in the doorway.

And T-Bone's hopping literally from one leg to the other, furious at the artwork that was his display of exotic soaps from far flung climes now dotted all over the Italian tiled floor. For five years he's kept Lulu from grabbing this collection and taking it in with him for his morning shower, a collection desecrated in as many seconds by Morrissey and not one of them has even hit the fucking target which may not sound too bad to Lulu but only compounds the injury so far as T-Bone's concerned.

'He finished it just over an hour ago.'

T-Bone flicks another switch, another beam of light picking out grout on the tiles, still damp to the touch although if Morrissey does actually touch it now there's going to be murder committed in this bathroom and it won't be by anything as inoffensive as exotic soaps.

'Lovely job he's made of it too.'

Which is a matter of debate, but Carmel's now leaning close, sniffing the wet grout which has a definite smell all of its own and she should know, DIY taking up pretty much all her spare weekends these days which is why she briefly contemplated breaking the cycle, in one way anyway, with Morrissey.

T-Bone keeps eyeing them.

'Which is why he was about to get a blow job when it isn't even his birthday.'

'Was I?'

Across the bathroom, Lulu's eyes soften, his groin stirring, the muscles hardening over his arms and shoulders which is one fuck of a horrible sight but T-Bone only has belligerent eyes for the wankers who've upset his display.

'So what the fuck was he supposed to be doing while he was in here grouting my goddess?'

Fomo's moving from pen to pen, adoring legs brushing up against him, the air humming with the sounds of contented felines

Cats don't give, which is what Fomo likes about them. They're not dogs, they deal with the world on their terms. They're independent, yet aware of the relationships they need to maintain to survive, making them clever, the highest form of life in the animal kingdom so for as a besotted Fomo is concerned, so it's really should only take a few seconds for Morrissey, Carmel and Lulu to work out one unalterable and cast-iron certainty set in any kind of stone you'd care to mention.

Even with all the riches in the world on offer, Fomo is never, as in ever, going to let his precious collection of pussies return to scavenging in the street while their lord, but never their master, hightails it for foreign shores.

Which is why the incoming threesome are already pausing as they head in through the door, before coming to a total halt as they see the absorbed Fomo in the middle of laying down saucer after saucer of dry food pellets along with individual cat sweets shaped in the form of different fishes, each one carved by Fomo himself each morning before he goes to work in Chang's kitchen, this being something of a daily treat.

Fomo doesn't even seen Lulu, Carmel, or Morrissey at first. He's in the closest state to beatitude he's ever likely to experience. But then his eyes clear and his state of grace quickly deflates as he turns and sees the new and unexpected arrivals.

'What the fuck?'

Which isn't exactly the question of course. The question's more like who the fuck, closely followed by where the fuck?

And Fomo's blankly enquiring face is telling them all they need to know right now which is they still don't have the answer.

Five minutes later, and with Fomo now well and truly returned to earth from the state of beatitude courtesy of his passport to pet school disappearing down a dark hole to crushing disappointment, the now not-so-fab-four are falling on each other in the time-honoured fashion of all such fallings-out.

'Course we've only got your word for it haven't we?'

Lulu stares at Carmel. In his book coppers are only step removed from the numerous villains he knows, in fact they're worse than villains because they at least operate by some sort of code.

'What the fuck's that mean?'

'This could all be a stunt.'

'Do I look in the mood for pulling fucking stunts?'

But Fomo also eyes Carmel, a lifetime spent paying off dodgy narks, bent health inspectors and minor hoods having also left him with a deep distrust of anyone remotely connected with authority.

'Lulu's right, you could have lifted that rock yourself.'

'Stole it from my own freezer, very fucking likely.'

'Then gone round to Morrissey's and played your injured Injun card.'

'Stole from myself and then reported it to one of the faces I stole it from, we could do with you in the filth, Lulu, you could be ACC by Christmas.'

But Lulu sticks with it.

'Before having it on your toes.'

'Apart from the fact I'm not actually on the next fast jet to go and join Biggsy on the beach in Brazil or hadn't you noticed?'

'He's back home isn't he?'

'Who?'

'Biggsy.'

'Or dead.'

Carmel shakes her head in despair, they're wasting time here which they haven't got.

Along with the rock.

'Which is exactly where I am.'

'Dead?'

'Home! Here! And do you really think I would be if I'd lifted that rock?'

Morrissey stares into the near distance, a new uneasy suspicion now beginning to claim him.

'Fuck.'

Carmel rounds on him.

'There's no point just saying, fuck Morrissey.'

Fomo nods. She's right.

'What do we do now, that's the fucking point.'

But Morrissey's still staring into that near distance. This lot may not be exactly reliable but they still all grew up together, and what slimy, shifty, unreliable little fucker would grow up with them only to go and shit on them all like this?

But even as he asks the question, he knows.

There might be one.

Which is why, for the second time in about as many seconds, Morrissey says it again.

'Fuck.'

53. A HIRED MUSCLE'S PINKY

The lap dancers are classy, maybe those students from the local school filling in again. OK, it's still the usual tits and tassels but there's a silky slinkiness to the way those tassels are being removed and it's drawing a fair old audience.

It's also drawing Billy. Normally he'd avoid these sorts of places like the plague, seeing as how anything Billy usually has to offer the enticing girls in front of him never normally guarantees him more than a quick flash of forbidden fruit and that's always tasted sour to Billy. What's the point of fruit if it's forbidden for fuck's sake? Fruit's juicy, ripe, and meant for sampling straight away.

Look and don't touch, that's fair enough. Look for roughly five seconds before some other punter carrying a bigger wodge blocks your view, that's something else.

But things have changed for Billy. Because Billy's suddenly become a front row merchant with a pile of the folding stuff in hand. And with a lap dancer's thigh now just an inch or so from his face, Billy ties a bluey to her suspender belt, and the lap dancer's already wondering about doing a few circuits around this particular saddo because this might just be her weekly supermarket shop all in one go.

A dreamy Billy closes his eyes, his face pressed so close to dreamland he can smell it, even if he can't touch it, and it's the sweetest smell in the world too and it's probably better than touching in truth because everyone knows what happens to all those perfect bubbles when you do actually touch them, they burst as the old song has it, then fade and die.

Which, in roughly five seconds, is what's about to happen to Billy.

For three of those five seconds, Billy's eyes are still closed so the incoming Morrissey, Carmel, Fomo and Lulu have the advantage. It takes another second for Billy's eyes to open and register four very unhappy-looking faces staring daggers across the floor at him. Part of the final second's taken up with formulating a plan which is several minutes less than Billy needs even at the best of times which this is definitely not. So all in all it's a good job Billy's face is still pressed up against the lap dancer's gyrating crotch and he's able to ignore the strict rules of the establishment and grab hold of one of her legs, shoving her, still tottering on her heels, smack bang onto her arse in front of the advancing bodies of his pursuers.

Morrissey and his companions stagger backwards as she crashes into them. The girl's not big but she's got legs to die for and if anyone connects with one of the sharpened stilettos currently attached to the end of each one there's an even chance of ending up on the wrong end of some needle and thread. And neither Morrissey nor any of his current companions remotely fancy a detour down to the local A & E, not when there's someone else to put there instead.

'Billy!'

Morrissey yells across at him, but the fast-exiting Billy isn't listening. He's chanced upon another obstacle which is about to become a diversion, a couple of pool players bored by the antics on the stage or, more likely, unable to compete for the lap dancers' attention by the likes of the suddenly flush Billy who's now charging into them, pool cues and balls going everywhere, those same balls rolling on the floor back towards the charging foursome who've now vaulted the lap dancer and her sharpened stilettos.

'Bil -!'

That's Morrissey again, even more threatening this time, at least for the time it takes for the first syllable to be yelled, the effect's a little spoilt by the time the second one comes out seeing as how Morrissey's then flat on the floor, face down on the carpet thanks to a small army of pool balls currently turning that floor into an ice rink.

'- ly'

Billy's already heading for the alley at the back of the club as Morrissey picks himself up, and as Fomo, Carmel and Lulu dance around the bobbing balls, and follow.

The problem being that the lap dancer might be out of the way, but Ugandan relations are still an issue as Billy now charges out of the rear door straight into a shagging couple on top of some dustbins, the woman's legs wrapped round her new companion's arse, one hand banging a dustbin lid up and down in rhythmic encouragement of his endeavours, the other gripped tight around his neck.

She gets the worse of it, no question, the bloke's towering over her as he pumps away so it's only natural he'd fall forwards when Billy cannons into them. For a moment she's thinking this is getting the wrong side of vigorous and doesn't he know what's in these dustbins? But then the back of her head crashes into the bin itself and suddenly her hands are clutched around the remains of two chicken vindaloos instead of his bobbing neck or arse. And now she's rapidly losing all interest in this shag, particularly when four pairs of running feet charge past, but her companion just keeps pumping away, chicken vindaloos not-with-standing, which says something about the difference between the sexes if Morrissey could be bothered to stop and ponder, but at the moment he's not stopping to ponder anything, all he's concerned with is killing a fleeing fuck called Billy.

Street theatre is Billy's next encounter. It's a local authority initiative, designed to brighten up the thoroughfares with music, poetry and song, a levy having been placed on all the grumbling local businesses to pay for it.

This particular example is a party of artists intent on recreating the halcyon days of mass entertainment back in nineteenth-century gay Paris. Not that there have been too many masses taking too much of an interest in it all, especially as this bunch of tosspots have opted for a mime performance that evening and most of the audience are beginning to think there's something wrong with their hearing only how can there be, they can hear themselves yelling at them to turn up the volume a bit, so why are this lot still opening their mouths but nothing's coming out?

But then the evening's rescued big-time as someone barrels into them from around a nearby corner and the fire-eater nearly swallows his stick. The rest of the company fall on him, scooping water from a nearby fountain into his smoking gob and the audience is really raising a cheer now because while it still may be difficult to work out what's going on, a stunt like that is well worth a round of applause.

Seconds later there's even more entertainment as four pairs of feet vault the stricken fire-eater, just about retain their footing on the now-soaking pavement and charge after the hero of the hour who's now making for an old warehouse about to be converted into upmarket apartments, its doors locked but the boarded-up windows open in a few key places, home to various local dossers and a place of refuge, or so Billy's fervently hoping, for himself right now too.

Billy struggles his way in through one of the partly boarded windows, the necessary delay just giving Morrissey time to grab his foot, but then Billy squirms out of his grasp minus his shoe but Billy's not giving a fuck about that, he's into the bowels of the warehouse and up the stairs even if he is now doing that Cinders-style.

Which is when Billy sees lights everywhere he looks, which is typical of the now-staring Billy's luck. He dives into a disused warehouse looking for a place to go to ground only to find something marginally less illuminated than Blackpool at switch-on time.

'What the fuck?'

Billy's jaw drops, partly in shock, but then partly in sudden shooting pain as a large hand belonging to an even larger hired muscle grabs his shoulder.

'Closed set.'

Billy blinks, his eyes now full of naked flesh, two blokes and one woman or at least he thinks that's what he thinks is currently writhing on the bed before him with arc lights picking out their every movement, it's a bit difficult to tell for sure who there is, how many there or who's doing exactly what to who.

'The set is closed.'

The hired muscle repeats the mantra which makes as little sense to Billy the second time round as it did the first.

'What the fuck are you talking about?'

'Go back down.'

'What?'

'Before I kick you back down'

Now Billy's brain beginning to kick back in gear, and while normally he'd have welcomed the chance to cop an eyeful of what's obviously some sort of porno shoot these aren't exactly normal times. He's got four pursuers on the warpath halfway up the stairs behind him and the last place Billy needs to be right now is heading back down to meet them.

So Billy springs forward instead only for that same hand to clamp down on his other shoulder.

'Didn't you hear me?'

Billy gasps.

'I'll shut my eyes.'

'It's a closed –'

But the hired muscle doesn't get any further because Billy's just bitten his left little finger, which as gestures of defiance go isn't much but it buys him a small amount of time at least.

The hired muscle howls, sucking his pinky as Billy charges across the set, not putting the performers off their stroke one little bit so full marks for professionalism. Behind the hired muscle, four more chancers now appear from the stairs and sore pinky or no sore pinky, he really is going to have to do something about this because he does have his reputation to protect, especially with the producer of this magnum opus now appearing from a side room doubling up as an edit suite. But before that producer can even begin to puff up what he's always thought of as his barrel chest, Carmel's deflated it by flashing what looks like a very convincing police warrant card and employing what sounds like very convincing police speak at the same time.

'Fuck off out of the way.'

'The performers, now revealed to be two women and a man, finally pause, limbs beginning to uncoil from limbs because strictly speaking no one really has any sort of official clearance for this. The hard-pressed producer was hoping no one might spot them in that disused warehouse in a wasteland of similar architectural blights, but now it looks like someone's tipped off the local cops which is going to play havoc with his already over-extended budget.

The producer approaches, arms wide, hoping to do some sort of deal, the boys in blue always being partial to a good porno on those quiet moments down the local nick and he's got a whole back catalogue on offer. But even that opening gambit's strangled at birth as Carmel and her entourage don't even break stride, just vault over the now frozen performers although one of them, a large body-builder type does grab one of the female performer's star-spangled thong as he goes presumably as some sort of souvenir, before they all disappear after the original sightseer who now seems to have hightailed it out of the nearest window.

The producer turns back to the hired muscle who's returned to sucking his pinky, to the female performers who only caught a tiny glimpse of all that preoccupied as they were with various bits of the male performer, and the producer's now really hoping like fuck his man is going to get his woody back and pronto with the official security guard all set to do his rounds in roughly forty minutes.

Meanwhile and now outside, Billy comes to a halt on one side of a mobile street cleaning machine, the street cleaner inside, and Billy's now seriously out of breath. He really can't keep this going much longer and he knows it, so he tries using his powers of reason, albeit staying very firmly on one side of that street cleaning machine as Morrissey, Carmel, Lulu and Fomo all gather around the other.

'I can explain.'

For a moment, Morrissey, gasping now too, just stares back at him, words failing him but only for a moment because Morrissey's already run a long way and through some very curious encounters for this.

'Not interested in explanations, Billy.'

'Please.'

'Not interested in anything you've got to say.'

'Just give me one minute.'

'All I am interested in is ripping your fucking head off.'

Inside the street cleaning machine, the cleaner takes a bite on his kebab, dimly aware of a developing commotion outside but not really taking any notice. Three years he's worked this shift, cleaning up puke, blood, every bodily fluid imaginable and some you really couldn't, and if he stopped to listen to every argument he's heard out on these streets in that time this not-so-little part of the city would be even filthier than it already is.

'I shouldn't have run, I know.'

'No, that's exactly what you should have done, run like fuck, because I would have done with what's coming to you.'

An incandescent Morrissey shakes his head.

'Just tell me you haven't already fenced it?'

Billy just looks back at him, his face Morrissey's answer.

'You're a tosser Billy, always have been, always fucking will be!'

Carmel lunges one way of the street cleaning machine tiring of verbals, Lulu lunging the other way, an out-flanking manoeuvre taking place and Billy makes a desperate grab at any diversion he can find right now which happens to be that street cleaning machine itself with the street cleaner still inside.

The street cleaner's actually had a couple of these sorts of experiences too, a gang outside a club deciding to turn him over, only he normally does get some sort of notice, but now his machine tips over with no notice whatsoever, no time even to take the kebab out of his mouth, his last aggrieved thought before he finally does the full one-eighty is that this is going to play total havoc with his digestion.

The diversion in place, Billy runs on towards the nearby train station. Why would be beyond even him if he'd stopped to think about it, even Billy knows he's hardly got time to queue for a ticket and ponder a choice of trains, but he does have one stroke of good fortune now in the shape of a large party of nuns just arrived for an ecclesiastical conference, or maybe it's fancy dress, all exiting the station in a flurry of black and hats, about to become a prone flurry of black and hats as Billy barges into them, scattering them in all directions, but mostly into the flailing arms of the pursuing Morrissey, Carmel, Fomo and Lulu who are beginning to wonder if this little shit doesn't have someone important upstairs on his side the amount of trouble they're having removing his head from his shoulders right now. Particularly when that same party of pious souls, outraged at their best bibs and tuckers being ruffled like that, decide to give their unwitting aggressors a good kicking and delay them even more.

Billy's vaulted the barrier by now and is heading for a goods yard at the rear of the station. He still doesn't have a ticket but there's not likely to be too many inspectors patrolling the few coaches of slag heading down to a quarry outside St Asaph which is just about the only activity taking place out of the yard that night. It's one fuck of a lot darker there too unlike that brightly illuminated porn shoot and all in all Billy's beginning to think that maybe this might just be a fair old result.

'Fuck.'

Which is the sound of one almighty fall from a state of all too temporary grace as Billy stumbles on the tracks as the points change beneath him, twisting his ankle as he does so.

But now Billy's keeping quiet despite his throbbing ankle as he sees Morrissey and his not-so-merry band of followers appear on the thin strip of land that separates the passenger station from the goods yard, trying to work out where that single and pained expletive came from because it sounded very much like a single and pained Billy-sort of expletive and they're all keen to hear some more pained expletives coming from those treacherous lips before this night gets too much older.

'Where is he?'

'I can't fucking see.'

'It came from over there.'

'I heard where it came from you fuck-wit, I just can't see 'cos it's pitch fucking black.'

Still silence as Billy keeps hugging his ankle, but not giving vent to any more of his feelings. He's done well so far as he keeps telling himself, double-well in fact, so don't fuck it up now. As quietly as he can he hauls himself to his feet, hopping off the track onto another track which is when all hell breaks loose in the shape of those coaches of slag now departing the sidings, lights suddenly blazing into life, air horns following suit a second or two later as the driver spots some local loony hopping over the rails in front of him.

Only Billy's not hopping anymore, Billy's out of there, dodgy ankle or no dodgy ankle, a hundred tons of rolling stock having sort of forced his hand.

But its blazing lights and blaring air horns have now, unfortunately for Billy but fortunately for Morrissey and the rest of the pursuers, well and truly identified his whereabouts meaning the chase is back on and the odds of Billy getting away are now significantly shortened given he's now carrying a knock which is going to be the least of the knocks he's going to have to worry about if lady luck finally stops smiling on him.

Billy zigzags across some more tracks, but he's triggered some security lights along the way, which means he's trying to evade detection in an area now more brightly lit than the nearby rugby stadium on international night. So Billy heads for the relative sanctuary of the goods yard itself away from the open trackside, making for the cover of the various stationary engines and coaches parked up inside, all awaiting maintenance and all extremely handy places of refuge.

Billy's still zigzagging, but he's triggering even more security lights as he does so, and Billy's hoping against hope they're on some sort of timer or something and that he's going to be plunged back into the darkness from whence he so recently came any minute, but Billy has three problems now.

Billy's first problem being that those lights are not on a timer, they're triggered by movement and the way Billy's dancing around right now they're going to be burning out their long-life light bulbs before much longer.

Billy's second problem being that his jigging figure is now providing even more of a visual target for his pursuers to follow and they're getting closer all the while thanks to them not jigging about at all, Morrissey, Fomo, Carmel and Lulu all sticking to the direct approach and gaining over him hand over fist.

Billy's third problem being the train.

This train's not any sort of Inter-City express, it's just a common or garden workhouse sort of train and there's not even any wagons attached to it at the moment as it's being shunted into the sidings from where it'll ply its trade the next day taking a few tons of ballast up the line to the water's edge where it'll form infill for yet another block of upmarket flats.

But Billy's looking behind, evermore desperate, at the pursuing foursome, up at the security lights praying for them to cut out, looking anywhere but in front of him which is doubly unfortunate because he now trips over another set of points which sends him sprawling to the ground again and now Billy's really panicking because that means any moment he's going to find four very angry and former mates standing over him.

But he's wrong about that too because he now looks up to find a train rolling over him instead.

It's not all of Billy that endures the attentions of the engine. It's just one part of Billy, but it's the part that's already been injured falling out of the Shogun and the part that was sprained in that fall a moment or so before, and so this really is adding insult to injury as it now rolls over Billy's left foot or, more accurately, Billy's ankle just above his Sunderland tattoo.

If Billy had been inclined to be a glass-half-full merchant, he might have reflected that he may never have to look at that testimony to his drunken antics up in Geordie-land ever again. But Billy isn't inclined to look on the bright side of anything right now. All he's thinking about is the sudden and lacerating pain in his lower leg as the wheel of that mini-leviathan all but removes his left foot from that left leg leaving him screaming on the trackside, the unheeding engine rolling on its way.

Moments later four faces appear above him just as he feared they would, but these aren't vengeful visages of evil intent anymore.

'Oh fucking hell.'

That's Lulu although it should by rights be Billy, but Billy's not saying anything right now because Billy can't. Any sounds coming out of Billy's mouth right now are pure agony and that's a sound beyond words.

Lulu turns away, retching, but Fomo's made of sterner stuff and bends to take a closer look. Two seconds later and now retching too, he realises he's not made of sterner stuff at all.

'It's crushed his fucking leg.'

'Billy?'

Morrissey stares down at him. A moment ago, Billy was on course for a right royal drubbing, one of the biggest he's had to endure in a life that's seen more than its fair share of those already, but he was never, as in ever, on course to suffer anything like this.

Billy's still not speaking because now shock's kicking in, which is some relief at least. He's no longer screaming his wordless imprecation to a God he's not sure is listening to stop a pain he's never before experienced, not even when he caught that football smack in the nuts at fourteen years old and had to hobble around for three whole days. But it's not really any sort of relief at all because all that means is he's now beginning to close down instead.

Morrissey looks at Carmel.

'What do we do?'

Carmel stares back at him.

'I'm a copper Morrissey, not Florence fucking Nightingale.'

Which is when Billy, now on the edge of slipping into unconsciousness, cuts in from the floor.

'Sorry, Morrissey.'

Four pairs of eyes stare in disbelief down at him. Billy's lying on the side of a railway track, one foot pointing in totally the wrong direction and already turning a putrid shade of purple and he's actually apologising.

Billy, don't say anything.'

'I shouldn't have, I know.'

'That doesn't matter, not now.'

'I just didn't think you'd mind.'

Four pairs of eyes stare at Billy again because while he definitely has the sympathy vote right now he is pushing it a bit by imagining Morrissey and his mates might just laugh off a two to three million quid sting.

'And it was only – you know – personal use.'

And now that old familiar cold feeling's beginning to creep down Morrissey's back again, although nowhere near as the cold feeling that's creeping up Billy's leg from a space that really shouldn't be there.

By some superhuman effort, Billy now reaches into his pocket and that cold feeling's turning to ice now for both Morrissey and Billy, for the latter because he's a man in serious need of some sort of specialist medical attention, and for Morrissey because he really doesn't think Billy's pocket is holding anything that looks remotely like a two to three million quid slab of the moon right now.

'I wouldn't really rip you off.'

Morrissey, Fomo, Carmel and Lulu look at the small wrap of exotic foodstuff in Billy's shaking hand, market value a few grand, tops, plenty enough to have a good few nights with a couple of local lap dancers, nowhere near enough to merit the near removal of a foot.

Morrissey looks back at Billy, but Billy's not saying anything else now, be that wordless screams or whispered imprecations, Billy having now passed out.

54. CHECKING FOR GAPS

Lifeless Larry's from Jamaican stock and has paid several visits back to the land of his forefathers over the years meaning he's seen some bad things in his time, his home country being no stranger to violent crime. So nothing really surprises him anymore, but even Lifeless is blinking a bit as he's presented with Billy, his foot hanging by a sinew, or whatever it's hanging by right now.

And for a moment Lifeless is wondering whether Morrissey's lost his mind as well as forgetting that Lifeless himself lost his medical licence to practice years before. And even if he hadn't, reattaching Billy's foot is the sort of surgical procedure that would stretch a team of specialists in a state-of-the-art teaching hospital let alone a back-street ex-doctor in a council flat within hailing distance of the edge of a muddy old wharf.

'This is a bit irregular, Morrissey.'

'Never mind that.'

'He should really be in the Heath.'

Morrissey nods.

'We know.'

'So why bring him here?'

'There's a problem.'

'I know there's a problem, I'm looking at it.'

Lifeless gestures down at the bit of Billy that's flapping right now.

'One very dodgy foot.'

'Another problem.'

'He's not lost something else as well?'

An appalled Lifeless sweeps his eyes over the rest of Billy's prone body, checking for gaps.

'If Billy ends up in hospital right now, it's going to get out.'

'What is?'

'What's happened to him.'

'What did happen to him?'

'That's what we don't want to get out.'

Lifeless pauses as comprehension starts to dawn, having spent enough time in his adopted country by now to have an educated stab at the answer.

'Looner.'

It's not a question, more of a statement, but Morrissey nods back anyway.

'He's going to start asking questions, looking in places we don't want him to look.'

Carmel takes it up.

'At people we don't want him to look at.'

Lulu chips in too.

'So the last, the very last thing we want right now is for him to start thinking some kind of falling out among thieves might have taken place.'

Lifeless looks back at them all.

'Because it has?'

'Never mind that, can you help him?'

Lifeless considers the prone and still unconscious Billy as Morrissey stares at him, urgent appeal in his eyes.

'I can help him.'

'He'll live?'

Lifeless hesitates, then nods.

'He'll live.'

Four relieved pairs of eyes stare at each other as Lifeless pokes his index finger at what was Billy's complete leg and is now Billy's not-so-complete leg.

'Can't save his foot though.'

55. WHY DOES IT ALWAYS?

Rain's pouring down on Morrissey, has been for the last couple of hours and according to the forecast it's going to keep pouring at least another few hours more It's soaking his skin, plastering his clothes to his body and his hair to his scalp but Morrissey doesn't even notice. All Morrissey's thinking about is that pathetic little stash in Billy's pocket.

Carmel's sitting with him on the wharf side, Fomo and Lulu there too, all of them also thinking about that pathetic little stash in Billy's pocket. No one's thinking about Billy's foot, or to be more precise every one's trying to think about anything but Billy's foot.

'He got you in scrape after scrape.'

Morrissey doesn't reply. Carmel's trying her best, but no one's going to make him feel any better about this.

'That parrot for starters.'

Lulu cuts in, nodding.

'What a fuck-up that was, and you paid Morrissey, big-time, more than two years you did under that three strikes rule, and all because Billy forgot it talked.'

Fomo nods too.

'That was harsh.'

'Double-harsh.'

'And all down to Billy.'

'The amount of shit he's landed you in over the years he was always going to cop some sort of payback.'

Morrissey cuts across.

'Not something like this though.'

Fomo, Lulu and Carmel look at each other. It's the first time Morrissey's actually spoken since leaving Billy with Lifeless.

Silence reigns for a moment as the rain continues to beat down on them and Lulu has one last stab

'He's still a Grade A fuck up though.'

Morrissey pauses, looking out over the sheet metal grey of the water, at the ghost-like abandoned wharves, at the two tower blocks just visible in the distance, but he's seeing something else now.

'He did one thing right.'

56. FRIED EGG SARNIE

Years before, Morrissey and Billy had been in a clinic, a few doors down from the old Whitchurch Hospital, all white walls and cubicles and functional furniture, very much not the sort of surroundings that lends itself to any sort of passion which makes it doubly, if not trebly difficult to have any sort of wank.

Which is what Morrissey and Billy are doing. Wanking. Or trying to. In separate cubicles, a couple of top-shelf magazines in front of them, Billy giving it his all, producing a lot of slapping and rocking backwards and forwards, but so far not too much by way of the goods.

Morrissey isn't doing too much slapping or rocking backwards and forwards and is even further away from producing any sort of goods.

'Come on Morrissey.'

Billy gasps in the next cubicle, exhorting not only his unwilling mate but his own equally unwilling and unresponsive member.

'I'm trying.'

'Try harder.'

'If something was harder there wouldn't be a fucking problem!'

'Think of the money.'

'I am.'

'Tenner a pop they're going to pay.'

'I know.'

But it's no good. Nothing's working although Billy's still trying to help matters along.

'That girl from the motor factors, Roath way.'

'I've tried her.'

All Morrissey can actually think about is the fried egg sarnie squatting in front of her on her desk as she knocked out a cylinder head gasket to him just three months before. At the time he nearly paid twice over the odds he was so distracted staring at her low-cut blouse and the treasures contained therein. Now all he can think about is her untouched breakfast and he barely noticed it at the time.

'Carmel from school.'

Even worse. Now all Morrissey can think about is Vesuvius and it's as if she's watching him right now. And she has that look on her face as if she knows exactly what he's doing which is very definitely not the sort of image Morrissey wants in front of his eyes with what he's got in his hand.

'Billy, shut the fuck up about school will you?'

In the next cubicle, Billy nods, miserable, knows exactly what's going through Morrissey's mind right now because exactly the same thing is going through his mind now too.

'OK, that one off the telly.'

'Which one?'

'The one who presents the footie.'

Aged punters with jutting chins from re-runs of Match of the Day flash before Morrissey's eyes.

'Or that women's rugby team we went to watch last year.'

Top marks for semi-naked flesh, bargain basement for sex appeal, most of them hadn't even shaved that day's growth from their upper lips, and now Billy's slowing as even he begins to accept the inevitable. This was his idea and it seemed a good one at the time, but this donation really isn't going to happen no matter how much the clinic's prepared to pay.

'And you know the worse thing?'

Morrissey nods back. He does.

'We're going to walk out of here and the first thing we're going to see is some real lush and that'll be that, we'll be pole-vaulting all the way back down Bute Street.'

Billy shakes his head, morose.

'It's just not fucking fair.'

But then Morrissey looks out of the nearby window which is when it happens. Well, not it, actually something better than it, something that takes his breath away as the whole world suddenly comes to a halt.

'Morrissey?'

Billy pauses, aware of the sudden silence from the next cubicle.

'Have you -?'

Still silence from the Morrissey cubicle.

'You sly scroat, how are you managing that?'

Still silence from Morrissey, and Billy shakes his head.

'Who was it, the girl the motor factors after all?'

But it's not the girl from the motor factors, not the one off the telly, not Carmel from school and not the bearded ladies from the women's rugby team either.

Kim.

Walking past.

On her way into work.

Not that Morrissey knows it's Kim, at least not yet and not that he knows she works in that very clinic because she's only just started, this being her first day in a brand-new job. All Morrissey knows is she's just very much done the trick.

And all Morrissey wants to know now is simple.

'Who the fuck is that?'

'Who?'

But Billy doesn't get a reply, Morrissey having even more immediate matters on his mind right now, like where does he claim his tenner?

57. DRINK

Half an hour later and Morrissey's alone, no Fomo, no Carmel, and no Lulu, just the same old rain battering on down, as back in his flat Lifeless works on Billy, patching and mending, making do as best he can, trying to put right yet another Morrissey fuck-up.

Morrissey looks out over the water and to his eternal discredit and he knows it, it's the moon rock and the stash that's in his thoughts now, Billy already edging away to the margins.

Because it's the simple story of Morrissey's not-so-simple life. Chances. They come along and Morrissey rides them, grabs them by the horns like a bucking bronco and sticks with them for all they're worth which can't be much otherwise why the fuck does it bounce him off all the time? And the worse thing of all is that he tries looking back, tries to work out all the wrong turns he's taken so can avoid them the next time around but he never does.

Just like he's looking back now, but he still can't see it. He not only never sees the fuck-ups coming, he can't even see where they come from. It remains as it always has been, bewildering and baffling.

How?

Why?

The two great questions of Morrissey's life are forever impossible to answer.

So he turns his back on that grey water and Morrissey does what he always does in times of crisis, Morrissey goes for a drink.

58. SHIP OF FOOLS

Two hours later, and even that's not working.

It's not helping that the three fellow travellers on Morrissey's current ship of fools have all had exactly the same idea and have all ended up in exactly the same shitty boozer in Mount Stuart Square on exactly the same errand of self-mercy to drink themselves into forgetful oblivion, their mutual presence now guaranteeing anything but.

Another hour on again and Morrissey drags himself into his home high-rise, the city spread out before him as he comes out of the lift. Morrissey looks out over it for a moment before he registers the open door to his flat. And for the first time in what seems a very long time, Morrissey actually smiles.

It may not be much of a smile but it's something. And Morrissey moves inside, shaking his head in wonder at the sort of chancer who's actually taken the trouble to break into a flat that even the local squatters wouldn't touch, in search of something to steal from a man with bladders. For that brief moment Morrissey's contemplating the prospect of meeting an even bigger dodo than himself.

Then that smile wipes as Morrissey walks into the flat to see Kim standing in the middle of the living room staring back at him.

'You really think you're the only one?'

Morrissey stares back at her.

'To want out from all this?'

Kim gestures out of Morrissey's window at the playground decorated with old mattresses, at the boarded-up shops with no boards, just gaps, at the shopping trolleys without wheels abandoned on each and every street corner, been there years, will be there for years to come because who's going to complain about them and who's going to listen anyway.

It's amazing that Morrissey's actually registering just what she's pointing at out there right now.

It's even more amazing he's actually hearing a single thing she's saying given that just behind her, stacked on his cheap and chipped Formica table, are some very familiar-looking packets of stash and an even more familiar misshapen piece of rock.

59. SIPPING PREMIUM SHAMPOO

'Why the fuck do you think I got that job in the first place?'

Morrissey, eyes blinking now like a camera shutter on fast forward, keeps staring back at her.

'I'd found out what was coming in, what was going out, and I was all ready to move too, all ready to finally wave bye-bye to this shithole.'

Kim eyes Morrissey, a look on her face he's seen many times before, a look that stretches back as far as time.

'And then what? Someone comes along and fucks it all up and guess what, it's the same slimy shitbag who always comes along and who always fucks everything up.'

Now Kim's almost weeping in frustration, and if Morrissey had that world enough and time again he might start thinking this sounds as much of a general rant as anything particular, more to do with all that's gone wrong between them over the years than the actual matter in hand, but Morrissey doesn't because he hasn't and he couldn't actually give a toss about any of that right now.

All he can think about is one thing and one thing only which is that fucking rock.

And Morrissey hits back hard.

'Fucks what up? I had everything sorted too, everything was smooth as fucking silk.'

Then Morrissey stops, getting way ahead of himself on this one because anger and accusations can come, what he's more interested in right now are rather simpler matters like an even simpler explanation.

But Kim's still very much in full flow.

'Just for once, once, Morrissey, could you not just have left well alone, couldn't you have come back five minutes after I was going to do my moonlight, not five minutes before, just give me some sort of fucking break?'

Morrissey cuts across in turn, trying to get back to basics here.

'So you took the rock?'

Which in truth is one fairly obvious statement of fact given it's actually here in Morrissey's flat and quite obviously delivered there by Kim.

'No, I fell over it on the fucking landing.'

'How the fuck did you even know about it?'

Kim just stares back at him, almost wonderingly at that.

'You really think you've been discreet?'

'What does that mean?'

'Getting Aidan to look up all that stuff for you on our computer for starters?'

Which is a fair point, but Morrissey's really not in the mood to be fair right now.

'So then you lifted it?'

'Like you lifted it in the first place you mean, Mr Moral fucking majority.'

'Getting us to run around like blue-arsed flies looking for it.'

'Tough.'

'Not to mention Billy's foot.'

Which does stop Kim in her tracks, that very definitely coming from the left side of any sort of field you'd care to name.

'What the fuck does that mean?'

But Morrissey's on too high a roll right now.

'You – you –'

'I'm what, Morrissey? I'm you. And Fomo and Carmel and Lulu and Billy, I'm holding right now, just like you lot were.'

'So what are you doing here? You said it yourself, you're holding, one dirty great hold as well, so why the fuck are you ten floors up in a shitty old council flat, why aren't you sipping premium shampoo ten thousand feet up above the clouds?'

'And that's typical of you too.'

'It's where I'd be.'

'So why aren't you?'

'Because you've got our rock, you dozy cow.'

'Why didn't you go before? When you did have the rock, when you were drinking down the community centre, trying to come onto me in the carsey, why weren't you hightailing it away then?'

Morrissey just stares back at her as Kim answers for him.

'Because you couldn't. Because you knew that every time you looked up from your pina colada there'd be a Looner-shaped fist waiting for you and that's if you were lucky, more likely that fist'd be holding a gun if you were half-lucky, a rocket launcher if you weren't lucky at all.'

Morrissey stays silent.

'Because you knew that crazy fuck would have dedicated his whole life to getting it back as well as ending the life of whichever lowlife had taken it.'

Kim hunches closer, warming to her theme.

'Which wouldn't have been any sort of life at all would it, armour plating the luxury motor, checking for piranhas in the swimming pool, laying down mines to protect the lawn in the penthouse?'

'Why would a penthouse have a lawn?'

'For fuck's sake, Morrissey!'

'All right, all right, point fucking made!'

'Same for me. Which is why I'm still here too. Because I don't want to be always looking over my shoulder, always wondering who Aidan's talking to, what's happening back here with Angel, has Looner found out and is he starting to take it out on whoever's left behind, I couldn't do it Morrissey, just like you couldn't, I need a plan too.'

'Actually, we had one.'

Kim looks at him.

'A plan?'

Morrissey nods.

'As in an actual, worked-out, thought-through sort of plan?'

Morrissey nods again.

'So what was it?'

Morrissey hesitates.

'We were going to wait.'

Kim stares at him and Morrissey shifts on his feet, uncomfortable. Somehow, that really didn't sound as feeble before.

'For Looner to start hitting on everyone, the state he'd be in it couldn't have taken long for him to get in some really serious shit.'

Kim keeps staring at him.

'So let me get this straight. You were just going to sit back and hope something might happen to him?'

'No.'

'What then?'

And now Morrissey's struggling.

'Well - yeah–'

A despairing Kim shakes her head, taking a deep, deep breath at the same time.

'There's no point sitting around hoping, Morrissey, he's got to be given someone.'

'What's that mean?'

'He's got to think he's worked it out even if he doesn't actually get his rock back, he needs a fall guy, a beard'

'Who?'

'Why the fuck do you think I'm up here in this shithouse talking to you? That's what I've been trying to work out, if I had I'd have gone by now.'

Then, Kim stops, Morrissey wheels round as there's a loud banging on the door and maybe it's Morrissey's over-active imagination but that knocking's sounding less like an invitation to open up and more like the chimes of doom.

Morrissey looks at Kim who's already moving into the actual shithouse across the hallway. Every face in a twelve-mile radius knows Kim's aversion to all things Morrissey these days and the last thing either of them needs right now are any awkward questions from stray callers like what the fuck is she doing here?

'Kim!'

Morrissey hisses across at her and Kim, her wits for once deserting her, returns, post-haste, retrieves the moon rock from Morrissey's chipped Formica table along with the bags of stash, retreating again as Morrissey moves to the door which is now being banged on again even more impatiently.

Morrissey opens the door to see Tonto looming in the corridor, looking back at him, grim. Working for Looner is a pain in the jacksy at the best of times but at least you get the evenings and weekends off, under normal circumstances anyway. The problem being these really aren't normal circumstances anymore and Tonto for one is becoming sorely tempted to pick up some stray rock from one of the local building sites and shape it to roughly the same shape and size.

'Looner thinks it's someone close to home who might have fucked him over.'

Morrissey looks at him, hardly daring to breathe, wondering why Tonto can't hear Kim's heartbeat thudding from the other side of that bog door because it's sounding loud and clear in Morrissey's shell-like right now.

'He wants everyone on the strength out there, looking.'

Morrissey starts to relax at the same time as a couple of metres away Kim's heartbeat begins to return to something approximating its normal rhythm and acceptable decibel level.

'We're starting with Standard Harry.'

60. SIZE FIFTEEN ITALIAN LEATHER

Standard Harry's the Firework King of South Splott as the large sign on the front of his warehouse proudly proclaims, or would if some of the letters hadn't dropped off. Why just south and why not the whole of Splott has always been something of a mystery though, because the manor's really not that big.

But there's more to Standard Harry than just fireworks, the balding perv having more strings to his bow than Robin and all his merry men. Standard Harry's also the main warehousing outlet for Looner and his ill-gotten merchandise, his once-a-year business leaving him lots of scope to branch out into other activities at different dates on the calendar meaning he's taken care of many a tasty load for Looner over the years,

And now Looner wants to know whether he's had it on his toes with one very tasty load in particular.

'I don't know what the fuck you're talking about.'

Right now, Standard Harry's clinging onto Looner's left knee as he kicks his way through the warehouse, turning over crates, packing cases and pallets, anything that might provide some sort of hiding place in fact for a small piece of rock.

'There's nothing here, nothing you don't know about anyway.'

Looner kicks on, one of his heels now connecting with Standard Harry's head. Not that it stops Harry carrying on with his pleading despite the new and stabbing pain in his left temple, because he knows all this is about to get a lot more painful if he can't make this obsessed loon see some sort of sense.

'I don't even know what's in half them packages you put in here.'

Looner leans close to the panicky Harry, that really not the wisest thing he could have said right now.

'So what about the other half?'

'I didn't mean it like that!'

'I fucking did.'

Standard Harry doesn't reply. He can't. His mouth's suddenly been filled by Looner's right boot, size fifteen Italian leather smashing his front teeth back down his throat with not a mark on the handstitched hide which has got to be classed as top-notch workmanship given the way Harry's teeth have just sheared into jagged pieces.

Squinting now, the world now turning red as blood runs down his chin, Standard Harry's still able to moan one last, desperate imprecation. He might get a nice little rake-off from Looner throughout the year for the warehousing, but by itself that doesn't pay for the nice motor parked round the back, the nice house well away from the grimy old water and the young wife who knows nothing about his penchant for tom and wouldn't give a flying fuck if she does, not so long as Harry keeps the money rolling in.

And there's only one way he's going to do that and its courtesy of the fireworks currently littering his warehouse floor which is why the sight of Looner with a lighted rag in his hand is making Harry forget even his mouthful of mashed molars right now.

Then Standard Harry stops as Looner's entourage, including Morrissey, Tonto, Diesel and Looner himself because the man might be mental but he's not totally dumb, suddenly turn tail and run like fuck because Looner's just thrown the lighted rag on Harry's stock, his reasoning being that it's going to be a lot easier searching for his little piece of heaven if there's just piles of smouldering ash to sift through.

The first rocket goes off ten seconds later only it doesn't go up because it's pointing sideways and it singes Tonto's arse as he makes it out of a side door. Moments later the first of the bangers announce their premature entrance into the big wide world. Five seconds after that and all hell really does break loose.

Up and down the street and up and down all the surrounding streets, doors start opening as everyone comes out to view this free floorshow put on by God-knows-who for fuck-knows-what reason, but who cares, all they need now are some toffee apples and maybe a nice flapjack or two and that's a dull weekday evening very much brightened up.

More and more rockets start to ignite, ascribing the sort of arcs their manufacturers very much did not intend as they snake across buildings, chase cars down streets and embed themselves in one instance in the top deck of a passing bus.

And that's just the rockets, the Catherine Wheels are soon doing handstands all over the adjoining playing fields, men walking dogs dashing out of the way because those things can inflict some serious damage. Add the bangers into the mix, and this is soon more resembling some sort of attack from aliens than a pleasant evening watching the sky change colour and most of the onlookers who'd come out to cop a gander a few moments before are already changing their minds and bolting back inside, battening down doors and windows, the sound of various rockets, Catherine Wheels and bangers thudding into those self-same doors and windows as they do so, not exactly tempting them to change their minds and come back out again.

Meanwhile Looner and his not-so-merry band of brothers are diving back into the various Shoguns that brought them over there for added shelter, praying that some spare bangers don't somehow find their way into the fuel tank, while Standard Harry just keeps sitting in the middle of it all in pain and in tears, his annual income going up in just a few moments and three months ahead of schedule and try explaining that to his insurers tomorrow morning.

Inside his Shogun, Morrissey sits with Kim who's also come along to help in the search. Tonto did try to get inside too but was repelled by Morrissey flicking the central locking and Tonto moved on into another of the Shoguns in disbelief, all this kicking off and he's still trying to get his rocks off with his ex for fuck's sake.

Morrissey and ex stare out at the dying embers of the free floor show which is actually where most of the fireworks have ended up, on the floor. Then Morrissey looks out at Looner in another of the Shoguns, at the now-moaning Standard Harry just visible on the floor of his wrecked warehouse, then out at the total mayhem before them.

Then he looks back at Kim.

'You're right.'

Kim looks back at him.

'We do have to give him someone.'

Morrissey nods at her and there's something of the old jauntiness back in that nod again now.

'And I know who.'

61. COCK OF THE WALK

Half an hour later and Morrissey is back with Lifeless, and this is a much more animated Morrissey than the last time he was with Lifeless and that's not just because Billy's recovering as well as he can with a now-severed foot, it's because Morrissey's got a plan which has actually got a lot to do with that severed foot.

The truth is that plans, scams, and schemes are what really make Morrissey buzz, they always have and always will. That moment when something shifts inside, when that charge starts somewhere deep in the pit of the stomach, spreads out in circles towards the arms and the feet until, and usually within seconds, the world's suddenly bathed in brighter colours and is pregnant with possibility.

It never lasts of course. Like most similar hits, it's usually followed by the most severe of come downs. But every now and again it works, every now and again Morrissey's faith in a suddenly bright future is rewarded and for a time, albeit brief, but life's short anyway, Morrissey is once again cock of the walk.

As he is right now. Thanks to Billy. Or, more accurately, thanks to Billy's foot.

Even if Lifeless really isn't too sure.

'This is very irregular, Morrissey.'

'Well Billy's not using it, is he?'

'That's hardly the point.'

'Call it a loan if you don't fancy donating it permanent.'

'Why the fuck do you want it at all?'

'I just do, OK.'

'If this is some sort of jape.'

'I just need to borrow it for a bit.'

A dubious Lifeless keeps eyeing him.

'If Billy feels that attached to it when he comes round and finds, well, that it isn't, I'll bring it back, cleaned and polished, I'll even make sure it has its toenails clipped if he wants, but please, just for a day or so, let me have that fucking foot.'

But Lifeless is still unsure.

'This is definitely not a jape?'

'Scouts Honour.'

'You weren't ever in the Scouts.'

'I'll swear on the Bible then, the Quran, the training manual for McDonalds, anything you like, but this is life and death stuff, Lifeless, my life and a lot of other possible deaths and if Billy could hear all this right now he'd say do it, with knobs on.'

Lifeless hesitates one last time, then opens his freezer, delving in amongst assorted pasties and pies and coming out with Billy's frozen foot, the Sunderland tattoo still visible even under the ice.

'I was going to knock it out to the medics in the Heath, their students were going to dissect it.'

'They still can. Four days. Five at the max. Then you can let them loose on it.'

Morrissey pleads.

'But in the meantime, just hand it over, yeah?'

62. CHANG'S SKIP

Everyone's more than a little wet again and everyone's staring at Morrissey again too.

But deep distrust is now etched over almost each and every face as well, and that's not just because he's put them through another dice with disaster journeying to that island on that now-infamous local park lake, it's because there's a strange face with them this time.

Kim's not exactly an unknown quantity. She's known this lot a fair few years, not as long as Morrissey's admittedly, but she has been more of a permanent fixture while Morrissey was away sampling the hospitality of Her Majesty at various state-run guest houses.

Most of them like her too, although Carmel's never been too sure. She and Kim have never really got on but maybe that's the price you pay for looking even more drop-dead gorgeous than she could ever manage and bagging what Carmel has to also grudgingly acknowledge is the most attractive man on the manor even if he was something of a part-time companion courtesy of all that generosity from the Queen.

But right now she's new to the gang, a. late attendee at the trough. And she has caused everyone a fuck-load of trouble too by lifting Looner's small piece of the heavens, not to mention costing Billy his foot in a roundabout sort of way. So all in all Morrissey's having to work extra hard to sell this new plan he's cooked up.

'Billy worked for Looner.'

Lulu cuts across.

'We all work for Looner.'

'I don't.'

That's Carmel.

'Neither do I.'

And that's Fomo. And while Morrissey has to concede Carmel, he's fucked if he's going to concede Fomo as well.

'Chang's in Looner's pocket.'

Fomo blinks as he works that through.

'So I do work for Looner?'

'You work for Looner.'

'Then I quit.'

'You can't and anyway that's not the fucking point, can we just get back to Billy for a minute?'

Not the first time where this motley crew are concerned Morrissey's struggling, this really isn't getting off to the best possible start.

'Billy worked for Looner.'

'You already said that.'

Morrissey struggles on.

'Now bits of Billy have been chopped off.'

'Meaning his foot?'

'Of course I mean his fucking foot, unless you've been taking off more bits!'

Fomo puts his hands up, surrender gesture.

'Just checking.'

'Morrissey stares at him, breathing ever heavier.

'And bits of Billy and yes that's the bits with toes and toenails before you fucking ask again, have been found.'

Morrissey pauses, drum roll time.

'In Chang's skip.'

A drum roll that's met by deafening silence and that's not the awed reaction of sudden converts to a cause, it's total and blank incomprehension.

'Why?'

Kim steps in.

'Or it will be.'

Kim hunches closer, filling in the blanks in Morrissey's sales pitch which is a good job seeing as how it's only those filled-in blanks that are likely to make any sort of sense of it.

'When we put them there.'

Three still-blank faces stare back at her now.

'We're going to put Billy's foot in Chang's skip?'

Morrissey nods.

'For starters. And more bits in other places too.'

'More bits of Billy?!'

'More bits, but not of Billy.'

'Who the fuck are they going to be then?'

'You're not volunteering one of us?'

Lulu stares at him, horrified.

'You've pulled some stunts in your time, but I am not donating any of my bits for anyone'

'They don't have to be bits of anyone, they can be bits of animals, stunt bits from a film fucking shoot, it doesn't matter, once he's clocked the foot he's not exactly going to be investigating too deeply is he?'

Lulu shakes his head.

'I don't understand a fucking word of this.'

'I'm starting to'

Morrissey looks across at Carmel. Thank fuck for someone with half a brain at least.

'And I'm starting to think we need to find you a fucking strait-jacket.'

Kim cuts in again, desperately trying to rescue what's increasingly looking like something terminal.

'So when Looner finds out a bit of Billy is in one of Chang's skips.'

But then Fomo breaks in.

'He's going to wonder why.'

Morrissey stares at him as Kim nods back. Wonder of wonders, someone else is actually starting to catch up.

'Why is Chang chopping bits off one of his drivers?'

Double wonder of wonders, Lulu is now too.

'What has Billy done to upset him so much?'

'Or what's Billy found out?'

'It has to be big.'

'Very big, to get his foot chopped off.'

'And not just his foot, look at all them other bits too, Chang must have done a hatchet job on him.'

Lulu looks at Fomo who looks at Carmel who's still eyeing Morrissey as Morrissey himself nods back at them, urgent.

'Looner is one paranoid fucker at the mo. He'd shoot his own shadow so imagine what he'd do to a face who knew all about that last load of coconuts, and who now's taking pot shots at his employees?'

'He'd go fucking ape.'

'Then Chang'd retaliate.'

Morrissey nods, encouraging them along.

'Then they both find some other bits and that leads them to Mac.'

'By which time Looner's twisting himself up into knots.'

'He starts shooting.'

'They start shooting back.'

'World War fucking Three breaks out.'

'Total fucking mayhem.'

Then there's silence again, Carmel, Fomo and Lulu now doing half-way credible impersonations of humans in thought, all examining this new notion from each and every angle, which is pretty rich as Morrissey reflects but doesn't actually point out given any other ideas regarding ways out of their current predicament are pretty thin on the ground.

'It might work.'

'Isn't that we what we said about taking that thing in the first place?'

'No, it's what Morrissey said.'

'I was talking about the stuff, and anyway it did work.'

'Which is why we're here sitting in the middle of a pond and why Billy's minus a foot.'

'OK, there've been complications.'

But then Carmel cuts across, bringing what might loosely be called this meeting to what might even more loosely be called some sort of order, having done a complete three-sixty now.

'It doesn't matter what we did or didn't do, what matters is what we do next and in the absence of anything better.'

Carmel nods at the faces before her.

'I say yes.'

And, slowly, albeit a lot more slowly than Morrissey would like, Fomo and Lulu nod back.

63. FAINT SCENT OF WOMAN

One hour later those three faces have long stopped nodding but they haven't had second thoughts either and they're now back on dry land, heading out over the gates at the far side of the park.

But Morrissey's taking the scenic route and that's not just because he wants to savour the taste of a plan well-formed and, with luck, about to be well executed, and it's not because he's drawing on an outsize spliff. He's also taking the scenic route because he's got a passenger in his small boat too.

'And if we put some of the bits in Looner's yard as well.'

Kim nods, drawing on the spliff herself now too.

'Making sure they're not too visible, but not too well hidden.'

'In some crates maybe, about to be chucked out.'

'Making sure that twat Tonto doesn't actually chuck them out.'

'Even if the police work out those bits don't belong to Billy that won't matter, it just means Billy was probably one among many.'

'They'll think some sort of gangland killing's gone down, so Looner's still stuffed.'

'Assuming he's not already got himself wasted going after Chang.'

Morrissey takes back the spliff, which is tasting ever sweeter now it's mixed with the faint scent of a woman and not just any woman.

'And we've still got the stash we can plant as well. OK, that's small-scale stuff given all the body parts that'll be floating around, but there's still going to be some pretty awkward questions if that starts turning up in the wrong sort of places.'

'Which it will if Carmel puts some in Mac's locker down the nick.'

'And Fomo puts some in a couple of Chang's Foo Yongs'

The spliff's still passing backwards and forwards, Morrissey's fingers brushing lightly against Kim's as it does so, Kim, for once, seeming to surrender herself to the rolling rhythm, and Morrissey's starting to hope.

Which is when, suddenly, he comes out with it.

'Come over to the flat.'

Kim doesn't speak, but it's a silence that's actually speaking volumes. If she hadn't been wondering the same she'd be staring at Morrissey, before wanting to know what the fuck he's talking about, what's that got to do with carving up Looner, Mac and Chang? But she isn't because she was actually expecting this and she's staying silent because she doesn't know how to answer.

'Just for half an hour.'

Kim stays silent. A day or ago she'd have hit back straight away, pointing out that's roughly twenty-eight minutes and fifty seconds more than Morrissey would normally need and that's after one fuck-load of practice, but now the cracks aren't being delivered, the put-downs aren't zinging, her eyes still staring down at that wood-bottomed boat.

'Quarter of an hour?'

Morrissey leans closer, cajoling, the spliff forgotten, smoke curling out across the water, a couple of warblers in the reeds destined for a happy old night because this is some seriously good shit that's being wasted right now. But Morrissey doesn't care and he doesn't care because he's still not been blown out.

'Ten minutes.'

Much more of this and he's going to be down to pleading for seconds, so Morrissey just keeps it simple instead.

'Please?'

Straight to the point.

Straight from the heart.

Kim, finally, looks up as the small boat now bumps against the shore. For a moment that lasts time she looks into Morrissey's eyes as he looks back at her.

Then Kim frowns as she looks behind him.

64.   DO PYTHONS HIBERNATE?

Morrissey wheels round as Kim keeps staring.

For one fearful moment Morrissey thinks the plan's already fucked, that Looner's standing there. And for that moment all Morrissey feels is the most intense irritation that his big moment has been spoilt rather than the more sensible reaction of total panic that his limbs are about to be separated from his torso, all of which is definite testimony to the power his current companion has over him and always will.

But it's not Looner.

Fatman's standing on the bank and Fatman's face is the picture of misery, mainly because that's exactly how the lovelorn Fatso's feeling right now.

'They've lost him, Morrissey.'

Morrissey stares back, totally blank.

What the fuck's he talking about?

'Look.'

Fatman waves an old shoe box stuffed full of banknotes in the still-staring couple's direction which isn't exactly any sort of aid to comprehension right now.

'I got the money, right down to the last penny, took it in to clear my debt and that's when he told me.'

Fatman's lips begins to quiver, a soul in genuine torment.

'He's gone.'

Kim looks at Morrissey.

'He being?'

Fatman cuts in again.

'My snake.'

Morrissey looks back at the staring Kim. It was breakthrough time just a moment ago or what was looking a fuck of a lot like breakthrough time.

'Fatman, this really isn't the time or place.'

'My snake that you took off me, Morrissey.'

Kim looks at him.

'Did you?'

'Not just me –'

Morrissey breaks off, nods back at him.

'Call round the yard, yeah? Tomorrow.'

'I've been all over that yard already. Searched high and low, but he's not there, so where is he?'

'He's probably hibernating.'

'Do pythons hibernate?'

Kim cuts in again and this is exactly what Morrissey feared, the focus is shifting now, the matter of the moment so far as Morrissey's concerned anyway fading fast so he makes one last effort to wrest back the initiative.

'Just fuck off will you, Fatman.'

'He wasn't just my pet you know.'

'I know, he was part of your act, so go and get something else.'

Inspiration strikes the evermore desperate Morrissey, painfully aware that the previous warm atmosphere is dissipating and fast.

'There might be an elephant coming along soon, ask Oz, maybe he'll let you borrow it.'

'Ten years we've been together.'

'That'll be an even bigger draw than some scabby old reptile.'

'Not a moment apart, not in all that time.'

And now even Morrissey's pausing.

'I took him in, fed him, watered him, looked after him, he never left me alone, never left my side, I don't know what to do now he's gone.'

Fatman turns imploring eyes on them.

'Something like that gets taken away from you, you can't think of nothing, do nothing.'

Morrissey looks at Kim who's now looking back at Morrissey.

'Help me, Morrissey, please? Help me get him back.'

And Kim keeps looking at Morrissey who keeps looking back at her.

65. TINKERS, TAILORS, SOLDIERS

Twenty minutes later, a human whirlwind is hitting the highways, byways, and alleyways of the old Cardiff docks.

Bemused locals emerge from inside as Morrissey bangs on every door, Kim following, Fatman bringing up the rear, adding his own considerable weight to his new champion's mission to reunite wrestler and reptile.

'Snake.'

'Fatman.'

'Missing.'

'Look.'

'Everyone.'

'Everywhere.'

'How far can it have got for fuck's sake?'

'Has to be here round here somewhere.'

And it's having its effect, like everything always does where an energised Morrissey's concerned, smiles are starting to replace initial scowls on all those disturbed faces as a community becomes mobilised and a manor sets out on the march.

Fomo, Carmel and Lulu are recruited back to the new cause, Aidan and Oz stirred from their sleep, Angel gets out the hearse, Diesel and Tonto are dragged from the pub, even Leanne dons her high heels and starts tottering around with a stick, cautiously prodding any stray stack of rubbish or slumbering tramp in case a six-foot python has decided to seek shelter inside or underneath. Taxi drivers join in along with all night bakery workers, security guards and street sweepers, followed by tinkers, tailors, soldiers, and probably spies as well, no one's counting anymore because no one's got that many fingers.

And Morrissey's at the very centre of it all, urging his makeshift army on while Fatman gets in his pet's favourite foodstuff which is very definitely not crisps, smoky bacon or otherwise, in eager anticipation of what has to be his imminent return with all this lot looking for him.

Meanwhile, what has now become Morrissey's mob take Looner's strong room apart, the place they actually stashed that python in the first place, but there's nothing there, just his usual collection of hardware, principally the type that fires bullets but there are ventilation shafts, holes in the unrendered breezeblocks, and while there doesn't look enough space to squeeze an earthworm through let alone Fatman's python, that snake got out of that strong room somehow.

Then Morrissey spots the disused car, far end of the yard, replaced some months before by the upmarket executive version to which Leanne has the one and only key ever since she found a red-faced Tonto in there, keks round his ankles, hastily stuffing some porno mags down the pan with some really sinister looking stains crawling down the recently white-washed walls.

Morrissey details Lulu to go and take a look. Lulu tells him to fuck off so Morrissey details Fomo who also tells him to fuck off. Then Morrissey looks round at a small sea of wary faces all now staring back at him too and Morrissey knows that no one's ever going to do anything but tell him to fuck off on this one.

So Morrissey advances towards the old carsey himself, everyone else hanging well back, and gingerly opens the door.

Nothing. Some old bog rolls, a very odd smell, paint peeling from the walls but nothing that even remotely resembles a six-foot snake.

Morrissey turns away which is when he realises the toilet lid is down. Morrissey stares at the shit-streaked lid for a moment, wondering if it's his imagination, but did that lid lift ever so slightly just then? Morrissey looks at the lid, back at the watching crowd, at Kim at the very front and Kim's looking at him and there's something in that look that is nowhere near hero worship but which faintly approaches approval, and that's good enough for Morrissey.

Morrissey takes a deep breath, then turns, opens the lid getting ready to run like fuck if the head of a python suddenly rears up out of it.

Nothing again, just a few tattered remnants of Tonto's old porno mags.

No snake.

Later that night and Morrissey's still looking, the net spreading wider all the time, even moving out towards St Mellons which has to be a no-no for man or snake, an armoured tank'd think twice about riding that particular road to hell.

Meanwhile, Kim on a break is back with Angel outside their front door, trying to sound casual, Aidan with them too, the young boy as fooled by his mother's casual-sounding tone right now as her sister who isn't fooled in any way, shape or form.

'It's just a talk, that's all.'

Angel and Aidan look at each other.

Believe that and they'd believe anything.

'Just so we can clear the air.'

Same reaction and the same expressions too.

Pull the other one.

'So we can put what happened behind us.'

Kim nods at them, desperate to convince herself as well as her sister and her son.

'Once and for all.'

So which one's going to break first, ditch the pretence, tire of the charade, but that's never in too much doubt, not with the ever practically minded Angel part of this particular trio.

'Here.'

Angel reaches out her hand, folds it over Kim's palm, depositing a small package inside, then Angel nods at her.

'Just in case.'

Kim's stares down at a packet of condoms, Aidan nodding beside his aunt. She looks up, about to protest, but then a shadow falls across them, both literal and metaphorical as Oz passes, heading yet another small posse but the light's fading now and the communal resolve is starting to fade as well.

'Looks like it really has gone.'

Kim looks at him.

'Can't find it anywhere.'

Oz moves on as Kim looks back at the packet of condoms in her hand, and as all around the light fades some more.

Meanwhile Morrissey's also taking a quick break up in his flat and is spraying his armpits with air freshener. It's not Old Spice and it's not Lynx but it'll have to do.

Morrissey sniffs his jeans before spraying them too, opens the windows and puts on some music before turning the lights down low but he's no choice anyway because there's only one single bulb so thank God for darkness because it hides multitudes.

But this is destiny or at least that's how Morrissey's seeing it. Fate. Something that just had to be and now will be. And once he's got his rocks off with Kim he'll go back out and resume the search for Fatman's pet.

Outside, Kim's now sitting alone on the playground wall. And she's alone because that's how she wants it, thinking, as she's been thinking ever since Morrissey came back, although she's never actually admitted that even to herself, but the part of her brain that can't be quietened has still been whirring away, turning everything over, worrying all those all too familiar torments to a pulp.

What does she do?

Does she do anything?

Can she?

Should she?

But now that's moved from a part of her brain she doesn't want to visit to right before her eyes and now Kim's doing what she promised herself she would never do, she's considering, she's debating, she's wondering.

Meanwhile Morrissey opens more windows and brushes the floor, only he can't find a brush so he uses a comb, using the sharp end to scrape out last night's supper and what looks like this morning's breakfast from the sofa because Kim may well not fancy the bed seeing as how Morrissey doesn't actually fancy the bed. The sofa's not a much more attractive option but it's better than the floor which really isn't looking too much fresher despite all Morrissey's efforts with the comb.

Outside, Kim looks down towards the water, distant lights on the horizon, ships heading for even more distant shores, looking out towards them just as she used to look out on them as a girl.

Back in the flat and with Morrissey's efforts complete, he's at the window, also looking out on the distant skyline just as he used to look out on that as a boy.

Then Morrissey looks at his watch.

One hour later and Kim's not looking out towards the water.

That same one hour later, Morrissey's still looking at his watch.

And one hour, one minute and forty-five seconds later, Morrissey's outside the front door of Kim's small links house again, looking at the ornamental lanterns either side of the door as he presses the bell, half of him telling himself to play this cool, bide his time, the other half knowing he's in for a whole night of watch-watching if he does.

And what if Kim's twisted her ankle, fallen down the stairs in her haste to get over to Morrissey's drum, there could be any sort of explanation for the no show, it doesn't have to mean there's been a change of heart.

Five seconds later the door opens and Kim, on both feet, no obvious evidence of any sort of injury, stands in front of him, not speaking, just staring out at him and there's an all too familiar challenge in that stare and Morrissey's beginning to get an all too familiar sinking feeling too.

By Morrissey's side a faithful friend hoves into view as Yorkie now squats next to him, somehow knowing as he always knows that he's probably going to be in need support right now.

'So this is just business, yeah?'

Morrissey keeps staring at Kim, filling the silence with words that aren't really needed but Morrissey needs to say them anyway just as he needs to hear something back even if it's only fuck off.

'You need money, I need money?'

Still just silence from Kim.

'There's nothing else to it, nothing more to the two of us working together than that?'

Then Morrissey stops and that's not because Kim's suddenly rediscovered her tongue, it's because Tonto's just appeared behind her on his way from the kitchen to the sitting room, a lager can in hand.

Morrissey stares after the apparition, an apparition who seems pretty much at home right now, definitely a damn sight more at home than the one man with his dog standing by the ornamental lanterns with no lager can in his hand.

'He passes the time.'

Morrissey turns those same staring eyes back on Kim.

'How long were you away exactly?'

And Kim just about holds his stare but it's not easy, in fact this is taking real effort on her part, which is good news for Morrissey in one sense but it is all more than counter-balanced by the undeniable fact she's sticking to her guns on this one.

The even worse news for Morrissey is that Kim now closes the door in his face.

Morrissey stares at the closed door for a moment as Yorkie looks up at him. Sensitive soul that he is, Yorkie just stays silent, doesn't even nuzzle his owner's leg. Sometimes the strong, silent treatment really is best.

Not that anyone's told Morrissey that.

'Kim!'

Morrissey begins banging on the door.

'Kim!!'

Morrissey stares at the still closed door in front of him.

'For fuck's sake!'

Then Morrissey pauses, just in case his voice might have carried a bit.

'Sorry Aidan.'

But Morrissey's not sorry for Aidan, he's sorry for himself and for Kim, for all they had, for all they'll now never have, for all the fuck-ups he thought they might have put behind them, for the incontrovertible fact of that closed door and the equally incontrovertible fact that they obviously haven't put anything behind them at all.

Then Morrissey looks up as an upstairs window opens above, perfectly happy to do his Romeo impression if that's what's now required, but it's not Juliet looking down on from a balcony or some bint with long flowing locks letting down her tresses so he can climb up. It's Angel looking from the carsey window, trying to offer her own little sliver of comfort.

'You're still the best shag she ever had, Morrissey.'

Morrissey looks back at the closed door before him for a moment, momentarily contemplating breaking it down but he won't and he knows it because he already knows there's no point.

Morrissey leans down instead, strokes Yorkie, receiving another slobby lick for his pains, then turns and walks away.

67. THE HOTS

The next morning Morrissey's walking towards Looner's collection of portacabins to get the latest gen on the increasingly unbalanced maniac's search for his small celestial orb.

It hadn't been the best of night's sleep for Morrissey, not that he'd been planning on doing too much sleeping anyway but that wasn't really the point. And he doesn't get to Looner's office either because Aidan's playing football and the ball suddenly crashes into his gut. Aidan's not exactly the best kicker of a football, much as Morrissey's not exactly the best thrower of soap, so he's not about to score any bragging points on that count. He just wishes he'd spotted the ball five seconds before it hit his gut rather than immediately after because Morrissey's got enough mental pain to deal with right now and he really doesn't need the physical variety as well.

Five minutes later a still-winded Morrissey is sitting with Aidan on the same playground wall as Kim those few hours before.

'Sorry, Uncle Morrissey.'

Morrissey rubs his stomach gingerly.

'Accident. Forget it.'

'Not the football.'

Morrissey looks back at him.

'That fuck-up with Mum and the computer.'

'Don't say fuck, Aidan.'

Morrissey hesitates, grimacing again now, and not just because of his bruised gut.

'Anyway, it was my fuck-up really.'

Then Morrissey pauses, trying to find some subtle way into all this.

'So is she really with that clown Tonto?'

And failing, spectacularly, on the subtlety front.

Aidan starts to grin. He may still be in short trousers, but he's well plugged into the angst of all adults around him, most particularly his Uncle Morrissey and that hopeless torch he carries around.

'I mean, that can't be serious can it?'

'You've really got the hots for her haven't you?'

'No.'

That same youthful smile's spreading all the while.

'We're mates, old mates, that's all, I just don't want to see her making a twat of herself.'

Still that same smile from Aidan.

'Me and your Mum were done and dusted years ago, so for the last time I have not got the hots for her.'

'Not seen you with anyone else though have we?'

'What?'

'Oz was saying it. Ever since you got back.'

'So?'

'So you can't help wondering, he said that too.'

'I'm just not interested.'

'Carmel is.'

Morrissey stops and stares.

How the flying fuck did he know about that?

'Oz said that too, it's obvious, the way she looks at you.'

Morrissey cuts across.

'Should we be doing this? A grown man discussing his love life with an eight-year-old, isn't there some sort of law against it or something?'

'You haven't got a love life, that's the whole point.'

Aidan grins even wider.

'Obvious you want one though. Obvious who with too.'

Morrissey shakes his head. What price dignity? He's sitting on a playground wall, an ache in his gut courtesy of a stray football, being pinned down on matters of the heart by a kid who's probably not even had his first kiss yet.

'Can we just change the subject?'

'Hit a sore spot, have I?'

'No, you have not hit a fucking -!'

Then Morrissey stops as he stands, makes to head away. Looner's yard now in his eyeline or more particularly Leanne's now in his eyeline, coming out of her portaloo, doing up her jeans.

Then Morrissey looks back at the still-grinning Aidan, his face setting, determined.

'You want to shag me?'

Five minutes later and Morrissey and Leanne are in a quiet, very quiet, part of the yard, Morrissey cutting out the usual preambles like drinks and conversation, just getting straight to the point.

'Yeah.'

Which isn't Morrissey's usual style but after that little chat with Aidan he's feeling he's got a point to prove right now and doesn't want to hang about too long before making it.

Leanne blinks, Morrissey's full-frontal approach having momentarily robbed even Mega-Mouth of the power of speech.

'For fuck's sake, Morrissey.'

'All I want is a simple yes or no.'

Then Morrissey backtracks.

'Actually, what I want is a yes, followed by a shag, but if it's going to be a no then tell me quick, yeah, 'cos deep regrets and all that, but there are other women.'

Leanne eyes Morrissey.

'I'm with Looner.'

'I know.'

'Looner as in loony-fucking-tune.'

'I know.'

'Psycho Looner.'

'I know who Looner is and I know you're with him for fuck's sake.'

'And you still want to shag me?'

'Yeah.'

Leanne eyes Morrissey, wonderingly.

'You are either off your trolley Morrissey or one seriously horny fucker.'

But Morrissey shakes his head.

'Phil the Travelling Greek?'

'I never shagged Phil the Travelling Greek!'

'I never said you did.'
'So what did you bring that lanky streak of piss up for?'
'Landed you in it with Looner though, didn't he?'
'Slimy fucker tried.'
'Told Looner you were playing away from home.'
'What fucking business was it of his anyway?'
'And what happened to him?'

69. BOUZOIKA

Phil the Travelling Greek believed in honour and he believed in telling the truth. He also believed that life's harsh realities should be bravely and honourably confronted, not swept under the carpet or cravenly ignored.

So when Phil the Travelling Greek discovered a pair of Leanne's lace panties in the Shogun he was driving for his employer, he acted on his principles. He knew that while it may cause short-term pain, that's a small price to pay for long-term gain.

Ten minutes after acting on his fateful decision, some very strange sounds were coming from inside Looner's office which wasn't all that surprising given that the man of honour in question was now being strangled with the strings from his own bouzouki.

70. GET OUT OF JAIL

Leanne's now staring at Morrissey in something approaching stunned wonder as she finally gets his point.

And just in case it needs hammering home, Morrissey spells it out.

'Looner shoots the messenger, everyone knows that. And no, we're not going to do this under his nose, but, yes, there is still a possibility someone may hear something, clock something, but even if they do, what total fucking idiot's going to walk up to him and say, guess what your squeeze has just been up to, Looner?'

And it's like the parting of the seas, shafts of light breaking through the darkest of clouds as a rooted Leanne keeps staring at him.

'You know what I am, don't you?'

Morrissey nods his head. He knows exactly what Leanne is, everyone does, everyone always has done.

'I'm the safest shag in the docks.'

No response to that from Morrissey.

No need.

A long considering look from Leanne follows which could be a last-minute show of reluctance, but the fact that look's moving all the way down Morrissey's body and ending at his crotch is giving Morrissey hope for at least a half-way happy ending here.

Then Leanne looks back up at him and nods.

'OK, Morrissey. Let's see what you've got.'

Which should be sweet. Because Leanne is a very tasty number with zero baggage, the unaware Looner excepted. And there's no risk of any sort of emotional attachment forming courtesy of that same unaware Looner because then he wouldn't be unaware and Morrissey wouldn't have the use of his limbs. A dream shag in short.

Only now this has actually started the same thing's happening again. That same sinking feeling in the pit of Morrissey's stomach, that same strange desire to be anywhere except where he is actually right now, the same feeling he had, in short, when he was confronted with the naked Carmel.

Only Leanne isn't Carmel and the fact Morrissey's now having second thoughts only seconds after he had his first isn't going to deter her even if she does suss his new reluctance, which she doesn't because Leanne's just been handed the keys to the sweet shop. Being with Looner's a one-way ticket to being kept under virtual lock and key most of the time, but Morrissey's just presented her with a get out of jail card and now Leanne wants and Leanne is going to get her shag. And if Morrissey's spirit is now flagging that's his look-out, it's his flesh she's interested in and his flesh she intends to well and truly sample.

But then, and just as all that's about to start in one of Looner's Shoguns, the Professor and his Mate come along.

And all of a sudden, plan B – shagging Leanne – suddenly connects to Plan A – shafting Looner.

'So we were on that bit of waste ground.'

'You and?'

'Parked up, back of Legoland. The music's on low, the heater's on high and she's wearing these heels, high.'

'How high?'

'Only now she's taking them off because they keep getting caught in the cloth.'

'On the seat?'

'On the roof.'

'Class.'

Morrissey looks at Diesel who's taking the bait just as intended even if this isn't exactly as it was meant to pan out. But that doesn't matter, from now on it should be rollercoaster time, first Looner finds out, then Chang, then Mac and then it's pack of cards time, mutual suspicion and even more mutual distrust as they confront each other, go up against each other just as Morrissey intended, everything shaking down super sweet.

A short time earlier, Morrissey had been updating Fomo, Carmel and Lulu and more than a little breathlessly because all this has just taken on something of a life of its own.

'Leanne's clocked the foot.'

Only Lulu's frowning because he's a long way from riding any sort of rollercoaster.

'Why did Leanne clock the foot?'

Which has always been Morrissey's problem which was why he needed Kim back on that island in the park because he always does it, is always jumping ahead of himself, not filling in the gaps, but there's no time for that now.

'Doesn't fucking matter why Leanne clocked the foot.'

Fomo cuts in, bewildered too.

'I thought Tonto was supposed to clock the foot when he emptied the skip.'

And Carmel's looking puzzled now as well.

'No, I thought Looner was supposed to clock the foot.'

Making her yet another convert to Morrissey's currently completely fucking stymied camp of followers, and now he's trying to go back to basics, set the scene, just like he did with Diesel before Slippery started pawing the stripper.

'No, Tonto was supposed to clock the foot, but Leanne clocked it first because the Professor and his mate had taken it out of a Chinese lantern.'

Which all seems crystal clear to Morrissey but he's clearly in a majority of one right now and that's not much of a majority.

'Why the fuck did the Professor take Billy's foot out of a Chinese fucking lantern?'

'What is this, Jacka – fucking – nory? Story time? Does it fucking matter, he just did!'

'Do not tell me we've got to split this with the Professor now as well as Billy?'

But something else is puzzling Fomo

'Who's the Professor?'

And now Morrissey's losing the will to live.

'And how come Leanne saw it?'

Carmel cuts in again and, too late, story of his life as well, Morrissey's sees that big trap door opening up in front of him, meaning it's time for some really slippy thinking to head off another great big fall, but then Lulu steps in having understood this part of the story at least.

'Because she and Morrissey were having a shag.'

And now all Morrissey wants to do right now is rip his head off, which from the expression on her face is much the same way Carmel's feeling right now about Morrissey.

'You were shagging Leanne?'

That expression says it all. Morrissey might have been in deep shit for refusing her, but he's in double deep shit for not having the same sort of scruples when it comes to taking on the docks bike.

'No.'

Morrissey struggles, trying to be scrupulously fair to all parties here, although mainly it has to be said, to himself.

'I was trying to shag Leanne.'

Then Morrissey breaks off, that obviously very much a distinction without a difference so far as Carmel's concerned.

'Look, none of this is the fucking point.'

Carmel keeps staring at him, her silent eyes clearly begging to differ.

'The point is, it's not happened like we expected it to happen but it has happened and now I've primed Diesel and he's taking the story back to Looner.'

Morrissey pauses.

'So it's still going to be OK.'

Three pairs of eyes look at Morrissey, just one thought in all their minds now.

Now where the fuck have they heard that before?

Roughly two hours later Chang had been visited and extracted from roughly four inches inside his waitress and Mac had been removed from his annual barbie.

And Morrissey can't get his head round this. So near and yet so far. Looner, Mac and Chang had been within ten seconds of blowing each other's heads off and they would have done if Tonto hadn't decided to treat them to his film buff act. But he had and he did and now everyone's back on Looner's yard.

Looner, Chang and Mac themselves are up in the office but their voices were clearly audible outside.

'None of us chopped up Billy.'

'Someone's just trying to make it look like one of us chopped up Billy.'

'Which means someone's trying to fuck us over.'

'Set dog against fucking dog.'

Meanwhile, at the bottom of the stairs, Morrissey, Fomo and Carmel were huddled together, their own intense little debate playing out, very much making sure this isn't audible to anyone apart from themselves.

'This is a fuck-up.'

'A complete and total arse.'

'Now what are we going to do?'

But no one says anything else because they don't get chance. The door to Looner's office suddenly swings open, Looner, Mac and Chang just as suddenly appear in the doorway and they're all staring down at Morrissey, Fomo and Carmel.

Then all three start walking down the stairs towards them, Looner leading the way, his voice positively fecund with menace.

'We're going to have to do a Mary Poppins.'

Morrissey looks across at Kim who's looking back at him, and this really could be it, last request time and all that, but even now Morrissey still wouldn't be too sure of that shag.

But Mac's looking at Looner.

'What, the bint who flew on a broomstick?'

Carmel's not listening to her senior officer, she's looking at Morrissey and cursing the stupid fuck who might just have robbed her of the chance of her own last shag.

Looner shakes his head, getting ever closer to Morrissey, Carmel and Fomo all the while.

'No, the bint who started at the very beginning.'

And Looner's now so close Morrissey can smell the onions he ladled on his steak last night.

'That was Maria Von Trapp.'

Then the smell of those onions waft past as Looner moves on, passing Morrissey Fomo and Carmel with Mac and Chang following.

'Who?'

'Maria Von Trapp.'

Morrissey opens his eyes, not realising he'd actually closed them.

'The Sound of Music.'

By Morrissey's side, Carmel begins to breathe again too.

'She was the one who started at the very beginning.'

Looner, Mac and Chang are now climbing into a Shogun, not even looking at their rooted audience, Looner now with another bone to chew on and he's giving it one fuck of a good gnaw now too.

'Not Mary Poppins?'

Mac shakes his head and he should know, he's had to sit through enough shite musicals in his time with Verity blubbing into her popcorn bedside him. The stuff a man has to put up with just to occasionally, very occasionally, get his rocks off.

'No, Maria Von Trapp.'

Looner snaps on his seatbelt, twisting round in his seat.

'But I've always said that. 'Let's do a Mary Poppins, let's start at the very beginning.'

Chang breaks in, growing ever more impatient.

'Doesn't matter how long you've been saying it if it's fucking wrong.'

Which is a fair point, but Looner's world seems to be under attack on all fronts right now, this being just the latest salvo and he's really in no mood to roll over.

'Let's do a Mary Poppins' sounds a fuck of a lot better than 'Let's do a Maria Von Trapp' for fuck's sake.'

Chang smashes the dash of the Shogun with his fist in frustration.

'For fuck's sake, we've got two feet and a finger in my skip, Mac's barbecue and my chippy's plate of ribs and you're talking Julie - fucking - Andrews!'

73. NOT THE LIZZIE VERSACE

Thirty minutes later one small part of Looner's brain is still brooding on a mis-heard catchphrase, but that's back of his mind time, something to be pursued later. The actual matter of the moment right now being an exotic ballgown currently being held in front of a staring Lulu, the tattooed man's pride and joy, one among several maybe, but ultra-precious nonetheless.

As Looner knows.

Making this leverage.

As Lulu also knows.

'See, you were the first to handle that load, Lulu.'

Lulu, eyes only for his ballgown, instantly switches into full-frontal aggression mode, attack always being the best form of defence, just ask any cornered rat.

'I handle every fucking load that lands on that fucking dock, so fucking what?'

Looner holds the thin material between two of his fat fingers, kneading it, stretching it almost to breaking point before kneading it some more, Lulu staring in appalled fascination all the while.

'So the way I see it.'

Looner's fingers keep rolling the cloth, backwards and forwards, out of shape, in shape again.

'If there has been any funny business.'

Lulu cuts in.

'That's a Julien McDonald, I bid a fortune for that on eBay.'

Looner's index finger slips through one of the seams, opening it up, only a small hole at first but getting larger all the while.

'You must know something.'

Then, and with a quick, savage, deliberate twist, that seam's suddenly a mishmash of frayed thread, the sculpted cloth in rags and Lulu howls a wail of protest.

'I don't know fucking anything! I don't know what the fuck you're talking about!'

Looner picks up another dress from the collection by his feet on the floor, Chang watching, Mac keeping his eye on an equally tearful T-Bone watching from the door in case he's tempted to launch some sort of kamikaze rescue act.

'That's a Lacroix.'

Witness to one of Lulu's greatest triumphs, the recent Diamonds gig down the community centre, the night that was meant to mark the upturn in all their collective fortunes after which nothing was ever going to go wrong again.

'No it fucking isn't.'

Lulu stares at Looner again. What's he talking about, the fat fuck couldn't even spell Lacroix, let alone identify a fake.

'Yes it is.'

'No.'

Looner smiles, evil, Lulu having just swallowed his feed, hook, line, and sinker.

'It was whatever the fuck you called it. Now it's – '

Lulu's next howl of protest almost drowns out the sound of more ripping cloth. Almost, but not quite. And Lulu pants, this doing absolutely nothing for his blood pressure, but even less for his frocks.

'Really love this stuff don't you?'

'And you can rip the whole fucking lot up too, because I'm still not going to tell you anything because I don't fucking know!'

'I'll just have to do it then. Rip the lot.'

'For fuck's sake.'

'And then maybe you'll know how it fucking feels'

Looner picks up another dress from the floor, just more skimpy material to the space freak, very much not just more skimpy material to the horrified Lulu and to the still staring and equally horrified T-Bone. And Lulu's voice is now so hushed it's barely a whisper which is odd seeing as how inside the big man's head it's sounding louder than a Jumbo during lift-off.

'Not the Lizzie Versace.'

His absolute pride and joy, six months wages blown in one single charity auction, Lulu putting up with one hell of a piss-take from just about everyone on the manor for blowing that sort of dosh on something held together with safety pins, only in roughly ten seconds time it's not going to be held together with anything at all, Looner's giant hams of hands getting ready to split it, shoulder to leg.

Which is when Lulu whispers, the pressure impossible to resist, feeling now as a mother might feel when faced with a threat to her young or at least that's how the miserable Lulu's going to justify it later in countless pubs up and down the docks, but it's not going to cut much ice not when the offspring in question is a dress that was pretty fucking naff in the first place.

'Sorry, Morrissey.'

Looner looks at Mac who looks at Chang who looks back at them both.

Then Looner stares back at Lulu, keeping his eyes cast down to the floral carpet, but the words are out now and they can't be taken back.

'Morrissey?'

74. DIAMOND OR THE PLOUGH

In times of crisis the very first lesson is don't deviate from the routine.

Which is why Morrissey's in a changing room, a dozen or so sweaty bodies next to him, trying to fit his size twelve feet into size ten boots, about to take to the local footie pitch for Oz's charity match.

Oz himself is striding amongst his flock, beaming broadly and pressing the flesh or at least those bits of flesh that don't wobble which isn't too many given this out-of-condition lot, as all the while Morrissey's tries to stay focused and pretend to be at least halfway interested in his coach's team talk.

'OK, we'll play the diamond, or maybe the plough, no, let's make it the diamond, pack the midfield, force them out wide whenever we can, three at the back, a sweeper, two roving wings and a target man, upfront, OK?'

A baker's dozen or more pairs of eyes stare back at Oz, the same puzzled expression on all their faces. What the fuck's he talking about?

Oz stares round, impatient.

'I'm just trying to get us all a little bit beyond a kick-about in the park.'

'This is a park.'

'And we are having a kick-about.'

'What's wrong with trying to put on a bit of a show?'

'Who for?'

'The punters.'

'Who's turning up?'

'Well, no one probably'

'So what's the fucking point?'

An increasingly flustered Oz turns, appeals to the only player who's stayed silent up to now.

'Morrissey understands, don't you Morrissey?'

But Morrissey's not listening because Carmel's just walked in and the grim expression on her face is telling Morrissey more eloquently than mere words could ever have managed that she's not arrived with a skip load of lemons for half-time.

'For fuck's sake.'

The player next to Morrissey grabs a pair of shorts, hoping to God she hadn't just seen him scratching his nuts like that. Not that Carmel's even remotely looking at him or his nuts, her eyes are well and truly fixed on Morrissey.

'Outside.'

Oz steps in.

'He's the goalie.'

'Now.'

Oz appeals to him again.

'Tell her, Morrissey.'

'Two minutes, Oz.'

'We're just about to go out.'

'Just two fucking minutes!'

75. JAMAL BACK FOR GOOD

One minute of those two later, Carmel and Morrissey are on the other side of the changing room door, the visiting team stumbling over the divots in the pitch as they have a warm-up, the referee already dreaming of his half-time pint, Aidan struggling with Oz's ancient ghetto-blaster which isn't called that anymore, trying to cue up an equally ancient cover of You'll Never Walk Alone.

But what Carmel has to say to him has nothing to do with the opposition who actually look half-tasty, divots or no divots or the referee or the state of Oz's audio equipment.

'Lulu's talked.'

Morrissey stares back at her.

'What about?'

'For fuck's sake Morrissey, what do you think? Oz's footie match, his elephant, climate change, the pros and cons of us joining the EU again –'

Carmel breaks off.

'He's fucking talked!'

'Shit.'

'He's told Looner all about the stuff and the –'

Carmel nods up towards the sky, not wanting to actually put a name to it either.

'Why?'

'Oh, let's stand around and hold an inquest shall we? Does it fucking matter why, he just has meaning he knows, Morrissey, meaning Mac and Chang know too.'

'Shit.'

Carmel stares at him.

'Is that the best you can do? Just stand there and say shit?'

'We have got to get of here.'

But now Carmel hesitates.

'Actually Morrissey, it's just you that's got to get out of here.'

Morrissey stares back at her, blank.

'It's only you Lulu's put the hand on. They don't actually know about the rest of us yet.'

And now there's an urgent appeal in Carmel's eyes and this isn't a fancy-a-shag sort of appeal, this is a life-and-death sort of appeal.

'My final court hearing's coming up.'

Behind Carmel, football players in various mismatched bits of kit begin to file out from the home changing room, but they could vanish into thin air and the pitch could subside around them and she's not going to take her eyes off Morrissey right now.

'I'm already proving myself with this crap fucking job, you should hear the Social Worker, I'm her right little success story, if I can get a house of my own, a proper home on top, that'll be that, I'll have Jamal back for good.'

Carmel nods at Morrissey.

'Keep me out of it.'

Morrissey stares back at a pleading Carmel.

'If you can.'

Morrissey doesn't reply because he can't. Two huge hands have just clasped his shoulders, levering him away from Carmel and those entreating eyes as Oz steers him towards the footie pitch and a set of goals.

'Two minutes you said, two minutes you got.'

Oz nods at Morrissey.

'For the next ninety, plus injury time, plus the half-time break, plus extra time, plus the penalty shoot-out if anyone's still standing by then.'

Morrissey looks back at Carmel but Oz yanks him on again.

'You are fucking mine, Morrissey.'

76. PUKKA GOALIE

Thirty seconds later Morrissey is still with Oz who's now giving his last-minute pitch side pep talk and being with Oz suits Morrissey fine and dandy right now because Oz can keep him for a fuck of a sight longer than ninety minutes plus stoppage time, plus tea breaks if he wants. In fact he can keep him at his side and in amongst these walking lumps of lard for ever, this being the closest Morrissey can get right now to a human shield.

'OK, now we may not look too good.'

A listening disorientated Slippery trips over a football that some inconsiderate soul has left, wonder of wonders, on a football pitch and Oz eyes the prone Slippery heavily. He's a non-essential component in his diamond formation it has to be said, but a component nonetheless.

'Or play too good.'

But Morrissey's tensing. A very familiar looking Shogun is now approaching, slowing as it comes within sight of the pitch and the players.

'But we have got some pukka tactics, a pukka good cause and a pukka fucking goalie, right Morrissey?'

Oz clasps Morrissey who ducks underneath his bear-like arms to hide from view. Across the street the Shogun's beginning to move again, picking up speed all the while which is the good news. But it's heading straight for the footie pitch which is the bad.

And Looner's at the wheel, which is even worse.

'Actually, Oz -'

'So let's kick off and bring the fucking sky down.'

But it's not the sky that's coming down, at least not yet although it might be in roughly a few seconds time if the murderous expression on Looner's face behind that wheel is anything to go by. For now it's one of the nets that's brought down as Looner doesn't bother with niceties like steering around it, just goes straight through instead.

'I might have a bit of a -'

Morrissey doesn't finish, but he doesn't need to. It's plain as the nose on anyone's face that Morrissey's got a bit of problem right now although judging by the way the irate Looner's now jumping down from the Shogun and kicking away bits of net and football post Morrissey has actually got one fuck of a problem.

77. BULLBARS

It's chase sequence again, which Morrissey didn't enjoy last time following that close encounter with the Porsche but at least back then there were only coppers on his tail.

The worst that was going to happen following that much-regretted and highly regrettable little interlude was a quick reverse trip back to the institution in which he'd been so recently incarcerated, and a big hello from the sour-faced old screw who'd drawn the lucky ticket in the sweep to predict just how long Morrissey was going to last in the great outdoors before Her Majesty decided she really was missing him too much.

If Morrissey had known how things were going to work out he'd have waltzed back in, hands up, hello boys, give me a hug and I wonder if they've taken my centrefolds down yet? It'd have been a breeze compared to having Looner on his back.

Not that he's actually on Morrissey's back as yet but it's fast turning into a close-run thing. In fact it's only the irate Looner's feet being still entangled in the demolished footie net that gives the Morrissey the tiniest chink of light by way of a breathing space. Which Morrissey takes as he hares off across the pitch, showing a faster turn of speed than he's managed in any training session so far, praying he's going to be granted the space to actually keep on breathing just a little longer yet.

Morrissey heads back into his old manor, which is history repeating itself again, only this time it should be a whole lot easier because he knows all the obstacles now, just keep them in his head and everything should be fine. Which is when Morrissey turns a corner and bangs straight into a bricked-up underpass, not a different bricked up underpass, exactly the same bricked up underpass, meaning he's fucked up already.

Behind Morrissey the sound of a Shogun screaming its guts out is heard, low gear engaged, engine screeching in protest but Looner's way beyond niceties like changing up, he doesn't give a fuck if he rips this engine of his apart so long as it's closely followed by ripping apart Morrissey.

Which is when Morrissey's brain finally begins to shift into gear. And for the next few minutes it actually keeps on working too as he runs on, all the dead ends successfully avoided, all the now closed and former escape routes swiftly circumnavigated, all the new rat runs exploited which is just as well seeing as how it's not just the incandescent Looner on his tail now, it's Chang and Mac as well.

But he's doing it. He's getting away, evading capture, is actually playing this one absolutely right, which makes it all the more irritating to slide down a wall only to see Looner's Shogun – and where the fuck did that come from? – cannoning towards him, bull bars aiming straight for his trapped and now-rooted chest, absolutely no way to evade the fast-approaching impact, nowhere to go.

Which makes this well and truly end game.

The final curtain.

Bye-bye Morrissey.

Nothing to do, just close those eyes.

'For fuck's sake, Morrissey!'

Morrissey opens those same eyes. There's been no impact which is the first pleasant surprise, although Kim behind the wheel of that Shogun follows pretty closely on its heels.

'Don't just stand there like some shop store fucking dummy, get in.'

Morrissey, not needing a second invitation, scrabbles in through the rear door, pressing his nose flat to the scuddy carpet on the floor, head well and truly down as Kim pilots the borrowed motor past the football pitch, past various police, Chinamen, and other assorted Shoguns, back to the rear of the high-rise that Morrissey once called home.

A few moments later, Kim's loading a holdall into the boot of the Shogun and Morrissey's trying to recover from the shock of those approaching bull bars.

'Nearly gave me a fucking heart attack, coming at me like that.'

'Never mind nearly, you'd have had one for real if that had been Looner.'

But Morrissey's still feeling aggrieved.

'Why pick one of his motors?'

'Because they're about the only thing that's going to be able to move round this manor today without getting fucking torpedoed.'

Kim nods across at the waiting Shogun.

'So take it.'

Then she opens the rear door.

'And take this.'

Kim stuffs a holdall inside.

'The rock's inside, it's wrapped in last night's Echo. Fence it, then lay low for a bit, then we'll all meet up again when everything's settled down.'

But Morrissey just looks at her, not moving.

'That's fence the rock, not the Echo by the way.'

Morrissey's still not moving.

'Morrissey, just fucking go will you?'

A police car's siren cuts across from no more than a couple of streets away by the sound of it, but Morrissey's still not moving and all of a sudden again, out it comes.

'Come with me.'

Kim stares back at him.

'Grab Aidan.'

Morrissey holds Kim's incredulous stare, steady.

'Come with me.'

'Just go Morrissey, OK, just get the fuck out of here.'

Morrissey leans closer, a last ditch, desperate, attempt to make that not-so-fat lady sing, to wake up, smell that coffee.

'Bring Angel too - and Oz - and Uncle Tom fucking Cobley, I don't care, anyone you want, just come with me and we'll start again, a brand-new life.'

But Kim just shakes her head because all she's hearing is the same old song, the same old, tired old, refrain.

'With the same old Morrissey.'

'I'm not –'

But Kim cuts across, her voice as urgent and impassioned as Morrissey's right now because this her last chance too, her last-ditch effort to make him see some sort of sense.

'You're always going to be the same old Morrissey and it was great when we were seventeen, it was part of your charm.'

Kim tails off, just looks at him, inches away but the other side of another unbridgeable divide and she knows it even if he doesn't.

'And I wish it wasn't true, I really wish I could look at you and think, yeah, he's different now but you're not and I can't and I've too much at stake these days to saddle myself with a fuck-up.'

And it's not the words, he can deal with them, he's heard them many times before, it's the tone, the obvious and clear regret, the ineffable sadness behind the eyes. If it was outright hostility he could fight it, but how can he even begin to fight something like this?

But Morrissey tries, taking refuge in attack and maybe making Kim's point for her, even if deep down he's no stomach for any sort of fight.

'Very trusting where fuck-ups are concerned aren't you?'

Morrissey nods back at the Shogun, the holdall on the back seat, passport to dreamland inside but it's a pretty hollow sort of dreamland on his tod. So now he's thinking maybe threats might work where pleas have failed, maybe making Kim's point for her all over again.

'What's to stop me shooting off on a one-way ticket to the lap of luxury myself, strictly solo?'

Which is a fair point Morrissey's now thinking, it has to be because Kim's taking a fuck of a long time to answer, but this new and sudden silence is nothing to do with his former lover being stumped for something to say.

It's all to do with Kim being on the verge of saying something she promised herself she'd never say.

But then she nods at him.

'You might stitch me, Morrissey, if you're hurting that much.'

And Morrissey is hurting that much right now and more.

'Yeah.'

'And I don't suppose you owe Lulu or Fomo or Carmel that much either.'

In front of her, Morrissey's still doing his impersonation of a nodding dog.

'Right.'

And now Kim's pausing again because this is a card she never thought she'd deal in a game she never thought she'd play, but she's not playing anymore and this isn't a game and it hasn't been for a long time, for eight years plus to be precise.

'But the way I see it, you'd never, in a million lifetimes, stitch your son.'

And now Morrissey suddenly stops nodding which is something of a relief to his neck muscles which were in serious danger of suffering serious strain. But that's definitely at the expense of his eyes which are now staring back at Kim on what Morrissey's old Nan used to call chapel hat pegs whatever they were.

And Morrissey's ears are suffering right now too because they're twitching away as his disbelieving mind runs some sort of check, making sure he is still hearing everyday sounds OK because he sure as fuck didn't hear that properly.

But his eyes seem fine and his hearing seems normal, but what Kim's just said still makes no sense. Aidan could never in a million lifetimes be Morrissey's son. For starters, and whichever way Morrissey looks at it this is one hell of a starters, Aidan was born more than two years into a three year stretch for Morrissey and he hadn't laid eyes on Kim for the whole of that time, never mind what else he'd have had to lay on her to get her up the duff.

So what the flying fuck is she talking about?

Which is when Kim cuts across, hissing at him now.

'Mac!'

Morrissey turns and sure enough there he is, just driven into the alley, a Lone Ranger for now but from the grimly anticipatory look on Mac's face as he picks up his mobile, not about to remain one for much longer.

But Morrissey looks back at Kim, only one thing on his mind right now and it's not that fat twat.

'What the fuck does that mean?'

'It means you're dead if you don't go, and that's as in fucking now.'

'I'm talking about Aidan.'

'This fucking minute you muppet.'

Further down the alleyway Mac's getting out of his car, the wailing whine of a Shogun still being driven way too fast in way too low a gear now sounding as it approaches.

Up in the tower block, Aidan watches from a top storey window, clocking Mac, clocking Morrissey with his Mum and clocking now too the fast-approaching and loudly protesting Shogun.

But Morrissey is still looking back at Kim, one last, silent appeal for some sort of answer, but even he can see he's destined not to be enlightened for now and maybe not ever if Morrissey doesn't get into the cab of that Shogun and quick.

Morrissey dives back into the cab, Mac with his mobile still in hand dives back into his cab too, Morrissey gunning the accelerator, spinning the rear wheels, desperately scrabbling for grip as he fishtails out of the alley.

Mac follows, gunning the accelerator too, spinning the rear wheels as well, also desperately scrabbling for grip, but then he slams on the brakes, his windscreen suddenly turning into crazy paving as a surgical collar hurled from the heavens hits it.

Or, more accurately, hurled by Aidan from that upstairs window of the tower block, another one of Angel's insurance props bouncing from the now-shattered windscreen back onto the road.

Still by the window, Aidan breathes a whispered imprecation.

'Go, Uncle Morrissey.'

Mac, now crashed into a concrete bollard, is now shouting venom up at a sky that's suddenly started raining surgical collars, but Looner arriving behind has the fast-exiting Morrissey in sight and he's got the turbo and tuned version of the entry level model that Morrissey's driving, and for the first time since he split all those coconuts and found empty spaces where no spaces should be, Looner's starting to smile.

Morrissey speeds down one street scattering flocks of pigeons in his wake, and soft-hearted fucker that he is, can't resist a look in the rearview mirror to make sure none of them have carped it only to see self-same mirror filled with a close-up of another Shogun and Looner now grinning evilly at the wheel, Diesel beside him. And Morrissey forgets all about possible casualties of the feathered variety and puts his foot down before he turns into one too.

Back in the pursuing Shogun, Diesel shakes his head, the unfathomable actions of his fellow human beings exercising what passes for his mind right now.

'So Morrissey had your stuff.'

'Fuck the stuff.'

Looner points towards the sky which is no mean feat seeing as how he's got a steering wheel in one hand and a rocket launcher in the other, all ready to unleash it on the hapless Morrissey just as soon as he gets his murderous hands on him.

Diesel nods.

'And your -'

Diesel points towards the heavens too as, ahead, Morrissey's still fishtailing his way down various alleys, short cuts, and side streets, not actually managing to put anything like fresh air between himself and his pursuers.

Meanwhile Diesel muses some more on the ineffable mystery that's suddenly become Morrissey.

'And your bird.'

Then Diesel freezes just one second after Looner freezes, the impossible just happened, Diesel having momentarily wiped the single overwhelming matter of the moment from the big man's mind.

Looner stares at Diesel, a cyclist wobbling out of the way as Looner mounts the pavement.

'Leanne and Morrissey?'

'Shit.'

Not the most articulate of responses from Diesel, but it's about all the suddenly panicky fuck can manage right now.

A crack sounds outside as the Shogun's front wing collides with a lamp post.

'Leanne and Morrissey?'

Looner's voice is rising in volume, Diesel looking anywhere but at those staring eyes currently boring into the side of his head, one face and one only before his eyes right now and that's Phil The Travelling Greek.

By his side, Looner's voice isn't rising in volume anymore because his own personal decibel limit has now been well and truly reached, it's just becoming lower, deeper.

'Leanne and fucking Morrissey?!'

Looner swings his rocket launcher to his left, originally destined for use on the fleeing Morrissey and still destined for use on Morrissey, but about to take a diversion along the way.

Diesel flips the handle, pushes open the door but the door slams back on his flapping hand as the Shogun careers into another lamp post and now the rocket launcher's pointing straight at him.

Looner squeezes the trigger just as Diesel gets the door open again and dives for the relative safety of the road, the missed shot taking out a shop window and everything inside as Diesel rolls over collecting an infinite variety of cuts and bruises along the way but remaining in possession of his head.

But thanks to the diversion Morrissey's now made a good few metres. Looner's detour via the pavement, assorted lamp posts and his fumbles with a rocket launcher having actually put something like clear air between them. Morrissey's eyes flick backwards and forwards from windscreen to rear view mirror, back to windscreen then back to rear view mirror again, but there's no wailing Shogun behind, just empty road.

Morrissey turns down a side street, ignoring the dangerous appeal of the high-speed link out of the sinful city in the near distance, opting for rat run routes closer to home.

Bad move. The high-speed link might be exposed and dangerous particularly as Looner has the faster motor, but that's nothing compared to the danger of being caught in another three-car stunt which is what Morrissey's about to be caught up in as he comes across an upmarket Jag, a frustrated driver at the wheel and he's frustrated because he's tailgating a very familiar, if not painfully familiar, invalid carriage.

Fuck!!

Morrissey twists the wheel of the Shogun just before the Jag's rear brake lights illuminate as the suddenly panic-stricken driver stabs at the stop pedal, the crunch of metal a moment later ample testimony to the fact it's too little too late for him but not for Morrissey who just manages to swing round Angel's latest bit of highway mayhem, albeit with inches to spare.

As he does so Morrissey just catches sight of a wailing Shogun turning down that same side street behind, engine revving higher in triumphal celebration, a quarry re-sighted.

Morrissey swings down another street but Looner's gaining all the while. Morrissey swings down another, but Looner is as close now to his rear bumper as the tailgating Jag was to Angel's just moments before.

Morrissey twists the steering wheel again, his Shogun now right on the limit of adhesion, tyres just about hanging onto the tarmac, careering down another side street as a suckered Looner buys the dummy, shoots past the entrance, brakes screeching, tyres flat spotting, as the big man struggles to spin round. Morrissey glances in his rear-view mirror, seeing clear air again, meaning it really is time to put metal to the pedal and get the flying fuck out of there.

Morrissey races for the end of the street. One second later Morrissey slams on the brakes again as the Shogun's front wheels stop one inch from a six foot drop down into a wharf full of water.

Morrissey looks left to see more water, looks right to see even more of the fucking stuff, looks behind at the only route into and out of this escape to victory which has turned out to be a more than spectacularly dramatic dead end, but the road's still clear.

Morrissey rams the Shogun into reverse just as his rear-view mirrors fills once again with Looner's Shogun who now stops, feet away from Morrissey's now stationary and trapped motor.

It's stalemate.

High Noon.

Except it's no sort of stalemate at all and Gary Cooper did have some sort of chance in High Noon.

Morrissey stares at Looner, now eyeing him from inside his cab, Looner savouring the moment and why not? A lifetime's dream about to be realised and, this a definite bonus on top, Morrissey's life about to end to the same time and quite right too seeing as how he's been boning his squeeze. Looner is going to relish every single, solitary, glorious moment of this.

Morrissey looks back at the wharf, wondering whether Jap technology might extend to vehicles floating on water. Then he looks back at Looner, now climbing out of his cab.

Looner puts the rocket launcher down which gives Morrissey momentary hope. Then he opens the boot and takes out an even bigger rocket launcher instead and that hope vanishes. He might still have the business end currently pointing down towards the ground because that is actually one fuck of a big rocket launcher, but something's already telling Morrissey it's not destined to stay pointing down too much longer and he's right.

Looner's ever grimmer smile is spreading wider all the while now, his brain desperately searching for some killer line before he carries out this much-relished execution, something he can re-tell back in the portacabins, before he decides not to bother and just blow bits of Morrissey all over that sheet-grey water before taking back his nicked Shogun and that most precious, most priceless, of objects inside.

Morrissey turns back to the Shogun, looking for anything he can lay his hands on, maybe a weapon of some description that Tonto or Diesel might have left lying around, just something to even up the odds a little, a scrabbling Morrissey trying the glove box, the various oddment drawers, underneath the seats.

Nothing.

Absolutely fuck all.

So Morrissey next grabs Kim's hold-all, maybe she'd put something inside, some sort of back-up in case Morrissey tripped across a complication like an incandescent Looner with a rocket-launcher, but Morrissey just takes out a half-eaten chocolate bar and some footie stickers discarded from Aidan's last training session with Oz.

Morrissey stares back at Looner as that rocket launcher now slowly rises from the ground, a dead weight for any ordinary mortal, but it's light as a feather in Looner's giant fist.

Morrissey looks back at the water, for just a moment contemplating a desperate swim before turning back again because that really would be the ultimate indignity, his head blown to pieces and soaked and freezing cold to boot.

Morrissey drops the holdall, which is when, from inside, comes a strange-sounding clunking sound. Morrissey hesitates, then reaches inside and takes out the Echo.

Inside the Echo is Oz's elephant poster.

And inside the elephant poster is the moon rock.

Morrissey looks back at the approaching Looner, who's now positively salivating.

And Morrissey has one shot at this and he knows it, one shot at postponing mortality, most particularly his own. But if previous experience is anything to go by, most particularly all those mis-fired the soaps in Lulu's bathroom, this is going to be one fuck of a long shot.

Looner's left eye is now fixed to the sights of the rocket launcher, Morrissey in the very middle, X marking the spot, Looner moving the barrel slightly this way, then that, debating maybe a flesh wound first just to prolong the sweet agony that little while longer, but then Looner frowns because something's glinting in Morrissey's hand now as it catches the light.

Then it glints again, and then there's a positive flash as if the sun's picked it out for special treatment or something.

Then there's more flashes as it leaves Morrissey's hand and begins to ascribe a long, slow arc all the way over to the now-staring Looner.

'What the fuck?'

Looner takes his eye away from the sights of the rocket launcher to get a better look which is a bad move on his part. Gun, quarry, imminent and unfriendly fire should be next on the immediate agenda, the last thing he needs now are any distractions but how can Looner not be distracted, because this is something he's dreamt of since birth, has coveted since infancy, this is what's been embedded in what passes for the fat fuck's soul ever since.

80.   CRUSHED BEYOND REPAIR

At six years old Looner was already growing out rather than up.

It didn't help that almost every other kid on his home manor were whippet thin and no wonder seeing as most of them were out kicking a ball on the nearby footie pitch from sunrise to sundown while Looner remained on the fringes, waiting, watching, and already starting to hate.

One day a stray ball kicked by a wayward boot landed at Looner's feet, and for one moment there was the glimpse of an opportunity with the other kids urging him on to kick it back, join in.

Looner picked up the ball, held it between what were already two large fists, then squeezed the life out of that innocent bladder of air, crushing it until it was punctured and distended beyond repair.

Dozens of pairs of small eyes stared at him but no one dared approach, the fate of that football a timely warning because if that can happen to hardened leather, then what the fuck would happen to flesh and bone?

Looner looked back at them, actually wanting to say sorry and suddenly wanting to cry too, because he had no idea why he'd just done that and now he's wishing more than anything that he hadn't, but Looner, already being Looner, didn't say a word, just turned, and went home instead.

But that night, lying in bed, looking out of the window, he does say sorry and he says it to that face staring down at him, the face up in the sky, and there's no judgement from that face, no censure, and there never will be.

And that face never calls him a fat twat either, not the face in that shiny, spooney, Juney moon.

81. THREE THOUSAND VOLTS

The moon rock keeps arching towards Looner in what seems like slow motion, sunlight reflecting from its every surface.

Looner's mouth is opening, his eyes widening, because now he knows just what this is, it's his gift from the Gods, the blessing he's waited for, actual, real and direct contact with that smiley face that's sustained him all these lonely years, something he can hold, keep near, that can be his comfort and his strength in times of trouble and all that bollocks.

Those few metres away Morrissey stares as Looner actually starts to smile as the lethal weapon he's just hurled cannons ever closer to his awestruck head. Looner closes his eyes for a moment, everything else forgotten, this moment to be cherished beyond all others. Never mind lowlifes like Morrissey and blasting him to Kingdom come, that can wait, this is Kingdom Come, this is the promised land, Christmas and all his birthdays wrapped up with a great big bow.

Looner opens his eyes again just as the moonrock smashes into the exact middle of his forehead, sending him spinning down towards the water of the nearby wharf.

But even then, even with a pain that intense and with his head nearly split wide open, there's only one thing on Looner's mind as his rock deflects up into the sky, he's just desperate to catch it on its way back down, to touch it, hold it, feel it.

Looner's feet scrabble on the slippy waterside, his hands a blur in front of his face as he sees the rock falling to earth just three feet from the dock and all of a sudden Looner's done it, it's in his outstretched palm and it's like a three-thousand-volt charge arcing through his system, almost fusing that precious rock to his skin.

Only that last bit is obviously only in Looner's fevered imagination because it doesn't fuse at all, it just bounces out of his outstretched palm and cannons away towards the water instead.

With a howl that would bring tears to the eyes of angels, Looner spreadeagles himself, grabbing out at the rock again to scoop it back to safety and he manages that victorious rescue too, but it's a victory destined to become more than a little Pyrrhic as the momentum of his rescue attempt now sends him over the edge.

Looner crashes down into the deep, dark, swirling water making one fuck of a splash along the way. A not-so-minor tidal wave in fact moves across the water, breaking on a small collection of now-fleeing goosanders some hundred or so metres away.

Then there's nothing.

A cautious Morrissey stares at the water. Then Morrissey looks back at the moon rock, just lying on the ground, a few inches from the edge.

Morrissey looks at the water again, waiting for the reappearance of Looner, but there's still nothing.

Then Morrissey reaches down, picks up the moon rock and holds it in his hand. He doesn't get a celestial charge coursing through him from the stars. But he also doesn't get a fat fuck coming back out at him from the depths of the dock either.

So Morrissey pockets the rock, gets back in the nicked Shogun, swings it past Looner's abandoned motor and heads home.

82. AIDAN?

Back on Morrissey's home turf, the football match is still going on even with one net smashed to pieces.

'That can't be right.'

The watching Kim turns to see Morrissey standing behind her again, trying to still that sudden lurch in her guts, trying to tell herself that one day it won't happen, that she won't get feel this way, knowing every time that she will.

But for now, there's a more immediate matter of the moment.

'Where's Looner?'

'Fuck Looner.'

'And where's the rock?'

'In my pocket and fuck that too.'

Morrissey stares at Kim, bewildered not even coming close.

'Aidan?'

Kim doesn't reply, just looks back out across the pitch, Oz now trying to extricate himself from the net that's half-up, half-lying on the ground, tying himself into more knots with each hopeless twist and turn, Kim knowing exactly how he's feeling.

Her and her big mouth.

'I mean, how?'

She'd kept quiet for over eight years for fuck's sake. Why not add on an extra eight seconds?

'Forget it.'

'Kim!'

'Slip of the tongue.'

'Kim!!'

And now it's deep breath time as Kim looks back at the floundering Morrissey.

'Thank Billy.'

83. NINE MONTHS LATER

All those years before, back in those adjacent cubicles in that private clinic, Morrissey in one, Billy in the other, a couple more struggling souls in two other cubicles further along too.

But Morrissey's speeding up now, faster all the time and he's going to go faster still if only that vision pausing outside the window to talk to her new mate in work will stay there just a few seconds longer.

And because it's a shitty little clinic and not a fairy tale she doesn't, but it doesn't matter because the memory of that vision is plenty enough to do what the wank mags were totally unable to do and that's take Morrissey well and truly over the finishing line in a final canter so memorable it makes him wonder, albeit briefly, whether he shouldn't be the one paying for this.

Spool forward.

Morrissey's visits and donations had become regular occurrences, even after he'd swopped the vision for reality and Kim had become his girlfriend. Morrissey had always needed the money and Kim never seemed to mind and now Morrissey's beginning to understand why.

A few years later again and with Morrissey now in one of his regular stints in stir, Kim lets herself into the closed and now darkened clinic, extracts one particular phial of white goo from the freezer and makes another visit to a very different and more than a little totally dodgy clinic the next day.

Nine months later . . .

Back in the present day, Morrissey's staring at Kim, mouth wide open, which is Morrissey's mouth, not Kim's.

'Ninety per cent of you is fab, Morrissey. Always has been, always will be.'

Kim pauses.

'The other ten per cent, that's a total and complete fuck-up.'

But Morrissey's barely listening because a golden glow's beginning to envelop the shitty steel-shuttered flats behind them that everyone's always said were scheduled for demolition but are still hanging in there somehow.

A bit, it seems, like Morrissey.

'I can't do anything about that, I've tried, for fuck's sake, and I can't, there's no point.'

Morrissey just keeps staring at her.

Now she's shimmering too.

'But I can with him.'

Kim nods behind Morrissey who stares across at Aidan, the young boy now dribbling the ball past a whole series of lunging legs and scoring a perfect goal, smack bang in the middle of the opposition net.

Morrissey doesn't say a word, but he doesn't need to.

His eyes are saying it all.

PART FOUR

'The happy end of God's correction'

Job, 6.

85. ONE MONTH LATER

One square mile of the old Cardiff docks is buzzing like a swarm of giant bees with the sort of turn-out on show usually reserved for victorious football stars on open top buses, or that returning semi-finalist from that shit TV talent show.

And right in the middle of it all, the cynosure of each and every eye, and there's a fuck of a lot of those right now and no wonder because it's not every day you get to see a real-life, in the flesh, actual elephant smack bang in the middle of a city square.

Oz is like a man reborn which is exactly how he's feeling after that disaster of a football match, Aidan's goal notwithstanding. But that's a distant memory now along with the demolished nets and a desire to kill Morrissey who seemed to have visited down on them that mayhem that day as well as depriving them of a goalie because Slippery just didn't cut it in the replacement stakes.

But that's now been replaced by an equally intense desire to give Morrissey and everyone else he comes across today the biggest bear hug he can, to squeeze those ribs until they pop in fact, because Oz's body might be in his home city right now but his soul's floating up on Cloud Nine or even Ten or however many more there may be up there.

'This is fucking mega, Morrissey.'

Oz paces up and down, energy pumping inside, doubling back, starting off again.

'They can evict people, no sweat.'

Oz pauses briefly.

'Correction. They have evicted people, no sweat.'

But Morrissey is only half-listening. His eyes are now on Aidan, just emerged from a small links home across the road.

'They've evicted half this fucking manor in fact but they will never, ever, in a million fucking lifetimes evict–'

Oz, drunk on the unaccustomed narcotic of new-found power, turns, stares at the apparition before him, so mystical, so magnificent but, and above all, so utterly and gloriously permanent.

'- a fucking elephant.'

And as if by way of a rousing chorus of agreement, the elephant suddenly bellows a triumphant greeting back at him, kids yelling as he does so, adults joining in, Slippery blinking in the daylight having just come out of the pub to see an elephant where the bus stop used to be, before looking skyward expecting at any moment to see pink pigs too.

But Morrissey, still with eyes only for Aidan, tenses as the door to that same small links house opens again and Kim emerges from inside, Angel with her, a holdall in Kim's hand.

Morrissey takes a deep breath, heads across. Angel melting away as Aidan moves towards Oz and the elephant, aunt and nephew both keeping their usual diplomatic distance as everyone always seems to when it comes to anything to with these two.

Kim pauses for a moment, her holdall now at her feet, as Morrissey nods at her.

'So when's the flight?'

'Six.'

Morrissey nods back, trying to stay cool, trying to seem casual, failing miserably as Kim nods back at him

'Yours?'

Morrissey hesitates.

'Don't know about that anymore.'

A few short weeks ago there was only one thought on Morrissey's mind and that was getting out of there, getting away, and he'd have done it too save for one very sneaky Porsche and a gob full of goo. Now Morrissey gestures around.

'This is home after all. And the place isn't looking too bad right now.'

Kim nods across at the new arrival

'Apart from the ton of elephant shit that's just come out of that thing.'

Morrissey presses on, dogged.

'The Council's starting to spread a bit of dosh around at last.'

'Extra street sweepers'll come in very handy.'

'Got to be better than living with some bunch of ex-pats, out Beni-way.'

Then Morrissey stops as Kim cuts across.

'This is window dressing, Morrissey.'

Even as she's saying it, she knows she should just keep her mouth shut, not rise to the bait, just get in the taxi that's just pulled up a few metres away and get the fuck out of there.

'This place is dead.'

'Not lying down though is it?'

'And I'm not either.'

Kim nods across the great divide at the new flats in the distance. then down towards the new bay and up towards the ever-expanding southern edge of the city, their home community being squeezed on all sides, Kim trying to get out before the pips squeak.

'How long do you think it'll be before the bulldozers arrive? Raze this place to the ground, elephant or no elephant?'

'Hang around. Wait and see.'

And Kim hesitates now, but not over Morrissey's all too familiar invitation. The only issue now is not when to leave or should she leave, but how to leave, how to actually say goodbye?

But there's only one way really.

Leaning forward, as gentle and as tender as she can, she kisses Morrissey, lightly, on the lips.

'Bye Morrissey.'

And that's it. And Morrissey just has to watch as she heads for the waiting cab, collecting Aidan along the way.

The taxi doors open, the doors close, the driver depresses the clutch and engages the gears and with one squeal, probably from a worn clutch release bearing, Kim's gone, Aidan gone too, one life over, another about to begin.

'You OK, Morrissey?'

Morrissey turns to Carmel, has just watched all that, as has Oz and almost everyone else too, but most of those eyes turn away as soon as Morrissey looks back at them, no one wanting to make this any worse by turning private grief into a public peep show.

And Carmel doesn't want to make it any worse either but she's not able to help herself, she and Morrissey so very nearly got it on after all and they would have done too if that picky cow hadn't been on the scene.

Morrissey looks back at Carmel, debating, briefly, whether to pretend he doesn't know what the fuck's she talking about, but then Morrissey's shoulders droop.

Carmel reaches out, massaging those now-drooping shoulders as if to keep their owner upright, keep him off the floor.

86. FOUR MINUTES, FORTY-EIGHT

One mile away, then two, and Aidan looks sideways at his Mum who's stayed silent for each of them, determined not to betray herself and very definitely not looking back the once, just staring straight ahead.

'I knew it'd all work out.'

Kim nods.

It has.

So why can't she trust herself to speak right now?

'Oz has got his elephant.'

Kim nods again, barely listening, trying to stop her eyes misting up.

'Everyone's rid of Looner.'

Kim looks out of the window still barely listening.

'And you've finally told Uncle Morrissey he's my old man.'

Whooooah!

Hold up, spool back, re – fucking – wind!

Kim, now well and truly listening, stares back at him, heart pounding, mind racing, no mist in front of her eyes now, Kim's hoping like fuck that some inner voice has just played a trick on her.

'Say that again'

But Aidan doesn't because he doesn't need to, he just looks at his mum instead.

Kim keeps staring at him.

'You know?'

Aidan nods.

'I've always known.'

'How the -?'

Kim stopping herself, just before the 'fuck.'

'Everyone's always known.'

The first of the signs for the airport, now just a mile or so away, flash past outside the window.

Aidan smiles.

'Well - apart from Uncle Morrissey.'

Aidan leans close, gives his Mum a warm, comforting hug.

'I'm so pleased I got your brains you know.'

Back on the Square, Morrissey looks at Lulu who's just appeared in a full ball gown and high heels, especially donned in honour of the occasion, a grinning Lulu giving Morrissey a big thumbs-up, Morrissey returning a smile wrenched from his guts.

Meanwhile and a few moments later, the taxi driver pulls up onto the concourse outside Departures and gets out, eyes a patrolling traffic warden, the warden programmed to compute a five-minute cycle for each and every new arrival, fingers primed to dispense a ticket once any stray vehicle lingers more than a millisecond outside its permitted waiting time.

But the driver smiles as he starts unloading Kim and Aidan's bags from the boot. He's a seasoned professional, has done this a million times before so he's not hurrying, in fact he loves this game as the minutes tick down under the Jobsworth's watchful eye. Getting down to three is strictly for wimps, getting down to four is more hardcore, four-thirty is definitely for the serious piss-taker, but his personal best is four minutes, forty-eight, just twelve seconds to spare.

In the cab, Kim, not moving, is looking at Aidan.

'And you really don't mind?'

'About Uncle Morrissey?'

Kim stares at her unconcerned son as he shakes his head

'I know he fucks up a lot.'

'Don't say fuck, Aidan.'

'But I like him.'

Outside, it's approaching three minutes and the driver's glancing across at the man with the stopwatch and the twitching ticket machine. His passengers are still making no move to get out, but he's not concerned, not yet, there's still plenty of time.

'I always thought it was for the best.'

Aidan nods back.

Back outside, standing by the bags unloaded from the boot, the seconds ticking on, the third minute now within sight of the fourth, the driver taps on the window, just a gentle nudge to make a move but keep taking your time for now, let this wanker of a warden sniff a win for once.

Kim doesn't even see him or hear the tap on the window.

'He always makes such an arse of everything,'

Aidan nods again.

'But he did get Oz his elephant.'

'Apart from getting Oz his elephant.'

'And he did get Lulu all his dresses.'

'And apart from Lulu and his dresses.'

The driver opens the door to the side of Kim, it's now four minutes, twenty and this is now getting a fraction on the tight side but Kim reaches out, slams it shut again.

'And he got Carmel her new gaff and she is going to get Jamal back now.'

'And apart from Carmel and her gaff and Jamal.'

Aidan pauses.

'And he did make me.'

Outside, the driver now tugs at the door, there's just ten seconds to go for fuck's sake, but Kim deadlocks it shut, the driver turning, staring in disbelief at the advancing and now-grinning warden, ticket already in hand.

Inside, Kim just keeps staring at Aidan.

87. CREAM

Back in the docks the procession's getting under way, slowly, as it would with an elephant at the front, especially an elephant more used to rolling hills than a sea of people and who's already taken the first of several delighted detours across gardens, through fences and up alleys which isn't exactly helping in the progress stakes.

But the cameras are clicking like crickets and by morning this not-so-little beauty is destined to be on the front of virtually every shit-sheet and red-top the length and breadth of God's own, or at least this little corner of it, and that's all yankee-doodle-dandy so far as Oz is concerned.

Morrissey, following along with the rest, looks round his home patch which is actually beginning to feel a bit like his home patch again and he's actually starting to feel as if maybe he isn't some outcast from a life less ordinary, or a strange being beamed down from somewhere the other side of Mars.

Morrissey looks across at Lulu who's booked in for his pre-op the very next day, at Fomo who's already put down the deposit on a cattery miles away on the western edge of Wales or somewhere, at Carmel who burnt her regulation blue serge and police warrant card in a great big bonfire the night before and is already looking at a nice little place in the country for herself and Jamal too, over Chepstow way.

And he looks at Billy who may be hobbling but who's already working up a mean old head of speed with those new state of the art crutches of his.

Then Morrissey looks across at the one piece of graffiti the Council never touched, that one word, CREAM emblazoned on the wall, five words underneath, Cash Rules Everything Around Me, and ain't that forever true?

Which is when he hears it.

Behind him.

'You've got one –'

Morrissey wheels round. If he'd spun on his heels any faster he'd be powering at least five of those turbines you can see on a clear day up on Caerphilly mountain.

'- and I mean one –'

Kim stares at Morrissey, Aidan behind her, grinning, giving him a thumbs-up, the silent signal clear.

Go for it Morrissey, you jammy old fuck.

'- last – '

Further down the street, the elephant trumpets as if in approval.

'- and I mean, last –'

From across the street, Carmel watches. Why could she never put that sort of smile on Morrissey's face?

'– chance.'

88. TIME WARP

The same boozer, now rebuilt after Slippery's close encounter with the stripper, Morrissey and Diesel sitting inside again and it could be time warp time, history repeating itself, only this time there's a note to Morrissey's voice, a tone no actor could reproduce no matter how many gilded Oscars might smile down on his endeavours.

A picture plays in front of Morrissey's eyes again, a Shogun, another Shogun, rocking gently on its wheels.

'So, I really did get the wheels.'

And that's Morrissey's wheels this time too, bought and paid for, and that's cash, not even bothering with a discount which is Morrissey's only regret because there's class and there's downright stupidity. But who cares, because no one and nothing is going to bring Morrissey down from these clouds right now.

'And I did get the music.'

Surround sound too, top of the range, wasted on a man who only really gets off on a long-haired, zoned-out retard beating holy hell out an old guitar and a set of even older amps, but Morrissey's past caring about that too.

'And I got the girl.'

And this is the real reason he couldn't give a flying fuck and the reason he'd have paid that dealer double if he'd had to, never mind negotiating any sort of kick-back.

'And the right girl this time too.'

Diesel nods back which just goes to show that even amoeba can connect on some primeval level with higher emotions.

Then Morrissey's face clouds, this the one fly in the ointment, although this one is a bit of a biggie.

'I just had one last problem.'

Morrissey isn't seeing this at the time seeing as how he's otherwise engaged, but outside the Shogun, Yorkie, faithful as ever, is seeing it all even if he's not believing the evidence of his eyes because this is one totally surreal sight right now.

Another Shogun.

Black.

With blacked-out windows.

Looking for all the world like one of Looner's very special, top of the range, personal Shoguns and for a very good reason.

Because Looner's at the wheel.

Which is a totally impossible sight, and even more to the point is a totally frightening sight, particularly as he's currently got another very tasty-looking rocket launcher perched on his lap but which, from the look on his face, isn't going to be perched there much longer. So all in all maybe it's a good job that Morrissey's more than a little distracted by other matters right now because this might have a seriously deflating effect on those other matters now literally in hand.

Yorkie stares, mouth open, tongue panting, eyes staring, one word etched all over his face, the canine equivalent of, fuck.

Looner doesn't even see him. He's just staring at the rocking Shogun, his face setting ever more grimly as he gets out from behind the wheel, before slowly bringing the rocket launcher up and taking aim.

Which is when Yorkie jumps into action, springing up and yelping for all he's worth, barking over and over at the closed door of Morrissey's new pride and joy.

Inside, Kim opens dreamy eyes, looks up at Morrissey.

'What's that?'

But Morrissey shakes his head, he's not about to stop if the whole of the Household Cavalry approach right now, let alone one single hound.

'Ignore him.'

Outside the cab, Looner's now bringing the rocket launcher up to shoulder level, taking all the time he wants, all that rocking in front of him telling him that there's no, as in absolutely no, need to rush any of this.

By the cab door, Yorkie's yelps are getting louder and more insistent all the while and inside, Kim's eyes open again.

'What's wrong with Yorkie?'

'Nothing.'

'Then why's he yelping like that?'

Morrissey curses.

'He won't be yelping at all if he does this to me again.'

Kim frowns.

'Again?'

Morrissey cuts across, hasty.

'Doesn't matter.'

Outside, Yorkie now freezes because that is one fuck of a big nozzle on that rocket launcher and at the moment he's right in the firing line and he is a loyal little soul, man's best friend and all that, but there's absolutely no point in staying just a metre or so in front of a deadly missile and Yorkie doesn't, he hightails it away, towards the other side of the Shogun. But then, working out that motor might shift a fair bit with the sort of explosive charge that's about to rip into its side, he moves a good couple of metres further away still.

Silence descends again inside the Shogun. Blessed peace and calm. Not that there's no sound at all but it's the sort of sounds Morrissey wants to hear right now, quick, urgent, breathing sorts of sounds.

Which is when Kim cuts in again.

'He's still doing it.'

And he is. From outside it's started up again, more yelps and barks now too, maybe a little more distant but just as insistent and just as anguished.

And now Morrissey really is about to lose it, is about to jump out of that Shogun and to appeal to whatever passes for fellow feeling in that mutt of his to put a fucking sock in it, just for the next few minutes, then he'll get a walk, a bone, anything he fucking wants in fact.

But Kim, who's obviously made of sterner stuff than Leanne, reaches up, runs her fingers through Morrissey's hair and tells him to stay exactly where he is.

Outside the Shogun, Looner smiles as the motor in front of him starts rocking again, all this so sweet, so, so satisfying.

Looner trains the long barrel on the rocking motor.

Inside that motor, the rocking intensifies.

Outside, Yorkie puts two paws over his eyes, because there's no way out of this one even for his great escape artist of a lord and master but at least the old fucker's going to die happy.

Looner squeezes the trigger, doesn't even bother putting his eye to the sights seeing as how he's so close now but he really should have done. Had he performed that simple task then he might have seen a six-foot python hiding inside the barrel, has been hiding in there since Morrissey and the gang stashed it in Looner's hardware storeroom in fact, trying to keep still, dreaming of the day he's going to be reunited with Fatman.

Inside, Kim lets out a big, long moan, as from outside the loudest blast this side of Armageddon nearly rocks the Shogun off its brand-new springs.

Morrissey struggles to the door a moment later, opening it to see Looner. Or bits of Looner anyway and a few metres away Fatman's python, and the python's surprisingly intact too, that blast from the rocket launcher having very definitely gone back rather out towards the front, thanks to the considerable obstruction in its way.

Which is when Kim's voice breaks in on him.

'Do that again, Morrissey.'

Morrissey looks back at Kim, her eyes shining in wonder.

'It moved, I swear, the fucking earth actually moved just then.'

Morrissey looks one last time at the devastation all around and at Yorkie now opening his eyes, then Morrissey closes the door, returns to the matter of the moment.

Across the waste ground, Looner's left eye slowly opens too.

Then closes again.

Then . . .

THE END

About the author

Rob Gittins is a screenwriter and novelist and has written for almost every top-rated UK network TV drama from the last thirty years including *Casualty, EastEnders, The Bill, Stella, Vera, Soldier, Soldier* and *Heartbeat*. Rob has also written over thirty original radio plays for BBC Radio 4, including the award-winning *Losing Paradise*.

More books from Fahrenheit Press

If you enjoyed *Cash Rules Everything Around Me* we think you'll also enjoy…

Black Moss by David Nolan

In April 1990, as rioters took over Strangeways prison in Manchester, someone killed a little boy at Black Moss.

And no one cared.

No one except Danny Johnston, an inexperienced radio reporter trying to make a name for himself.

More than a quarter of a century later, Danny returns to his home city to revisit the murder that's always haunted him.

If Danny can find out what really happened to the boy, maybe he can cure the emptiness he's felt inside since he too was a child.

But finding out the truth might just be the worst idea Danny Johnston has ever had.

"As one would expect from a writer with the skill and experience of David Nolan, this haunting book deals with very difficult issues in an incredibly sympathetic manner while at the same time throwing a light onto one of the most complicated and shaming areas of our society - the failure to protect those who are the most vulnerable."